ALSO BY CLAYTON SMITH

APOCALYPTICON

DEATH AND MCCOOTIE

PANTS ON FIRE: A COLLECTION OF LIES

ANOMALY FLATS

For Amanda,

Since Margaret already
gave you all the
best, hopefully this book
can at least give you a
few laughs.
(watch out for mustaches)

Copyright © 2015 by Clayton Smith

Printed in the United States of America

First Printing, 2015

Library of Congress Control Number: 2015916082

ISBN 978-0-9965121-1-4

Dapper Press
www.DapperPress.com

For Tom, Patrick, Percy, Jordon, Tara, Tobben, Kelly, Tim, Serbus, Shipley, Shawn, Jenny, Jon Hamm, John Goodman, Mark Twain, Vincent Price, Harry Truman, and everyone else who knows what Missouri's really all about.

ANOMALY FLATS

CLAYTON SMITH

CHAPTER 1

THE ROAD WAS CLEAR, and the drive was smooth…until the bridge over the Missouri River decided to collapse, plunging two cars, three people, and one ton of concrete into the frigid water below.

Mallory rolled the car to a stop before the line of flashing blue and red lights of the Saline County Sheriff's Department patrol cars. One of the deputies signaled her with a slow wave of his flashlight. He held up a hand and approached her Impala.

"Shit," she whispered.

Mallory grabbed the purple Jansport backpack from the passenger side floor and stuffed it into the backseat. She gave herself a nervous glance in the rearview mirror. She looked like she'd just crawled out of a cave that doubled as a hurricane in its spare time. Maybe he was into that. She shook out her hair so it covered half of her face.

The deputy tapped his finger against the window, and she rolled it down, trying desperately to conjure up the Mallory Jenkins of fifteen years ago and smiling what she hoped was a coy, flirtatious smile.

She had a feeling it was more of a tired, crooked snarl in execution.

"What's the problem, officer?"

The deputy leaned down and spat a stream of brown liquid onto the highway. "Bridge's out," he gargled over the huge, wet glob of tobacco in his cheeks. "Gotta turn around."

Mallory peered across the tops of the patrol cars, at the gaping maw of empty air where there should have been a bridge, and the empty road beyond.

She sighed. "What's the best detour?"

The deputy leaned a pudgy hand on the window frame. The whole car groaned and lurched downward. "Depends," he said, glancing around the inside of her car. "Where you headed?"

Good question, she thought. She shifted in her seat, swiveling her shoulders in an attempt to block his view as his eyes slid slowly over the Impala's interior. "East," she guessed.

The deputy spat again. A trickle of brown dripped onto the car door. He wiped it away with his sleeve. "This road heads north."

Mallory's grip on the wheel tightened. The leather creaked under the pressure, and her heart skipped. "I'm...taking the scenic route," she said.

The deputy snorted. He lifted his hand from the window frame and slapped it on the hood of the car. "Turn around, take this highway to Marshall, jump onto 65, it'll take you to 70 West." Another pair of headlights appeared around the bend behind her as the deputy waved her on. "Go ahead." He rubbed the back of his hand against his stained lips. "Be safe, now."

"Thanks," she mumbled. She raised the window and made a U-turn around the officer. She couldn't say for sure, but as she drove away into the dying light, she thought she saw him grip the radio at his shoulder and speak into it, his beady eyes following her car—and her license plate. She held her breath and sped around the bend, and she didn't exhale until the red and blue flashing lights had faded behind the trees.

"Not good," she told the Mallory in the rearview mirror.

"Worse than not good," the mirror Mallory replied.

A new road opened up on the left, and she pulled the wheel. The Impala squealed against the pavement and cut off down the backwoods highway. The road wound deeper and deeper into the heart of nowhere; the trees loomed high above and crowded her in, blotting out what little sunlight was left. For the hundredth time since leaving Ladue, her fingers itched to turn on her phone and check the Google map. But phones could be tracked, and she didn't know if anyone was keeping an eye on her signal. She didn't want to find out the hard way. She wasn't even sure that turning the phone off made it untraceable. *NCIS* had been mixed on that point. "Thanks for nothing, Mark Harmon," she grumbled.

She knew she should probably just chuck the thing and be done with it, but she couldn't quite bring herself to do it. For one thing, it was *hers*; she'd been able to bring so few of her own belongings, it was weirdly comforting to hold the phone, even if it was just a cold, dead, plastic rectangle that was two whole models shy of being trendy. And for another, it had three years' worth of photos stored on it...pictures of her sister, whom she loathed, and her nieces, whom she thought were always a little too sticky to be very endearing, but still. They were family, and who knew when she'd see them again?

Or *if* she'd see them again...

So the phone sat uselessly in the cup holder, and it mocked her with its black, silent screen.

"Shut up, phone," she muttered.

The highway twisted through the woods, and Mallory started to feel uneasy, passing through what felt like two solid walls of trees. "This is the Midwest," she said aloud, frowning at the tall, dark shapes that spread out on either side of the road. "Where the hell are all the fields?"

She rounded a curve and saw a sign at the edge of the highway that read ANOMALY FLATS – 2 MI, with an arrow pointing to the left.

Flats, she thought. *Flats sounds fieldish, right? Flats sounds good.*

She turned on her blinker, slowed down the car, and pulled onto the road that led to Anomaly Flats.

CHAPTER 2

THE WELCOME SIGN FOR ANOMALY FLATS could best be described as odd. It was huge, for one thing, the size of a billboard, though it was propped up not two feet above the ground by a trellis of weathered wood that sagged and struggled under the weight of it. The woods had thinned out at this spot, but they hadn't disappeared altogether; the sign was just stuck in among the trees, partially hidden, as if it had grown there like a weed. It was painted with a quaint village scene: houses, a steeple, and a water tower, all nestled against the crook of a gently sloping rise, giving way to a field abundant with corn. A blue, cloudless sky stretched above the little town, and a big, round sun beamed down in cheery yellow and orange rays.

But the sign was old…1950s old. And it hadn't been kept up along the way. The color had faded unevenly, and the paint had peeled and flaked, and there was almost more weathered wood visible beneath the little village scene than there was actual village. The sign was lit from above by a trio of unreliable light bulbs screwed into rusty light fixtures that hooked over the top of the billboard. It was just enough to illuminate the words NOW ENTERING ANOMALY FLATS painted across the sky in looping cursive letters, and the span at the bottom, below the town's modest skyline, where it read, WELCOME HOME.

Mallory drove on past the sign, and as she did, her dashboard lights flickered strangely. For a moment, the inside of her car matched the fluttering dimness of the billboard. Then she smacked the palm of her hand against the top of the dash, and the lights brightened to a full glow once more.

"I should've bought a Toyota," she mumbled.

The trees continued to thin as she traveled. By the time she left the forest, the sun had set, and the night sky twinkled with stars; millions of stars, *hundreds* of millions of stars...more stars than Mallory had ever seen before in her life. She craned her neck and gazed up through the windshield in awe at the softly pulsing points of light. There was the Big Dipper. And there, just below, its little twin. She could see the three stars of Orion's belt marching across the southern end of the sky, and the five points of the regal Cassiopeia sparkling bluish-white against the darkness just above. So many constellations...so many stars she'd never seen, that she'd never known existed...so much beauty...such a swirling, dizzying, glorious universe, quiet and beautiful and wonderful and cold. The stars almost seemed to swirl across the sky, spinning in easy, graceful patterns...turning, twisting, each constellation bowing to the next, asking for a dance, whisking its partner in light, airy steps across the blanket of darkness. The stars were captivating, mesmerizing, beguiling. Hypnotic, even.

"So beautiful..." Mallory whispered. She reached up toward the stars with both hands. Her fingertips brushed against the glass of the windshield...she tried to push past it, push *through* it, to let her hands dance and sway with the constellations above, to join them in their ethereal ball—

A truck horn blared, and headlights exploded onto the road, flooding the car with violent yellow light. Mallory screamed, and her hands flew back to the steering wheel, jerking it to the right. The tires squealed, the car lurched, and she missed the oncoming pickup by just inches. The truck honked angrily as it passed, and the driver yelled something obscene out the window, but Mallory didn't hear it. She couldn't hear *anything* over the sound of her heart hammering, trying to break free of her chest. She stomped her foot on the brake, and the car screeched to a halt in the soft, grassy shoulder of the road.

"What the *fuck!*" she screamed, slamming her hands on the dashboard. Her blood surged through her veins; her lungs couldn't pump fast enough to cycle the air she heaved in and out. When she lifted her hands again, she saw that they were trembling, and they weren't alone; her entire body felt like it was set on *vibrate*.

"Calm down," she said, trying to soothe herself back to normalcy. "Calm down. You're fine. Calm down…"

But *was* she fine? Nearly plowing headfirst into a truck because she was looking at the *stars*? Since when did she get emotional over *nature*? She *hated* nature. It was all bug bites and poison ivy and heat stroke and sweat. It was only beautiful when enjoyed from indoors, at a distance, in an air-conditioned room, with no fewer than one drink in hand. She hadn't looked at so much as a single star since she was a Girl Scout, much less swooned over them—and she'd only done it then because it was absolutely required. Truth be told, stars and the idea of space in general made her feel nauseous. Sometimes, it gave her hiccups.

"So what gives?" she said aloud. But she knew what gave. She was crashing hard after a full day of adrenaline. Her body was freaking out, and her brain was making too much dopamine, or serotonin, or whatever the hell it was that made someone stare up at the stars like a drooling idiot.

She took a few more deep breaths, closed her eyes, and waited until her hands stopped shaking. Then she shook some life into her head, put her hands on the wheel, and pulled the car back onto the road.

The highway (and it still was technically a highway, according to the road sign ahead, though it looked more like a half-tarred horse trail) curved around to the right. Mallory rolled cautiously along, wound around the curve, and crested a small hill as the town of Anomaly Flats melted forth from the darkness ahead. The word that instantly popped into Mallory's head was "quaint." She'd never called *anything* quaint before, but there was no denying it: Anomaly Flats had quaintness in its blood.

The highway unfurled through the center of town, lined with old, low, brick buildings that seemed almost alive with warm, watery light. Lantern-style streetlamps shone down on the street as couples walked beneath them, enjoying the cool air. A bakery with a pink-and-white-striped awning had closed up for the night; a small line formed at the Anomaly Bijou ticket booth, the patrons glowing green beneath the marquee's neon lights. There seemed to be a crowd gathering at the Dive Inn, which was just a smoky little bar, judging by the buzzing neon beer signs in the window. Mom and Pop's Grocery was locked up tight, but big blue letters and a flashing blue arrow welcomed one and all into the Nite-Owl Diner.

If the American Dream were a town, Mallory thought.

Just then, the interior lights of the Impala flickered again. "Son of a—come on," Mallory said, slapping the dashboard. "Come *on!*" But instead of coming on, the lights went out. The panel went dark, the engine cut out, and Mallory's car rolled to a dead stop.

"No, no, no, no!" She put the car in park. She turned the keys back, then forward again, but the engine only clicked. "Please start...pleeeeease!" she pleaded, turning the keys back and forth. She pumped her foot on the gas pedal in case that might help, and she put her other foot on the brake, because, what the hell? But despite her begging and pleading and turning and pumping, the car refused to start.

Mallory slumped forward and knocked her forehead against the wheel. "This is the weirdest day I've ever had," she declared.

She glanced over at her phone. If ever there was a need, this was it. But she couldn't take the risk...and besides, who would she call? Everyone she knew was now everyone she'd once known; that was one of the rules. And it wasn't like she belonged to AAA, because who needed reliable 24-hour roadside service when you had all of the Internet in your cup holder?

"I hate you, phone," she decided. "You're useless and dumb, and I hate you."

Saying it out loud made her feel a little better.

She leaned back in her seat and sighed. "Well," she said, "time to mix with the locals." She glanced over her shoulder at the purple Jansport in the back and frowned. "Yeah," she finally decided, reaching back, "you're coming with me." She grabbed the pack, stepped out of the car, locked the doors, and headed across the street to the Nite-Owl Diner.

A little bell above the door clanged softly as she entered, and everything inside the diner stopped. Conversation ceased, forks froze in midair; chairs scooted and squeaked as the diners turned and swiveled to stare at the woman who'd walked through the door.

"Um…hi," she said, giving a little wave.

A man near the back of the diner cleared his throat. No one else moved. No one else responded.

Everyone just stared.

"Park yourself on down anywhere that looks comfortable," the woman behind the counter said, breaking the silence like a hammer against a pane of glass. She was old—or old-*ish*—with frizzy gray hair and wrinkles under her eyes. She wore a pink smock with a white pocket at the chest and white trim around the edges of the short sleeves. The white apron tied around her waist showed years of grease stains and soda spills. Her nametag said TRUDY. "What'll you have?"

"I'm not eating," Mallory said, leaning forward against the counter. The Formica surface was tacky under her palms with a lifetime of spilled syrup. "Is there an auto shop in this town? I'm having car troubles."

Trudy smiled. "Can't trust cars," she said, shaking her head with a chuckle. "Leaded or unleaded?"

Mallory raised an eyebrow. "My car?"

The older woman grabbed a mug from the shelf behind her and set it down on the counter. "Your coffee."

Mallory raised her hands defensively, as if the mug might spring to life. "I don't want coffee, I need a mechanic. A 24-hour one, ideally." She glanced uneasily around the diner. The other patrons continued to stare. A fly buzzed about the drooping mouth of a man at the far end of the counter and came to a rest on his bottom lip. The man didn't flinch.

Trudy grabbed a coffee pot with an orange handle from a burner near the stove. "Seems like you're plumb worked-up as it is, honey. It's decaf for you." She poured the steaming coffee into the mug. It fell out in a thick, viscous stream and piled up in heavy layers.

Mallory recoiled from the gloopy mess. "No, please—really...I don't need any coffee. I just need to know where I can find a mechanic." She shook her head. "And I'm not worked up," she added.

Trudy reached across the counter and patted her hand. "It's kinda late for full-on leaded anyway," she said kindly. She clasped Mallory's wrist, the tips of her fingers digging into her skin. "Drink your decaf, sweetie," she said, the kindness on her tongue tinged with steel.

"But I don't—"

"Drink it," Trudy instructed firmly.

"Drink it," the man with the fly on his lip agreed.

"Drink it," said an old woman, her mouth filled with a half-chewed piece of waffle.

"Drink it," intoned a middle-aged man with a syrup-coated chin at a table across the room.

"Drink it," his elderly parents chanted in unison.

"Drink it," Trudy said again, taking Mallory's hand and placing it around the mug. "You should drink it."

Mallory tried to pull her hand free, but the older woman's grip was hard as stone. "I'm really not—I don't—"

Trudy leaned in across the counter so she was close enough for Mallory to smell her perfume. It smelled of gingerbread and honey, and something about it made Mallory feel calmer somehow. "Drink it," Trudy urged yet again, in a gentle whisper this time. "Okay, honey? Just…drink it."

Mallory looked down at the coffee in the mug. It sat there in its sloppy, uneven pile. "It…looks old," she said doubtfully. "And solid."

"It's fresh as fresh is," Trudy whispered. "Drink."

"Drink," the man at the other end of the counter whispered.

"Drink," the woman with the waffle in her mouth whispered.

"Drink," the man with a syrupy chin whispered.

"Drink," his parents whispered together.

Mallory nodded. "Okay, okay," she said, wriggling free of Trudy's grip, "I'll taste it, okay? I'll taste it." She lifted the mug to her nose and sniffed it carefully. It smelled like burnt tires.

She lifted the mug to her lips, closed her eyes, and took a sip… which was really more like a bite. The thick goop spilled over her teeth and coated her tongue. It seemed to expand in her mouth, taking on a life of its own. But it wasn't unpleasant. Not really. It tasted a little sweet, and a little smoky, like blueberries roasted over hickory. Mallory relaxed, the tension melting from her shoulders. She smiled as she set the mug on the counter. "It's…good."

The other patrons broke their stares and returned to their plates, chewing and slurping and talking in hushed tones.

Trudy smiled. "Now that weren't so hard, right?" she said. She slid a menu across the counter and patted it twice. "Take a gander; see what looks good."

Mallory sighed. "Honestly, I'm not hungry," she said, even though she hadn't eaten since breakfast, and now that Trudy mentioned it again, the smell of waffles and syrup was definitely stirring something in her stomach. She thought about the sheriff's deputy standing in front of the collapsed bridge, speaking into his radio and watching her drive away. "What I really need is to get my car fixed...I have to get going."

Trudy shook her head. "There *is* an auto shop, but it's closed now. Don't open 'til 9 tomorrow. Might as well make yourself at home." She patted the menu again. "Take a look. I'll be right back." She shuffled off down the counter to refill the coffee cup in front of the man at the other end, who had resumed his chewing, even though the fly still clung to his bottom lip.

Mallory sighed and sat down on the stool. She let the backpack slide off her shoulders and tucked it between her feet. She slid the menu over; it showed a blue owl wearing dark sunglasses perched on a tree branch with the name of the diner carved into the wood. She flipped the menu open. The pages inside were blank, except for one line in the center of the right-hand page. It read, *Nite-Owl Waffles with Field Mouse Syrup.* There was no price, no further description, and not a single other item on the page. Mallory frowned. "Excuse me," she said, holding up the menu. "Is this everything?"

Trudy squinted at the page from the far end of the counter. "Bless me!" she called, laughing. "Sorry 'bout that, sweetie." She swayed back over to the stack of menus and plucked a new one from the middle. "I gave you the breakfast menu." She slapped the new menu down next to the other. This new cover was nearly identical to the first, except the owl was no longer wearing sunglasses; instead, his eyes were wide open and bloodshot, and there was a mouse tail wriggling out from the side of his beak. "This here's dinner."

"Appetizing," Mallory muttered. She flipped the menu open. The inside was perfectly identical to the inside of the breakfast menu, with the same item listed: *Nite-Owl Waffles with Field Mouse Syrup.* She looked quizzically up at Trudy. "Is this a joke?"

"Come again?"

"Where's the rest?"

"The rest of what?" Trudy asked.

"The menu...where's the rest of the menu? You know—bacon, hash browns? Steak? Club sandwiches with stupid little toothpicks?"

Trudy put her fists on her hips. "You don't like waffles?" The other patrons put down their forks and turned to stare once more.

"No—I do," Mallory said. Then she said it again, louder, so everyone else in the diner could hear. "Really, I do!" They turned slowly back to their plates and resumed eating their waffles. "It's just that...is it all you serve?"

Trudy shrugged. "We tried adding eggs and grits back in '93. It ended badly."

"How can eggs end badly?" Mallory asked.

Trudy sighed. "Ask the seventeen folks who died that day."

Mallory squinted suspiciously across the counter. "Seventeen people died because you served eggs?"

"We don't talk about it with strangers, Trudy," snapped the man at the other end of the counter. He glared at Mallory until she was sure his pupils would burst into flame.

Trudy leaned in close. "One of 'em was Rolly's brother. He gets real touchy about it. Matter of fact, he's the one led the charge to kill every chicken in the township the very next day."

"*What?*"

Trudy nodded. "Every single one. Killed 'em for what their off-spring did to our friends and family. To this day, you won't find a single chicken in Anomaly Flats. If you do, it's an illegal, and you can bet on the body count going up, up, up until someone finds it and breaks its neck."

"Wait, how..." Mallory began.

Trudy pushed on. "Mob tried to burn down the diner, too, like *I* knew what the eggs'd get up to! Hell, I ain't even sure it weren't the grits that done those people in. But it was a bloodbath, you know, and people, when things go sour, they want revenge. The mayor stepped in, though, thank the Lord, said wouldn't no one be burning down the Nite-Owl Diner, home of the best waffles in the quad-counties." Trudy clasped her hands in front of her throat and beamed up at the general direction of the Lord. "The mayor loves my waffles something fierce."

An uncomfortable blanket of itchy-wool silence settled on the diner. The patrons stared at Mallory, and Trudy stared at the air, and Mallory stared down at her menu. "So it's just the waffles, then."

"No one complains much."

"'Cept you," Rolly chipped in sourly.

Mallory shook her head at the two different menus. "Seems like you could've saved on printing," she pointed out.

Trudy cleared her throat and crossed her arms. "Do you want the waffles or don't you?"

Mallory sighed. In spite of her protest—and undeniable weirdness of this place aside—she *was* hungry, and, as a general rule, she *did* like waffles. She wasn't a monster.

"All right," she conceded. "Hit me."

Trudy knocked on the wall above a square opening that led to the kitchen. "Blue plate!" she hollered to whoever was manning the griddle in the back. She glanced over her shoulder and considered Mallory for a few moments before adding, "Hold the extras."

"What extras?" Mallory asked. But either Trudy didn't hear her, or she just ignored the question, and she swished out from behind the counter instead to check on the customers at the tables.

Mallory propped her elbows on the counter and laid her head in her hands, scrubbing her fingers through her increasingly wild hair. "What a nightmare," she muttered. She sat up, swiveled around, and peered out the window at her car, hoping maybe it had fired back up on its own and might be waiting patiently for her to finish eating her coffee and drive it away into the night—out of Missouri, up through the plains, and into Saskatchewan, to Lenore's place, where everything would be okay.

Instead, it just sat there, dark and cold and resolutely broken-down.

"Order up!" Trudy sang out, grabbing a plate from the kitchen window and skimming it down the counter.

Mallory swiveled back and pushed the menus aside as her waffles arrived. There were two of them; crispy, golden-brown, and distinctly of the Belgian variety. A pad of butter slipped over the waffles' little square pockets as it melted. The steam wafted up and teased its way into her nose. It smelled of childhood Sundays.

"They do look good," Mallory admitted, picking up her fork and knife.

Trudy grabbed a half-full syrup dispenser and took the liberty of covering the waffles in field mouse syrup. "Like I said: best waffles in the quad-counties," she repeated proudly. "Enjoy."

And Mallory did enjoy them. She hadn't had waffles in ages—probably twenty years, at least—but the sweet, sticky, buttery flavor brought her right back to spring mornings at her grandmother's farmhouse. She could practically hear the cows and smell the cornbread.

These waffles are magical, she thought.

But they weren't magical enough. They could help her remember, but they couldn't make her forget. Had the deputy back at the bridge recognized her? Had her car been flagged? She'd been careful, but even so...

"Trudy," she said, swallowing down a mouthful of waffle, "that repair shop...you said it's closed until morning?"

"That's right, hon. But no matter the trouble, I'm sure ol' Rufus can fix it in a jiff. Boy's got more heart than brains these days, but I swear, whatever he's got in his head, it's shaped like an engine block."

"What about a dealership? Maybe a used car lot?"

"Gracious! In Anomaly Flats?" she laughed. "I think you've got us confused with Kansas City."

Mallory frowned. "Do you know anyone who's selling a car? Or anyone who *would* sell their car?"

Trudy raised an eyebrow. "Lord, girl. You're anxious to get wheels underfoot, ain't you?"

"I'm..." Mallory paused. "I'm in a hurry," she said finally.

Trudy made a strange noise in the back of her throat. "No matter." She shook her head. "People in this town ain't really much for automobiles."

"What do you mean?" Mallory asked, sliding a piece of waffle around a pool of syrup.

"We don't got much call for 'em. Most people just walk to work, or take the bus, when it decides to run. Probably ain't more than, oh, say, a few dozen or so vehicles total in the Flats. And most of 'em spend more time in Rufus' shop than a cat spends in the sun. We just don't hold for cars 'round here."

"This is insane," Mallory said, more to herself than to her waitress. "What sort of town is this?"

Trudy wiped her hands on the front of her apron. "I know it's none of my business, honey, but you know, Anomaly Flats is a... well, it's a special place. Unique. I don't know why you're in such a twist, but I wouldn't be so quick to leave it behind if I was you. Give it a day or two." She gave Mallory a smile and a cold little wink. "Our little town might just grow on you."

Mallory swallowed down the last bite of her waffle and pushed the plate across the counter. "Sounds like I might not have much of a choice," she said.

Trudy shrugged. "We'll just keep you however we can." She smiled again and cleared the plate and silverware back to the kitchen window. "Seeing how you'll be here for at least the night, you'll want to head on over to the motel. Finest one in Anomaly Flats... the *only* one in Anomaly Flats, too. Just down the block, and right on Aberration Lane. You'll see the sign." She leaned on the counter and whispered conspiratorially, "Tell old Maude I sent you."

"Thanks," Mallory muttered. She picked up her backpack and unzipped it, digging for her wallet, but Trudy held up her hand.

"No charge," she said. "First one's on the house."

Mallory looked up, her eyes skeptical. "I probably won't be back."

Trudy just smiled. "Oh, trust me, darlin'...you'll come back," she said. "And you'll keep coming back, too."

Chapter 3

MALLORY TURNED DOWN ABERRATION LANE and stopped dead in her tracks. "You have *got* to be kidding me."

The hotel wasn't a hotel at all, but a stately Queen Anne-style mansion that perched on a little hillock, looming over the dark street below. It stood three stories tall, and while most of the house was constructed of rough, pebbly blocks of quartz, two towers rose through the stone, edged with smoothly-carved, utterly dark wood. They seemed to have been built from the strongest, darkest trees dragged from the Black Forest and dropped in the middle of Missouri. Antique gaslights were visible through a collection of small windows, set into the house in an odd arrangement, as if the architect had worked on the manor one piece at a time and had never examined the entire picture until he was finished. Floodlights staked into the ground shot streams of harsh light up at the house; its ledges and eaves threw tall, ominous shadows that went leeching up the walls and looming across the roof.

A tall sign rose from the grass just beyond the manor's green wrought iron gate, similarly lit by a too-bright flood lamp. It bore the name of the house in polished iron letters tacked onto a darker metal background.

The finest motel—the *only* motel—in Anomaly Flats was named Roach Motel.

Mallory briefly considered going back to her car and holing up in the backseat for the night. The Impala was comfortable, the locks worked, and there was nothing roachish about it. "But I'm not a hobo," she said through gritted teeth. And that settled it.

She shuffled up the path, which curved from the sidewalk to the front door and was lined on either side by unevenly spaced weeds with long leaves and small bunches of tiny white flowers. The weeds were wild and tangled, but there was a strange sort of or-dered chaos about them…they seemed to have been planted there purposefully. A rich and generous bedding of fresh mulch insulated each plant, and the bed had been recently watered. Given Mallory's attitude regarding nature and her insistence on avoiding it as often as possible, she wasn't terribly keen on the various species of plant, and she didn't know this particular weed from a dandelion. Fortu-nately, a small identifying plaque jutted out from among the thin stalks near the front of the walk, just barely legible in the darkness. It read, "Conium Maculatum (Poison Hemlock). Ingest At Own Peril." Mallory snorted. "Well, worst case scenario, I can off myself and be done with it," she grumbled. And she decided that particu-lar fate truly would be preferable to spending one night covered in skittering, rattling roaches. The thought sent a shiver through her whole body. She considered snapping off a bunch of the little white flowers, just in case the Roach Motel really did live up to its name. "No. Be strong, Mallory," she whispered, patting the Jansport back-pack. "You can live with anything for one night."

Somewhere deep inside, a small part of her wondered if that were actually true.

A tiny bell jingled above the door as she entered the house. The entryway was spotless; the windows sparkled with reflections of a brass gaslight chandelier that hung gracefully from the high ceil-ing; a low bench to the left was upholstered in deep red velvet that had been recently brushed; the maple wood floor had been pol-ished to a high glow. A withered old woman stood primly behind a stately oak counter on the opposite side of the foyer. Her bones were wrapped in wrinkled, papery skin, and her long, silver hair was pulled back into an oppressively tight bun. She wore a deep red crepe dress with a high collar buttoned to the throat. The flickering light of the chandelier threw dark, hollow shadows into her gaunt cheeks and cast a sinister glow in her eyes, dull brown in color, but sharp as steel. She clasped her hands in front of her waist, her long, thin fingers intertwining like gnarled tree roots. "Can I help you?" she asked. Her voice was wind blowing through a tunnel.

"Do you—" Mallory began.

The old woman cut her off sharply. "Close the door."

"Oh. Sorry." Mallory shut the door and turned to begin again. "Do—"

"Lock it."

Mallory hesitated. "Lock—lock it?" The old woman said nothing. "It wasn't locked when I…" Her voice trailed off. The look in the woman's eyes left no room for argument. "Okay," she said, throwing the bolt. It slid easily into place with a *click*. "Are you closed now, or…?"

"The Roach Motel is *never* closed," the old woman intoned. "There are things in the yard tonight that are best kept at bay. Did you not hear them coming up the walk?"

Mallory smoothed down her hair and brushed off her t-shirt, suddenly feeling self-conscious. "Uh…no. No, I didn't." She clutched her backpack tighter.

"They must have been watching you very intently," the old woman said, narrowing her eyes. "I wonder why that would be."

"I…I don't know." Mallory crossed the foyer uneasily and approached the desk. "Do you have a room available? For the night?"

"All of the rooms are available, and have been for some time," the old woman said. "We don't entertain many guests." She spoke almost suspiciously, as if the thought of Mallory's money were somehow off-putting.

"I can't imagine why…everyone's been so hospitable," Mallory said, rolling her eyes. *Easy, easy*, she reprimanded herself. *This woman is going to have keys to the room where you sleep tonight.*

"Most people pass this town by," the old woman continued. If she caught Mallory's sarcasm, she didn't let on. "But not you."

Mallory shrugged. "Nope. Not me." Then she added, "Just lucky, I guess."

The old woman raised an eyebrow. "Are you?"

Mallory blinked. "Listen, I'm sorry, it's been a really long day. Do you think I could get my room key and head up? Or down—or wherever you keep the guests?"

The old woman sniffed at this but turned to the wall behind her just the same. It was dotted with a dozen wooden pegs. Each held a ring full of keys. "How many nights?" she asked, running her hands along the keys as if feeling for the perfect set.

"Just one."

"Hmm…" The woman's hand stopped at a particularly dusty ring on the bottom row. "This one, I think." She grabbed the keys off the peg and laid them before her guest. "Thirty dollars a night. If you stay more than three nights, you have to pay a week's deposit up front. Otherwise, you pay when you check out."

"That'll be tomorrow."

"We'll see." The old woman picked up an old ledger, an old-fashioned ink pen, and a full inkwell from somewhere below the counter. A cloud of dust puffed into the air as she opened the ledger. She waved it away and turned to the next blank page. Then she picked up the pen and dipped the nib into the ink. "Name?"

"Mallory Jenkins," she said automatically. Then she winced. *Fake name, idiot,* she chided herself. *Use a fake name, for crying out loud.*

"I'm Mrs. Roach," the old woman said, writing Mallory's name down in the book.

"Oh! Ha. *Roach* Motel," Mallory said, suddenly smiling. "That makes me feel better."

"It shouldn't. The cockroaches are nicer than I am," the old woman muttered, slamming the book shut. "Or so I'm told." She eyed Mallory's backpack warily. "Luggage?" she asked.

"Just this," Mallory said, hiking the Jansport higher on her shoulder. The old woman narrowed her eyes in disapproval.

"We prefer not to welcome transients," she said sharply.

"*Transients*? I'm not a *transient*." She shifted the weight of the bag. "I'm...just an efficient packer."

The old woman made a strange sound in the bottom of her throat and slid the ring of keys across the counter. "You're in Room 205. Up the stairs, down the hall, to the left. The linens are fresh. The washroom's at the end of the hall. Don't make a mess of it. Any questions?"

"Which key is it?" Mallory asked, picking up the ring.

Mrs. Roach straightened her back. "All of them."

Mallory furrowed her brow as she did a quick count. "There are...seven keys on this ring."

"And there's a piece of chalk on your desk, with instructions on how to draw the protection runes."

Mallory tilted her head. "Did you say protection runes?" she asked.

"Draw them right, or they'll be less than useless," she said. "Or don't draw them at all. Makes no difference to me."

"Seven keys and a chalk drawing. Sounds a *tad* like overkill."

"Overkill is precisely what I'm trying to avoid," the old woman replied. "There's no telephone in the room. If you need anything, you'll have to come down here and ask for it. Lights out by 10:00, please. It's in less than an hour."

Mallory snorted. "I think your clock might be fast," she said, glancing down at her wristwatch. "It's only..." She stopped mid-sentence, and her eyebrows knitted themselves together in confusion. Her watch marked the time at ten past nine...but how was that possible? She'd sat in the diner for no more than half an hour, and the sun had just set when she reached Anomaly Flats. At this time of year, that should put her at 7:00 at the latest. "Huh," she said, more to herself than to her host. "I must've lost track of time."

"See that you find it again soon," Mrs. Roach snapped. "Checkout is at 11:00 am sharp. If you miss it for any reason, you'll be charged for a second night."

Mallory rubbed her forehead with one hand and jangled the keys in the other. Her body seemed to tilt and swim with disorientation. She was usually so good about time...how had it gotten away from her? "11:00. Got it. Thanks." She turned and headed up the staircase, into the flickering gaslight flames of the second story.

The old woman's lips curled into a smile as she watched her go.

CHAPTER 4

THE SECOND-STORY HALLWAY of the Roach Motel was tidy, and clean, and utterly disturbing. Mallory couldn't quite put her finger on it, but something about the hall seemed off somehow. Maybe it was the flickering lights casting harsh, wavering shadows that stretched across the walls. Maybe it was the two orderly rows of doors, standing strong and solid, like silent sentinels. Maybe it was the fact that there was nothing but emptiness behind those doors, and she was alone in a new and unsettling house in a new and unsettling town.

"Or maybe it's the fact that the carpet is ugly as shit," she muttered aloud.

It was dark brown, which was the main source of awfulness. But it wasn't the *only* source. Mustard-yellow paisley dotted the brown plush runner, and threads of pale pink were inexplicably woven in throughout the pattern. The flickering lamps did all they could to hide the awful thing in shadows, but Mallory couldn't help but think that the flames might be of better use setting fire to the whole carpet and ridding the world of its hideousness altogether.

Room 205 was located halfway down the hall, on the left. There was nothing particularly notable about the door; it was solid, surely, with a small brass number plate. It held only one keyhole.

"Of course," Mallory sighed, staring miserably at the seven keys in her hand. "Because why not?"

She picked out the right key on the third try, an old-fashioned thing with rectangular teeth and a bow that was molded into a flourishing brass wreath. It fit snugly in the lock, and it took a bit of coaxing, but soon the key turned, and Mallory opened the door to her room. It was modest, but it appeared comfortable enough. It contained a four-poster bed that looked as if it should be draped with some sort of linen, but instead, the posts stood empty and naked. That was fine with Mallory; she was prone to claustrophobia anyway. There was also a nightstand, a dresser, and an armchair that looked stiff and uncomfortable. It sat next to a window with plain lace curtains overlooking the unremarkable side yard of the house.

Mallory breathed a sigh of relief. After the day she'd had, she'd half-expected the room to be coated in moss or writhing with worms. Instead, it appeared recently cleaned and properly made up, and that was somehow refreshing.

She set the keys on the dresser, tossed the backpack onto the bed, and did a quick search of the room, hoping to find a safe. "No such luck." She picked up the backpack and tucked it under the bed. "You stay down there," she warned, "or we're going to have problems."

Exhaustion crept in on her, so she tested the bed. The springs creaked a bit when she sat down, but the mattress was firm, and it would serve for a decent night's sleep. "One night," she reminded the flower-patterned wallpaper. "I'll be fine here for one night."

Even though she had no pajamas to change into, she decided to freshen up before bed. She grabbed the ring of keys and started for the door, heading for the washroom.

That was when she saw them—the seven individual locks.

Mallory frowned. "Now where did you come from?" she asked. She opened the door and inspected the other side. Seven separate locks now ran in a vertical line above the handle. Mallory shook her head and sighed. "I'm losing my mind."

It wasn't really all that surprising, under the circumstances.

She stepped into the hall and closed the door behind her. Then she locked just the one lock—the one nearest the handle, the one made to fit the old-fashioned key...and she wasn't entirely sure even *that* one was necessary, considering that it was just her and Old Lady Roach in the house. If her bag went missing while she was out, there wouldn't be any great mystery as to who was responsible.

She swung the keys on the ring as she trod down the awful carpet, whistling a tuneless little nothing and making a mental list of the things she'd do when she finally reached Lenore's place.

A bath first, with bubbles. Fancy bubbles. The fanciest bubbles Canada's got. And a bottle of something expensive. Champagne, probably. Or Scotch. Or Champagne and Scotch. A bottle in each hand. Yep. Then, a feast. Not a dinner; a fucking feast. The main course should be something endangered. Bluefin tuna or a Bengal tiger. A Bluefin tuna stuffed inside a Bengal tiger. And roasted over rain forest wood. After that—

Her thoughts were interrupted by a loud *WHUMP!* from the door to her right.

Mallory jumped and threw herself back against the wall. She gasped, clutching at her heart. "Hello?" she said, but her voice caught in her throat, and the word died as soon as it left her lips. She summoned her courage and said, louder, "Hello?"

She crept closer to the door. She could hear nothing but the buzzing in her own ears. *Must've been a tree or something. Outside.* She eyed the door suspiciously. Room 210. "There's no one else here," she reminded herself. "Just Mrs. Cockroach and me." She placed her palms against the door, leaned forward, and pressed her ear to the wood.

WHUMP!

Something slammed into the door from the inside, rattling the thing in its frame.

Mallory screamed. She sprinted to the washroom and slammed the door behind her. She turned the lock and leaned back against the wood, shaking and panting and wiping sweat from her palms. "Holy hell," she whispered, trying to catch her breath. "Come on,

Mallory. Get a grip." So Mrs. Roach had lied about the hotel's occu-pancy. So what? It was weird, but it wasn't a big deal. "I'm just going to murder her, is all."

She shook out her hands and stepped up to the pedestal sink. The mirror hanging above it was a simple oval, big enough for her to get a full view of herself. "Woof," she sighed, dragging her hands through her hair and pulling at the dark circles under her eyes.

"Life on the road does *not* agree with you," said mirror Mallory.

"Shut up," said Mallory.

She noticed a bump on her forehead, just above her right eye… but she couldn't remember how she'd gotten it. "Stress is eating my brain," she decided. She touched it gingerly. It only hurt a little, and it didn't look particularly irritated. She counted that as a win. Then she turned on the sink tap, and brown water spurted out of the faucet.

She sighed again.

She waited for the pipes to clear, rolling a rubber band from her wrist and tying her hair back, inspecting for grays along the way. There were more today than yesterday—no doubt about it. She grunted and closed her eyes, then leaned over and splashed a hand-ful of water over her face.

Tap water had never felt so good.

With the first splash, she forgot all about how a sky full of twinkling stars almost became an accessory to her death. With the second, the memory of waffles and mass poultrycide melted com-pletely from her brain. With the third, even the thoughts of a door with seven locks and a mysterious thumping from a room that was supposed to be empty seemed to drift off into the ether. After a few more rinses, she was just Mallory—driven, lovable, crazy old Mallory, out in the world, just a step or two removed from her reg-ularly-scheduled life.

Then she opened her eyes and saw a cockroach squirming out of the drain, and that pretty much ended the fantasy.

Mallory jumped with a cry of disgust and instinctively pulled the stopper closed. She pulled hard; the metal plug slammed down against the drain, slicing the cockroach in half.

"Oh, God, I'm gonna puke." She threw a hand over her mouth, hurried over to the toilet, and threw open the lid. But the vomit didn't come. It seemed to lodge itself somewhere in the upper parts of her soul, her nausea burning through her chest and souring the further reaches of her stomach instead. "Well, I just want to die," she decided.

The water was still running. As she reached over and turned off the faucet, some part of her—some sick, twisted, sociopathic part—wanted to see the half-roach drifting in the pool of water, if for no other reason than to lord her dominance over the recently-murdered pest. A nuclear blast couldn't kill a cockroach, but Mallory Jenkins could. There was a special sort of pride in that.

She steeled her roiling insides and took a deep breath. Then she turned and looked down at the half-roach as triumphantly as she could. Her glory was slightly dampened by the fact that the half-roach was still moving. No...not just moving; *squirming*. It writhed through the bowl of steaming water, curling and uncurling and thrashing softly in the depths. Mallory's eyes grew wide with fascinated horror as she drew nearer the disgusting scene to get a better look. With her chin just a few inches from the surface of the water, she realized that the thing she'd sliced in the sink wasn't a cockroach at all.

It was something else entirely.

It was small, and black, and shaped almost like a cone. It seemed smooth and slippery, except for the underside, which was pocked with tiny circles that seemed to be able to grip the smooth, sloping sides of the sink bowl. It looked like the arm of a small, black starfish.

"Not an arm," she whispered, peering down into the water. "A tentacle."

And even severed from its host, the slimy little thing was still alive.

Mallory threw open the door and half-ran, half-stumbled back to her room. She plied the lock with shaking hands, threw herself inside, slammed the door shut, and managed to lock all seven locks in what was probably record time, under the circumstances. Then she gripped the doorknob and gave it a good twist. Thankfully, it held fast, as if cemented in place. She pulled and shook and heaved at the door, but it staunchly refused to budge. There were seven large, metal bolts holding the thing in place. It would take a hell of a lot more than a thump of a tentacle to burst through the damn thing. Even so, she decided not to take any chances. She rummaged through the dresser until she found the piece of white chalk resting atop a handwritten note on Roach Motel stationery. The small, tight scrawl at the top of the page read, "Elder Futhark Protection Symbols." Mallory didn't typically go in for the occult…but she didn't typically go in for tentacles slithering out of sink drains, either. She sketched the provided runes onto the door, three concentric circles of esoteric nonsense just below the peephole.

She backed away, chalk in hand, and considered her work. "Just one night," she reminded herself, her voice trembling. "You can survive anything for one night."

She closed the curtains and was about to climb into bed when she noticed something she hadn't before: a bottle of wine stood innocently on the nightstand, though Mallory was certain it hadn't been there when she'd arrived. She picked it up and inspected the label. It boasted an illustration of a silver flying saucer sucking up an oversized bunch of grapes in its tractor beam. "Neptune Norton," Mallory read. "U.F.O. Vineyards." According to the fine print, U.F.O. stood for Unidentified Fermented Object. The bottle was tied off around the neck with a small tag that read, *Welcome to Anomaly Flats. Enjoy a little local flavor.* It claimed to have a surprisingly high alcohol content—18%, which Mallory decided might be just enough. She peeked beneath the bed to make sure the backpack was still safe and sound, then she climbed into bed, fully clothed, and screwed off the cap. She propped herself up on the pillows, clutched the blanket to her chest, and took a few slugs of Neptune Norton straight from the bottle. It tasted like cherries and plums and oak and tar, and it made the tips of her ears tingle with warmth. *That'll do*, she thought.

Between the exhaustion of the day and the wine in her hand, it wasn't long before a bone-weary sleepiness crept in on her. She scooted down into the sheets and lay back against the pillows. She tried her best to block out the last 24 hours and to focus on the next: waking up, checking out, getting her car fixed, leaving Anomaly Flats, and chalking it all up to a particularly lucid fever dream.

Yes, she decided, *tomorrow will definitely be better.*

CHAPTER 5

MALLORY AWOKE with a start.

Watery sunlight filtered in through the curtains, and despite the extremely convincing nightmare she'd just woken up from, when she looked under the sheets, all her various parts and pieces were accounted for, and she was one whole Mallory.

She glanced over at the nightstand and, with no surprise at all, saw that only a few inches of Neptune Norton remained in the bottle. She yawned, and she stretched, and she said, "Ah, what the hell," as she picked up the bottle and finished it off.

She groaned her way out of bed and rubbed some life into her cheeks. Between the wine and the sleep, her breath was a horror. But she hadn't packed a toothbrush ("Because who has time for necessities, dummy?" she chided herself), and even if she had packed one, returning to the washroom was completely out of the question. The world would just have to deal.

She grabbed her backpack from under the bed and unzipped it to make sure she hadn't been robbed by phantoms in the night. Everything was accounted for. She closed it back up, slung it over her shoulder, and grabbed the ring of keys. As she made her way to the door, she noticed that the entire first circle of Elder Futhark runes and part of the second had faded into a smear of chalk dust, as if something had been rubbing away at them with its sleeve while she slept. "Good riddance," she muttered, emboldened by the daylight, or maybe the alcohol. She smeared the rest of the runes with her hand, unlocked the seven locks, stepped into the hall, and ambled down the stairs. She didn't bother to close the door behind her.

"Sleep well?" Mrs. Roach asked, standing stiff as a board behind the counter. She wore the same crepe dress, and her hair was still pulled back tightly. Mallory wondered if she'd moved so much as a finger through the night.

"Eventually," Mallory said. "You have squids in your drains."

The old woman snorted. "Squids, yet. They're not squids, girlie. They're something else entirely. And they keep the rats away."

"Well, one of them lost a finger."

"It will grow back."

Mallory shook her head, bewildered. Morning wine or no morning wine, this was too much. "You have something with *tentacles* living in your *plumbing*, and you're totally fine with it?" she demanded.

Mrs. Roach narrowed her eyes at her guest. "There are worse things in the world than tentacles."

"No—there aren't...that's the point! There is nothing worse than a mutant squid living in your walls!"

The old woman smirked. "You must not be from Missouri."

"I *am* from Missouri," Mallory said stubbornly, "the part of Missouri where weird-ass shit comes in the cable package and not in through your front door." She slammed her backpack down on the counter and pulled out her wallet. "How much?"

"Will you be staying another night?"

Mallory stared at her. "Are you kidding me? I'd rather eat your hemlock."

"Be careful what you wish for," the old woman said, her papery voice rustling across the desk. "Your bill is thirty dollars."

"Any breakfast recommendations?" she muttered, pulling a few bills from her wallet and tossing them down, along with the keys.

"Try the Nite-Owl Diner."

Mallory shook her head. "Hilarious. What else you got?"

"The Nite-Owl is the only breakfast establishment in town."

"How is that even possible?" Mallory balked.

The old woman shrugged. "There used to be a restaurant called the Blue Bottle, a few years back. It imploded."

"It *imploded*?"

"Yes…sucked itself into a tight little ball of drywall and metal."

Mallory squinted. "An entire building did that?"

"The town council warned them not to build a restaurant on a gravitational deviation. Too bad, too…the Blue Bottle served eggs—*proper* eggs, mind you, not the abominations that we do not speak of."

Gravitational deviation… Mallory shook her head. "And there's nothing else?"

"There's a Chick-fil-A in town, out on Route 83. It doesn't open until 10:00."

Mallory started. "You have a Chick-fil-A?"

It was the old woman's turn to squint. "Yes. Out on Route 83. But it doesn't open until 10:00."

"Right." She sighed and stuffed her wallet back into the bag. "Well, thanks for the hospitality." She threw the backpack over her shoulder and headed for the door. "Oh," she added dryly, "the guest in 210 has violent tendencies. You might want to have housekeeping check for incidentals."

The old woman cocked her head at an odd angle. "There are no other guests," she said, following Mallory to the door and latching it shut behind her. Mallory could just hear Mrs. Roach's final words through the glass: "No one else has been here for years."

No one but the tentacle monsters, Mallory thought.

She groaned as she rounded the corner of Aberration Lane and saw the sign for the Nite-Owl Diner again. She considered skipping breakfast altogether, but the early morning wine wasn't exactly sitting well in her stomach, and she had almost two hours to kill before she could get her car to the mechanic. The waffle from the night before couldn't tide her over forever. *You survived the night,* she thought, continuing toward the diner. *You can survive a few more hours.*

A metallic screech pierced the air. Mallory screamed and leapt at the sound. Above her, fixed to a tall wooden pole, was an old loudspeaker. It was shaped like a bullhorn and had once been mint green, but now it was mostly brown with rust. Mallory clutched her heart, which thumped heavily in her chest as the speaker squeaked and crackled to life.

"Attention, Anomaly Flats." A sharp, female voice crackled through the speaker. *"Today's Air Quality Index color is periwinkle. Be advised that breathing may cause irregular life conditions. All citizens breathe at their own risk. The Walmart is having a sale on canned tuna this week, three cans for $2.49. The Walmart would like to remind you that the canned tuna is in Aisle 3, not in aisle 8, and it is perfectly safe there. Attention, Anomaly Flats: Do not go into aisle 8 in the Walmart. Do not go into the Walmart. Do not ever go into the Walmart."*

The voice cut out, and after a few last squeaks and pops, the speaker went dead. Mallory stared at it, her mouth hanging open. Finally she sighed, shook her head, and headed down the block. "I've *got* to get out of here," she mumbled.

On the way to the Nite-Owl, she passed her poor, broken-down Impala on the side of the street.

It was even more broken now than it had been when she'd left it.

"Oh, no no no no! What the *fuck*?!" Her hands flew to the front passenger door, which now bore a deep, crumpled gash that started below the mirror and continued almost all the way to the handle of the back door. The silver paint had been scraped and ground away. "What the *fuuuck?*" Mallory cried again for emphasis as she ran her hands along the gash. "Were you attacked by a bear?!" Her face burned red with anger. She didn't know which inbred, meth-head, hillbilly kid in this upside-down town had done this to her car, but she sure as shit was going to find out.

She burst into the diner so hard, the door slammed against the wall and rattled the windows.

"Well, look what the cat dragged in!" Trudy beamed from behind the register. "Welcome back, honey. What'll it be today?"

"Did you see who did it?" Mallory seethed through clenched teeth.

Trudy frowned. "See who did what?" She set a cup and saucer on the counter and trotted off to fetch the coffee.

"Some asshole kid smashed up the side of my car!"

Trudy chuckled a bit. "Oh, I doubt that very much."

"See for yourself." Mallory pointed a vicious finger out the window toward her car.

Trudy returned to the counter with a pot of coffee, craning her neck to get a good view. She nodded slowly. "That's a dinger, all right. Caffeinated okay? We don't brew the unleaded 'til about 10 or 11 most days."

Mallory was in no mood for coffee talk. "A dinger? A fucking *dinger*? It's practically a *trench*! I'm going to find the kid who did it and run him over like a dog," she growled. "Once the fucking car is fixed."

Trudy paused, coffee pot in hand, as if she wasn't quite sure Mallory needed an extra jolt of caffeine today. "You run over dogs?"

Mallory collapsed onto the stool and buried her face in her hands. "It's a figure of speech," she said.

Trudy planted her free hand on her hip. "I've never heard it." She poured the coffee. "You take it slow with this, hear?"

Mallory rubbed her hands down her face and slapped some life into her cheeks. "I'm sorry," she sighed. "It's…been a long 24 hours."

"Seems like it," Trudy agreed. "I don't know how your car got scratched, but I can promise you it weren't no kids."

"Oh yeah? And how do you know that?"

"'Cause there *ain't* no kids in Anomaly Flats. We haven't had any births in almost thirty years."

Mallory started. "How is that possible? Don't people—you know…" She made a strange looping gesture with her hand. It wasn't biologically accurate, but the point was clear enough.

"Course we do. But everyone in Anomaly Flats is sterile."

Mallory choked on her coffee, and a fine brown splatter of thick globs shot onto the counter. She wiped her mouth with her arm. "*Everyone*?"

Trudy smiled as she grabbed a towel and mopped up the coffee. "Oh, don't worry, hon, it's all voluntary." She thought for a minute, then asked, "Do you *not* want to be sterilized?"

"No!"

"Hmm…" She picked up Mallory's coffee cup and dumped its contents into the sink. "Better wait for the decaf, then." She picked up a menu and slid it beneath Mallory's downcast eyes. "Now, what'll it be for breakfast, sweetie?"

Mallory glanced up at the waitress. "Are you serious?"

"Well, sure. Ain't you gonna eat?"

"Sure, Trudy. I'll have the country fried steak and eggs over easy, with a side of hash browns and a bowl of fruit."

Trudy frowned. "We don't serve eggs. Not since—"

"I know, I know. Not since '93." Mallory laid her palms flat on the counter and resisted the urge to ball them into fists and smash them straight through something. "Guess I'll just have the waffles, then."

"Good choice," Trudy winked. She whirled away and handed the order through the kitchen window, leaving Mallory alone at the counter to die a little more inside with each passing second.

X

"I have to get out of this town," Mallory said to Rufus, the mechanic. "Do you think you can fix it?"

Rufus was a tall man, lean and wiry, and his age was impossible to determine. He was completely bald; he had no hair on his head, or on his arms, or anywhere else Mallory could see. He had smooth ridges where his eyebrows should have been, and it creeped Mallory right the hell out. He pulled the lever on the antique tow truck and lowered the Impala down to the asphalt. The mechanism whined. "I can fix it," he replied. His voice was deep and hollow, a voice that would have been right at home in a cartoon about bored ghosts.

"You haven't even looked at it yet...are you sure?"

Rufus nodded. "I'm sure."

Mallory breathed a sigh of hopeful relief.

A little line of drool spilled over Rufus' jaw and dribbled down onto the parking lot below. If it bothered him, he didn't show it. "Your alternator's out."

Mallory looked disgustedly at the stream of spittle as it continued flowing from Rufus' mouth. "Umm...oh. Good. Wait—*is* that good?"

Rufus shook his head. "No. It's bad." The tow truck's high-pitched whirring stopped, and the Impala settled on the parking lot as he went to work unhitching the car.

"But how do you know it's the alternator if you haven't looked?" Mallory prodded.

"It's always the alternator."

"Always?"

"Yup." Rufus drooled on the bumper, but was polite enough to wipe away the little puddle of spit with the hem of his shirt.

Mallory waited for more information, but none seemed poised to sally forth. "And...why is that?"

Rufus opened the car's door to pop the hood. "Magnetic fields." Mallory cringed at the thought of his drool pooling on the floorboard. He circled back and opened the hood, then went into the tow truck and came out with a little yellow box with a circular dial. Two cords snaked out of the bottom, one black and one red.

"Magnetic fields," Mallory repeated. It became abundantly clear that the mechanic wasn't going to give up any information without a fight. "You *have* them? Or you *need* them?"

Rufus tucked himself into the engine and started clipping the little red and black cords to a big block next to the battery. "We have them. Strong. Way too strong for computers." He fiddled with the yellow box for a few seconds before unclipping the cords and closing the hood of the car. "Yep…it's the alternator," he confirmed.

Mallory stuck her hands in her pockets to avoid having them splashed as he swung his head around. "Okay. So how long will it take?"

Rufus rubbed his jaw thoughtfully. His hand came away wet. "Shouldn't be more than two or three days."

Mallory started. "Two or three *days?* No, no, no, no, no…I have to get out of here *now*—like, *today!*" She noticed that he wasn't wearing a wedding ring and considered flirting her way to faster service. But historically speaking, her attempts to come across as coquettish and sexy usually ended up with her tripping and falling, and that was unlikely to help. So instead, she clasped her hands beneath her chin and said, as sweetly as she could, "Please can you fix it faster than that?"

Rufus shook his head. "Takes a while to build one. Two, three days."

"*Build* one?" Mallory was no mechanic, but she was a reasonably good Capitalist. "Couldn't you just buy one?"

Rufus slurped at the drool spilling out through his bottom teeth. "No one delivers out here. Got to make one."

"Come on," Mallory said. "No one?"

"No one."

"Surely *someone* does. You get mail, right? And UPS? And FedEx?"

Rufus tilted his head to let a small lake of spittle run out the side of his mouth. "You-pee-what?"

"UPS! I love logistics! What can brown do for you! Ultimate Package Service! UPS!"

Rufus shook his head. "Doesn't ring a bell."

"But you get mail at least," she insisted.

Rufus shrugged. "Nope."

"What do you mean, 'Nope'? You don't get *mail*?"

"Not since the 90s." He scratched his ear. "We *do* get messages by government-sponsored drone."

"Whoa, whoa, whoa. You have government drones?"

Rufus nodded. "For messages."

"How do *they* not get their alternators scrambled?"

"Don't know," Rufus shrugged. "Part of what makes the government so terrifying."

Mallory's brain felt like it was developing a stutter. "This is ludicrous," she said. "No outside mail or deliveries since the 90s? How do you *get* things?"

"We don't get things," he said, stowing the little yellow box back inside the tow truck. "We make them."

Mallory shook her head and started pacing the parking lot. "Insane," she grumbled. "Buy an alternator online—Amazon Prime or Google Express! Have *them* send it by drone!"

Rufus whipped a greasy handkerchief from behind the seat of the truck and used it to wipe off his hands. It caked his hands with more dirt than it removed. "What's that?" he asked.

"What's *what*?" Mallory wondered if anyone had ever died from total exasperation, or if she'd be the first.

"Amazon Primer Google Express."

Mallory gaped. "Are you kidding me right now? You don't know what *Google* is?!"

Rufus wiped his wet lips on his shoulder. "Nope."

"Do you even own a computer?"

"No. No computers in town," he said. "Magnetic fi—"

"Right, right," Mallory waved him off. "Magnetic fields." She stopped pacing and leaned against the fender of her poor Impala. "So no one ever comes through here? No one drives into town and says, 'Whoops, made a wrong turn, now I'm in weirdo hell'?"

Rufus shrugged. "You did. Other than that…"

A thought occurred to her. "What about emergency vehicles?" she asked. "Fire trucks or ambulances? Or police?"

"We don't have any fire trucks or ambulances. You get injured or burned down in Anomaly Flats, you're on your own. We do have a sheriff. But I reckon he's unconnected from outside police, what without a phone and all."

Mallory furrowed her brow. "Your sheriff doesn't have a phone?"

"Wouldn't do much good."

"Magnetic fields," they said together. Mallory crossed her arms and considered that. "Huh." If the sheriff lived in an informational bubble, maybe Anomaly Flats wasn't such a bad way station after all…

But still. It was no Saskatchewan. It was no Lenore's. She'd stumbled across the town; surely a motivated police force could do the same. "Listen, Rufus: I'll pay you a million dollars for your tow truck," she said.

"Nah. Couldn't find a new one old enough."

"That…doesn't make sense."

"Does too." There was practically a river of drool streaming down the asphalt and spilling into the street now. "The only vehicles that work with any reliability are the ones made before computers, like ol' Fanny here." He patted the antique tow truck and left behind a handprint of mucous. "I sell her to you, I got to buy a new one that's old enough."

"I don't care about any of this," she sighed quietly. "I was joking, anyway."

"Sounded pretty serious."

"About the million dollars, I mean."

Rufus shrugged again. "Don't matter either way."

Mallory couldn't argue anymore. "No. I guess it doesn't."

"I can probably have it running for you day after tomorrow," he told her. "I'll try, anyhow. I can fix that door, too. Pop it out, touch it up, if you want. Won't cost no million dollars, either. You want me to do that?"

Mallory rolled her eyes. "No, thanks...I like it like that."

Rufus grimaced. "You do?"

"No, obviously I don't like it like that. Who am I, Jed Clampett?"

"Jed who?" Rufus asked.

"Never mind...just add it to the punch list," she said, swirling a finger through the air.

"Will do." Rufus tipped his head back, and Mallory could hear the soft gulping as he swallowed a bucket of his own spit. "Anything else I can do for you?"

Mallory sighed. One way or another, she was going to have to face it: she was stuck in Anomaly Flats, at least for a little while.

"Yeah," she said, closing her eyes and shaking her head ruefully. "Got any tips for killing time in this town?"

CHAPTER 6

THE BUILDING HAD BEEN A PIZZA HUT in some former, failed life. It retained all the telltale signs: sad, brown, clapboard siding accented by sad, brown brick; red wooden shutters, at least half of which had fallen off and rotted away; a wide parking lot of faded blacktop that was more weeds than asphalt; and, of course, the uniquely-shaped red tile roof that looked like a giant fedora designed by a troll. But time had marched on, and it had left stuffed crusts and P'Zones behind. The Pizza Hut had long since gone out of business, and the signage had been taken down and replaced with a hand-painted banner that read, "Anomaly Flats Department of Tourism."

The structure sat back about a quarter-mile off the main drag, surrounded by nothing but the vacated lots of similarly-doomed chains—the husk of a Del Taco; the crumbling shell of a Circuit City; the collapsing ruin of what might have once been a Chuck E. Cheese. It was in a prime location for being completely ignored, which Mallory supposed was probably fine, since tourism didn't exactly seem to be a booming enterprise in Anomaly Flats.

It was hard not to notice the flies as she approached the building. They buzzed around the entrance in a small, black cloud. She swatted her way through them, her stomach turning a bit as she felt their little bodies bump up against her hands. They scattered a bit, but didn't seem too intent on going far from the tourism office. There was a smell in the air, too, something a little sweet…and also a little sour. "If something's dead in here, I'm going to napalm everything," she swore.

She stepped up to the door and peered in. Florescent lights buzzed and flickered, and a woman slouched behind a folding table that served as a makeshift desk. For a second, Mallory thought she might actually be dead. But then her chest rose and fell with breath, and she decided that the woman was probably just bored.

She gave the flies one last swat and pushed open the door. The decorator hadn't done much to cover up the skeleton of the old Pizza Hut. Half of the brownish-red tile floor was covered by a dark, thin, threadbare carpet. The kitchen area was closed off by a series of shower curtains hanging from a clothesline that stretched across the south end of the building. The tables and chairs had been cleared away, but the salad bar remained, though thankfully the salad and fixings had been removed at some point in the last ten years. Now the buffet was host to a litany of pamphlets on Anomaly Flats' finest tourist traps. There actually seemed to be quite a few.

There was even a lone travel poster tacked up on one of the walls, over by the restrooms. It boasted a faded illustration of a fast food restaurant. The big, bold lettering read, *VISIT THE ANOMALY FLATS CHICK-FIL-A! YOU HAVE TO; IT'S THE LAW.*

"No wonder you never get visitors," Mallory muttered.

The woman behind the table was smallish in size, with curly brown hair that appeared to behave with quite a bit of autonomy; it went in every direction but down. She wore a blue Hawaiian shirt that was two sizes too big, and her bare feet peeked out from beneath the table. She was reclining as much as her hard metal folding chair would allow. Her eyes were closed, and her hands were folded against her chest.

"Excuse me?" Mallory said, leaning her hands down on the folding table. "Miss?" She snapped her fingers, but the woman did not wake up. "I'm desperate to know about all the creepy glories your town has to offer. Preferably the ones not near main highways or sheriff departments. And also, within walking distance," she added. "That's important." The woman in the chair didn't stir.

Mallory put her fists on her hips and frowned. Then she yelled, "HEY—WAKE UP!"

The woman started. The chair threatened to tip over, taking her with it, but a quick windmilling of her arms set it back down with a *thud*. She blinked her eyes open, and Mallory gasped. The woman had no irises...just two pupils swimming in two pools of milky white.

"I...like your eyes. The contacts," she said, trying to keep her voice from trembling. "Very...something." She didn't know why she was letting herself be so affected by every bizarre turn her life took in this town. Shouldn't she *expect* the woman behind the table to have pure white eyes? Hell, shouldn't she be more surprised that she had any sort of eyes at all? "Rufus sent me over," she continued, tugging self-consciously on the shoulder straps of the backpack. "He said you'd know some good sites to see..."

The woman stared with her pinpoint eyes. Her palms rested flat on the table, and a fly landed between them.

"So then," Mallory said, wondering why she'd even bothered in the first place. "Got any good recommendations, or...?"

The woman nodded. Then she opened her mouth, and her jaw fell open wide...*hugely* wide—so wide that it couldn't possibly open so completely without unhinging itself. It fell and fell and fell, and her mouth stretched and stretched and stretched, until it was wide enough to fit a football, end to end, between her top and bottom teeth. She hissed, a dry, rattling sound from the depths of her throat, and Mallory heard a loud buzzing. A massive swarm of flies exploded from the woman's mouth. They poured out from between her teeth in a black, buzzing tidal wave, crashing over her chin and gushing into the air. The office became so thick with flies that Mallory couldn't see the woman anymore. The buzzing jackhammered against her ears. She screamed and swatted wildly, pushing against so many flies with each swing, she could have swum through them. They covered her like a blanket as still more poured out of the woman's mouth. A thick knot of flies flew into Mallory's own mouth, wide open and screaming. She clamped it shut, spitting and retching and clawing the insects away from her face.

She ducked her head and ran blindly toward the door. She smashed into it, bounced hard, then lowered her shoulder and rammed it again, throwing it open. She tripped over the jamb and tumbled out onto the overgrown parking lot as the flies that broke free spiraled up into the sky, leaving her heaving and writhing on the ground.

A pair of hands reached down and seized her under the shoulders. She screamed as hard as she could without opening her mouth and thrashed at the arms that gripped her, running her nails down them and drawing blood.

"Ow! Hey—come on! Cut it out!" It was a man's voice, soft and gentle. He sounded genuinely wounded.

Mallory opened her eyes and scrambled to her feet. She came more or less face-to-face with a man in a white lab coat—more or less, because Mallory was almost a full head taller than the man, even though she was wearing sneakers. "Geez. Are you okay?" he asked.

Mallory opened her mouth to answer, but another loud, metallic screech cut her off, and a loudspeaker fixed to the roof of the tourism office blared to life. The same woman's voice pierced the air again:

"Attention, Anomaly Flats: Rain will begin in two minutes and thirty-seven seconds. Seek shelter immediately. Rain will begin in two minutes and thirty-five seconds." Then the speaker went dead.

"Whoops," said the man in the lab coat. "We'd better get you inside."

"No!" Mallory yelled, throwing her hands up and clawing the air frantically, her eyes wide with fear and disgust. "I'm not going back in there!"

But the man in the lab coat shook his head. "No, not in there. In *there.*" He pointed to an old Winnebago that sat idling in the parking lot.

"Oh," Mallory said. She bit her lip as she considered the welts already springing up on his arms where her nails had raked his skin. "Sorry about…all that."

"Don't worry about it." He hurried over to the RV and opened the rear door. "Come on in. Trust me, you don't want to be out here when the rain starts."

Mallory shook her head. "No offense, but I have a strict rule about strangers and vans. I'll take my chance with the rain." She turned toward the street and started hurrying away.

"Your name's Mallory, right?" he called out after her.

She stopped cold in her tracks. How did he know that?

"I think I can answer some of the questions I'm sure you have, Mallory."

Dammit, she thought. *Just keep moving, just keep moving…* But her brain and her mouth were misfiring, as usual, and without turning around, she hollered back, "What questions?"

He paused for a moment, then he said, "All of them?" as if maybe he wasn't very sure himself. But he sounded hopeful. "Definitely some of them."

Mallory turned and crossed her arms. "Go on."

The man in the lab coat gave a worried little sigh. He checked his watch nervously. "Have you seen any tentacles? I can tell you about those." He pointed at the Pizza Hut. "And Marcy! I can tell you why Marcy shoots flies out of her mouth." He frowned up at the darkening sky and shifted his weight anxiously from one foot to the other. "We *really* don't want to get caught in the rain."

Mallory set her lips into a firm line. She *was* curious about the tentacles, and about the flies, and about a few other things. Like magnetic fields and waffle obsessions and keys and runes and the complete and total absence of Google. And chicken genocide… mostly, she was curious about that. Besides, the man in the lab coat was comically small, and she was pretty sure she could overpower him physically, if it came to that.

And he had a good point about the rain. She hated getting wet.

"All right, fine. I do have tentacle questions. But try anything, and I'll make sure you shit blood for a week."

The man gasped. "Well…wait," he said, holding up a hand. "Now I'm not sure I *want* you to come in," he said seriously.

"Oh, shut up," she said, and she pushed past him into the RV.

The inside of the Winnebago had been custom retrofitted into a mad scientist's playground. The cooktop had been ripped out and replaced with two rows of Bunsen burners. There were white racks bolted to two of the walls, snugly securing dozens of beakers of various sizes. A counter in the rear held three different centrifuges, and there was a blue box next to the tiny bathroom that held no fewer than five different types of scales. A small refrigerator stood next to that, the type that Mallory had had in her college dorm room, once upon a life. Microscopes were scattered all around the space, and a jumble of canisters, jars, flasks, and retorts were stowed wherever room could be found. Most of them held various liquids of bright and unusual colors. A dark blue fluid dripped slowly out of the flute of one retort near the Winnebago's cab, and each little drip smoked and sizzled into the floorboard. A giant fume hood hung from the center of the ceiling, and a poster of a bear wearing lab goggles hung on the back wall. It read, *ONLY YOU CAN PREVENT BAD SCIENCE.*

"Whoa," Mallory said. "This is…pretty weird."

"Glad you like it," the small man grinned. He hopped inside, closed the door, and wiped his hands nervously on his lab coat. She took a good, long look at him. He wore a green-and-yellow-checkered shirt under the lab coat topped with a pale blue bow tie. His shirt was neatly tucked into a pair of pressed khakis, and a pair of old Keds tennis shoes covered his feet. His light brown hair was short and a little hectic, and his square-rimmed glasses seemed to not quite want to stay on his nose where they belonged. Sizing him up, Mallory guessed that he wasn't used to having company…especially company of the female persuasion.

"Would you like something to drink?" he asked.

Mallory looked doubtfully at the brightly colored liquids in the beakers. Some of them seemed to be bubbling of their own volition, even though they were nowhere near a direct heat source. "I'm fine," she said. "I had breakfast wine."

The man in the lab coat looked at her strangely and shrugged. "Suit yourself." He picked up a beaker from the Bunsen burner counter and filled it with an amber liquid from a canister marked with a giant X. He took a long sip.

"Um…what is that?" Mallory asked, preparing herself to be disgusted.

"What? This?" The man nodded down at his beaker. "It's tea." Then he sniffed the liquid. Then he sniffed it again. "I *think* it's tea…" He sounded genuinely concerned.

Mallory rolled her eyes. "All right, Dr. Honeydew. Let's hear those answers."

"Mm! Dr. *Burnish*," he corrected her, swallowing another sip and extending his hand. "Dr. Lewis Burnish. You can call me Lewis," he added with a little blush. He looked away shyly, becoming suddenly very interested in his beaker of tea. "So what would you like to know?"

"We can start with the flies." Mallory's arms prickled with goose bumps at the memory. "What is *that* all about?"

"Well…" Lewis said uneasily. He cleared his throat and hemmed and hawed a bit. "I…may have lied. I mean, I did. I did lie. I have no idea why she shoots flies out of her mouth. But isn't it *fascinating?*" he beamed. "*Everything* in Anomaly Flats is fascinating!"

"Okay," Mallory said, throwing up her hands. "It's been fun." She moved for the door, but just as she reached for the handle, something solid pinged off the roof of the Winnebago. Then a second something struck, then a third, and a fourth, and soon the RV was being positively pelted from above. "What is that? Hail?"

"No; it's rain," Lewis said. He set down his beaker of tea and rubbed his hands together excitedly. "You're going to love this." He reached over and pulled the cheap curtain that covered one of the windows. "Look!"

Mallory peered out. What she saw made her gasp.

"Is that...*metal*? Falling from the *sky*?"

Lewis nodded excitedly. "It's nickel!" he said. "It rains nickel here! Isn't it wonderful?"

Mallory shook her head in bewilderment as the world outside was pelted with a cascade of hard metal bits. "What *is* this place?" she shouted over the din.

"Ah!" Lewis shouted back, pointing a finger into the air triumphantly. "Now *that*, I can answer!"

CHAPTER 7

"ANOMALY FLATS IS...well, it's an anomaly," the scientist said, clearing a family of test tubes from an overturned milk crate and gesturing for Mallory to have a seat. "Or a series of anomalies, to be exact. Let me ask you; how did you arrive here?"

"I drove," Mallory said dryly.

"Yes, of course, I understand that. But what I mean is, how did you *find* Anomaly Flats?"

"I followed the road."

"And how did you find that road?"

"What, are you serious? I saw a road, I turned onto it. How does *anyone* find a road?"

"Hmm...very interesting." Lewis pulled out a notebook and pen from one of the crates and began scribbling some notes. "Why did you turn onto that particular road?"

Mallory exhaled with exasperation. "I don't know! I saw a sign, I turned."

Lewis' eyes grew large. "You saw a sign?" he asked. "What kind of sign?"

"A road sign."

"Yes, but what *sort* of road sign?"

"Look," Mallory yelled over the sound of the raining metal, "what the hell does it matter what sort of road sign? I was on the road, I saw a sign for Anomaly Flats, I turned, and here I am—and absolutely adoring every second of it," she said sharply.

"Hmm…" Lewis clicked his pen a few times as he let his hidden thoughts tumble about in his brain. "And how do you feel now that you're here?"

"Goddamn irritated!" Mallory cried.

Lewis nodded. "Subject shows signs of emotional distress," he mumbled as he wrote. Mallory swiped at him and knocked both the book and the pen from his hands. "Hey!"

"I'm about to give you all *sorts* of emotional distress…I will *drown* you in it. Why are you asking me all these questions?"

"Because you're the only other outsider I've been able to study!" he said excitedly. "Er, meet. I meant meet. You're the only other outsider I've been able to meet."

"With your social skills, that's an incredible surprise," Mallory snorted.

The scientist shook his head. "It's not like that. I mean you're *literally* the only other outsider I've met. I'm curious about the town's effects on you. You see, Anomaly Flats is a sort of nexus of oddities. One of those oddities is that most people can't find it. Even if they look."

"And lucky me, I just stumbled across it," she said.

"Yes, exactly my point. The chances of that are so slim as to border on impossible. The town seems to use its geographical secrecy as a sort of defense mechanism."

Mallory rubbed her forehead. The beginnings of a headache were throbbing to life somewhere in there. "I thought you were just going to answer my questions," she sighed.

"I'm trying to," the scientist insisted. "It's all part of it. Don't you see? A town that camouflages itself is, in my experience, *highly* irregular…and it's one of the least irregular things about Anomaly Flats. I've been working out the 'whys' of its unique properties for some time now, and I've only cracked the surface. At first, I thought the strange things that happened here had to do with the area's peculiar magnetic properties. The magnetic fields in this area are… extraordinary."

"I've heard," Mallory sighed over the sound of raining metal. She shrugged out of her backpack and shoved it beneath her knees. "My alternator paid the price."

"Yes, exactly!" Lewis cried. "Not just your alternator, but *every* computer! I don't have to tell you how difficult it's been to carry out experiments without the help of a computer," he said with a little chuckle.

"Does this truck have an alternator?" Mallory asked, looking around the Winnebago. It was a complete scientific mess, but it looked to be fairly new.

Lewis smiled shrewdly. "It does. I constructed a superconductor casing of iron oxyarsenide for the RV's computer systems. It blocks out nearly 98% of all magnetism," he said proudly. "That was my Year Three project."

"Year Three? How long have you been here?"

"Let's see," Lewis said, tapping his chin thoughtfully. "I guess it's been...geez...over twelve years now." He seemed genuinely surprised by this. "Time does fly," he said, shaking his head. "Here more so than most places."

"You've been studying this place for twelve years, and you don't know why the Director of Tourism vomits flies?" Mallory said, raising an eyebrow. "That's one strike for scientific progress."

Lewis waved off that little insult. "There is so much of Anomaly Flats to explore—so much to *analyze* and *discover*—that Marcy's esophageal aberrations haven't been high on the list. But they *are* on the list," he assured her. He rifled through a pile of notebooks on the floor of the RV behind the passenger seat and came up with a spiral-bound journal with a holographic lizard on the cover. Mallory remembered having something like it when she was in grade school, almost three decades ago. Lewis flipped the book open to a marked page and held it out for her. "See?"

The page showed a long list of items, written in four columns. About a fifth of the items—including *magnetic properties, sharp snow, hypno-stars,* and *mutant cornfields*—were crossed off. Others—*Clone Lake, volcanic activity, drones,* and *aisle 8* among them—were not. There were similar lists on several pages, each with four full columns. *Marcy's flies* was among the items on the third page, and it was not yet crossed off.

"I'll get to it eventually," he promised. "What were we...oh! Magnetic fields! I thought those were to blame for the strangeness at first, but they're just a *symptom,* not the *sickness.* The root cause of Anomaly's anomalies seems to be something more...dimensional."

Mallory's brow furrowed. "Dimensional?" She wasn't much for science-fiction.

Lewis glanced at her uneasily. "The things I'm about to tell you...they're not for everyone's ears."

She snorted. "What, you think I'm gonna grab a beer with the Lord of the Flies in there and gossip away all your secrets?"

Lewis nodded. "Good point. I just...this is sensitive information. I'd like it to remain between us. Can you promise that you won't tell anyone else?"

Mallory shrugged. "Sure."

This seemed to satisfy the scientist, at least a little. He nodded again, and began. "Anomaly Flats seems to be some sort of...well, I guess you'd call it a dimensional way station. Like a complex highway interchange—except the highways are other times and places. To be honest," he said, lowering his voice as if he were afraid of being overheard, even over the clattering nickel rain that fell outside. "I'm not entirely sure that we're actually in Missouri anymore at all."

"Someone had better tell Google Maps."

Lewis looked confused. "What's a Google map?"

The quaintness of Anomaly Flats was really starting to grate on Mallory's nerves. "It's just a map...thing."

"But you see, that's exactly what I'm saying! Anomaly Flats isn't *on* any maps. Not one! Not one that I've found, anyway."

Mallory shrugged. "So? This is Missouri. It's like fifty thousand square miles of write-off. We're lucky they even put St. Louis on maps."

"It's more like seventy thousand square miles," Lewis said. "But that's not—listen, do you know, I've been here for over a decade, and not a single other outsider has so much as set foot inside these city limits. Not a single passerby, not a single visitor, not a single tourist."

"Well, hey, it's not exactly Branson."

Lewis shook his head. "I'm serious. Do you understand the enormity of that? I mean, no one else has driven through. No one else has taken the wrong road. No one in town has family from out of town who comes to visit. No postal workers, no deliverymen, no county service trucks...nothing. I was the *only* person to arrive in Anomaly Flats for over twelve years. And now, suddenly, you." He thought for a moment., "It's almost as if you don't access Anomaly Flats; Anomaly Flats accesses you."

Mallory had to admit, it was strange. But "strange" seemed to be the norm for this place. "Well, how did *you* get here?" she asked.

Lewis smiled at the memory. "I received a letter. It told of a wonderful, extraordinary, scientifically baffling place where a curious mind could spend his entire life seeking out answers to improbable questions and never even scratch the surface. And it came with a map."

"But you just said it isn't on any maps."

"Not on any regular maps, no," he said, grinning shrewdly. "But it's on this one." He reached into the pocket of his lab coat and produced a folded sheet of paper, yellowed with age and lightly frayed around the edges. He handed it to Mallory. "See for yourself."

She unfolded the paper gingerly. On one side was a handwritten letter; on the other, a crude, hand-drawn map with directions to Anomaly Flats. The map showed the town surrounded by a body of water. In the estimation of whoever had drawn this, Anomaly Flats was an island. "I'm no cartographer, but this seems inaccurate," she said.

"Twelve years ago, when I arrived, this place *was* an island. In the center of a massive body of water that had no business being in the Midwest. Isn't that strange?"

Mallory looked doubtfully down at the map. "If no mail goes in or out of Anomaly Flats, then who sent you this?"

Lewis smiled hugely. "I did."

Mallory blinked. "I'm sorry?"

"Look at the signature." Lewis grabbed the paper and turned it over. It was signed *Lewis T. Burnish, Ph.D.*

Mallory stared up at the scientist, her mouth hanging open. "You sent this to *yourself*? From a place you'd never been?"

"You can see why I was so intrigued."

"How is that possible?" she asked.

Lewis shrugged. "I have no idea. A dozen years later, and I haven't even written that letter yet, much less figured out a way to get it to myself in the past. But I'll come up with something." He snatched back the letter and waved it triumphantly in the air. "This is proof enough of that."

"And you haven't left?"

Lewis laughed out loud. "Leave? Why would I leave? This town is a scientist's dream! The research I'm doing is completely unparalleled! I'm the first person ever to study inter-dimensional anomalies in a setting this intimate," he said proudly.

Mallory gripped the milk crate beneath her with both hands, so hard the plastic dug into her skin and made her fingers go numb. "So you're telling me I drove my Impala into…another dimension?"

Lewis smiled. "Well. Not exactly. Whatever Anomaly Flats is, it *does* seem to be at least *rooted* in Missouri. Most of the soil and water samples are consistent with what you would find in this part of the state. There are just…some additions."

"That's absurd. You know that, right?" She shook her head. "That *all* of this is completely absurd?"

"It is, isn't it?" he said, his voice filled with glee. "But that doesn't make it any less true."

"So a dimensional nexus. That's where we are; that's what this town is. A place where dimensions mash themselves together."

"It explains the tentacles, doesn't it?"

"Does it?" In spite of all she'd seen, Mallory couldn't quite bring herself to believe it. "Sorry, Poindexter. I don't buy it."

Lewis fiddled with the buttons on his lab coat. "You don't have to buy it," he said. "It's empirically true, whether you recognize it or not."

Mallory closed her eyes and rolled her head around, stretching out her neck. "Look, Lewis—" she began.

"Listen," he said, cutting her off. "I know it's difficult to believe. But think about what you've experienced since arriving. Have you noticed any time jumps since you arrived?"

Mallory's eyes narrowed. "What do you mean by 'time jumps'?"

"I mean, does it seem like time has gotten away from you? In a very real and literal sense?"

She squinted suspiciously at the little man. "Time *did* seem to move really fast last night," she admitted, letting her thoughts trickle out slowly through her lips. "But I just lost track..."

"And your hotel room," Lewis said, interrupting again. "Did you use the chalk to draw the runes on your door? You did, didn't you? You must have."

"I did," she said, nodding gently. "Why do you say I must have?"

"Because you're still alive."

"Oh, come on. You're saying I'd be dead right now if I hadn't drawn those stupid circles?"

"Or something worse than dead," he confirmed. "I bet the runes were smeared when you woke up this morning, right? Like something had spent the entire night trying to wipe them away?"

Mallory noticed her palms had gone clammy. She wiped them on her jeans. "How do you know that?"

"Because this is Anomaly Flats, and that's the sort of thing that happens here."

"This is the dumbest dumb thing I've ever heard," she decided. Even so, there was no denying the complete otherworldliness of the town. If it wasn't a dimensional nexus, *something* was wrong with it, all right. She shook her head in disbelief at what she was about to say. "All right; so *suppose* this is all true...it's not, but let's just *suppose* we're actually in the middle of a time-and-place tornado. *Supposing* that's true, when my car is fixed and I'm finally able to leave...will I drive back into Missouri? *My* Missouri?"

Lewis thought about that for a bit. "Yes, I think so," he finally decided. "As long as you take the right dimensional off-ramp."

"Great," Mallory groaned. "And how do I find that?"

"In theory, it should be the same road you came in on. If it brought you in, it should take you out."

"Should?" Mallory asked pointedly.

"Should," Lewis confirmed.

"And what if it doesn't?"

Lewis frowned. "Then given the evidence of what exists beyond some of our borders...you'll probably wish you'd stayed."

CHAPTER 8

EVENTUALLY, the onslaught of deadly rain subsided, and Mallory peeked out through the Winnebago's window. The parking lot was covered by almost a full inch of little bits of nickel.

"It does this every time?" she asked. "How do you get rid of it?" She pictured a small army of masked men storming in on Hummers, sweeping the metal away, giving all onlookers a threatening hand gesture and swooping out just as quickly and mysteriously as they'd come.

"It melts. Then it washes away and runs into the storm drains, like any other rain would. It eventually makes its way to the town's treatment plant." He paused. "You…might not want to drink the water while you're here."

"The water is made of nickel, the coffee makes you sterile…"

"Only the regular," Lewis quickly pointed out. "Not the decaf."

An awkward silence fell between them. Mallory checked her watch. Unless it was somehow really 1:37 in the morning, the stupid thing had completely stopped working.

"Listen," said Lewis, fiddling with one of the Bunsen burners. "It usually takes Rufus a day or two to work out a new alternator… and I don't know if you…I mean…do you want to…maybe…" He cleared his throat and tried again. "Mallory, would you like to come with me on my rounds today?" He nodded toward the notebook with the holographic cover. "Help me cross a few things off the list? Just tag along? Not in a romantic way," he blurted, a little too quickly.

Mallory grimaced. "Why would I think it was romantic?"

"You wouldn't! And *I* wouldn't! I *don't*! It's not! It's just...science!" His hand slipped, and it knocked into the starter mechanism for the burner. A blue flame whooshed to life out of the pipe, nearly singeing Lewis' lab coat.

Mallory sighed. She did have time to kill...lots of it. And if her choices were to spend it with the locals or spend it with another outsider, she should probably stick with the outsider. "All right," she said, throwing up her hands in defeat. "Where to?"

"Excellent!" Lewis beamed, jumping into the driver's seat. "First stop: Plasma Creek!"

X

The lime green creek of plasma ran along the western edge of town, about ten miles beyond the downtown strip. "It curves down to the south after Rubber Rock," Lewis told her with a weirdly high level of enthusiasm. "That's this huge outcropping of rock, and the tests all say that it actually is rock...but guess what it's really made of, primarily?"

"Uh...rubber?" Mallory guessed.

"Yes!" he squealed. "It's a rock that is *also* rubber! My tests show that it's both things at once! Isn't that *bizarre*?"

Mallory blinked far too many times. "I had a tentacle in my drain last night, and this morning I saw a woman exhale a swarm of flies, just before the sky rained metal...but yeah. Sure. That's bizarre, too."

Lewis beamed. "*So* bizarre!"

He pulled up alongside the creek and took the Winnebago off the highway, through a drainage ditch, and into a grassy meadow. As they bumped and bounced along, Mallory held on for her life. "I think you missed the road!" she shouted.

"Less walking this way," Lewis said, holding tightly to the wheel and jerking it to maneuver the RV around the larger rocks. "It's best to spend as little time outside the lab as possible, generally speaking. There are all *sorts* of neat things that can kill you out here."

Soon, they came upon a few dozen circular burn marks in the grass. Lewis slammed his foot on the brake and threw the RV into park. "This is really exciting stuff," he informed her, squeezing into the back of the truck and gathering an armful of supplies. "Now, be careful out there, okay? Step where I step, and *don't go wandering*."

He opened the back door and stepped out of the RV, holding a small plastic wand in front of his face. Mallory glanced nervously over at the Jansport. It was still tucked safely next to the milk crate, but the thought of leaving it behind made her palms itch. She wasn't sure that taking it along was such a good idea either, though; as a rule, burn marks and things you didn't want to burn weren't a great combination. She chewed indecisively at her bottom lip.

"Are you coming?" Lewis called.

Mallory picked up the milk crate and dumped out the flasks inside. A few of them cracked. One of them even shattered. She didn't care. She flipped the crate over and set it down on top of the backpack, so it was caught safely inside Jansport jail.

"There. Camouflage."

She squeezed out of the RV after the scientist. "What is that?" she asked, nodding at the wand.

"It's a thermometer. Highly sensitive."

Mallory squinted over his shoulder and read the digital dial near the base. "It's broken," she observed.

"It isn't!" Lewis said excitedly.

"Yes it is. It's not 109 degrees out here."

"Oh, yes it is. It just doesn't *feel* like 109 degrees. But it's definitely 109 degrees. The thermometer says so." Then he cried, "Science!"

Mallory rolled her eyes.

Lewis continued. "The sun may feel temperate here, but it's actually surprisingly strong. Haven't you noticed how tan everyone is in Anomaly Flats?"

"Oh, come on," Mallory said. "That's absurd."

"You want proof?" Lewis turned and stuck the tip of the thermometer into his mouth. He bobbed his head a little as he waited for it to read the temperature. After about twenty seconds, he pulled it out and showed Mallory the display.

It read 97.9 degrees.

Mallory shook her head. "How can it be 109 degrees but feel like 70?" she demanded.

Lewis shrugged. "Who knows? It's an—"

"Yeah, yeah," Mallory interrupted. "It's an anomaly. You know, for a scientist, you don't seem to know too much about science."

"Hey, come on," Lewis said, clearly hurt. "Cut me some slack. I'm the first scientist in the field of anomalogy. There's bound to be a learning curve." He cut in front of the RV and headed away from the creek.

Mallory stopped. "Hey, the creek's this way."

Lewis turned, confused. "Yes, I know."

"Why are you going that way?"

"Because that's where the science is happening."

"Okay, first of all, I've taken biology, okay? Science happens everywhere. And second, are we not here to study the plasma?"

Lewis frowned. "Why would we study the plasma?"

"Because it's *plasma*. In a *creek*."

"But I've already studied it."

"All right," she said, taking a few deep breaths and crossing her arms. "Unravel for me the mysteries of Plasma Creek."

"It's a creek," he said, nodding toward the slowly flowing, neon green channel. "And it's full of plasma."

Mallory ran her fingers into her hair and pulled, just a little. *Maybe I was wrong about going with the other outsider.* "Are you *really* a scientist?" she asked suspiciously.

"Of course."

"Where did you go to school?"

"Look, do you really want to hear the minutiae about the plasma in the creek—that it's an electrically neutral semi-solid medium of unbound positive and negative particles? That its density is 1032 m-3 in particles per cubic meter? That its average daily temperature is 273.16 Kelvin? That its velocity distribution is non-Maxwellian? Is that the kind of thing you want to know?"

Mallory blinked and thought for a second. "Science is boring."

Lewis rolled his eyes. "Fine. How about this: Any organic material immersed in the plasma turns into a completely different collection of organic materials."

"Well, yeah, obviously," Mallory said.

"Obviously," Lewis agreed.

They stood in their shared obvious knowledge for a while before Mallory finally asked, "And that means...what, exactly?"

Lewis smirked. "Here, look." He plucked a long blade of grass from the meadow and cautiously approached Plasma Creek. He leaned over the edge and beckoned Mallory forward. They squatted on the bank as the plasma bubbled and gurgled below them. Lewis held the grass by one end and dipped the other end into the creek. When he drew it back out, the grass that had been submerged was no longer grass, but had become a flopping, silver-scaled fish tail instead.

Mallory's eyes popped open wide. "Holy shit!"

Lewis nodded. "Fascinating, isn't it?"

"It turns things into *fish*?" Mallory cried.

"Well, not *always* fish. Other things, too; eggplants, worms, cedar trees, gasoline, bark. You name it. One time, Emily Bainsbridge dipped her feet in, and they turned into a pair of miniature dachshunds." The color drained from Mallory's face as the neon green creek burbled happily along. "Oh, and it's hard to see in this sunlight, but the plasma also makes the matter glow. Which is pretty neat. Still, though...best not to get any on you."

"Don't touch the plasma," she said, backing away from the bank. "Got it."

"Now are you ready to do some *new* science?"

Mallory nodded. The idea of putting some distance between herself and the glow-inducing mutation juice seemed pretty solid. "What are we here to study?"

"Those." Lewis pointed at the cluster of burn marks in the grass. The singed circles were scattered all across the meadow without any discernible pattern, each about two feet in diameter. "Stay close. Step only where I step."

Mallory crept into the field on the scientist's heels. Lewis held the thermometer aloft like a magic wand, ready to defeat any unexpected forces of evil with the magic of his digital display. "What are they?" she asked.

"I've been hearing reports of people spontaneously evaporating. Isn't that curious?"

Mallory raised her hands in defeat. "I'm out," she said. "Walk me back to the Winnebago. I'm locking myself in my hotel room and not coming out 'til my car's ready."

Lewis put a finger to his lips. "Shhh…it may be triggered by decibel level. You should keep your voice down."

He reached the first burn mark and squatted before it, staring down in wonder. Mallory stood helplessly behind him, flapping her arms like a frustrated bird. "*Lewis*," she hissed, but he was too rapt in science to hear. She was stranded in a spontaneous-evaporation minefield, with only two sure paths through: the one back to the creek, and the one forward to Lewis. She cursed under her breath and approached him slowly…carefully. Quietly.

"Look here," Lewis said excitedly as she drew near. He kept his hand where it was and tilted the thermometer, lowering the tip toward the burn mark without breaking the plane of air directly above it. The digital display went haywire, flickering like a zoetrope as the numbers climbed at an alarming rate, to alarming heights: 109; 829; 1,480; 4,902; 12,373; 28,937; 110,873; 874,441. And then the display reached its limit of 999,999 degrees, and a little plus sign appeared in the top right hand corner.

The air at the edge of the circle was over one million degrees Fahrenheit.

"Now it's *definitely* broken," Mallory murmured.

"Maybe," Lewis said. "The thermometer's not melting. So that's strange."

"Yes...*that's* the strange part."

"This was definitely a person at one point," he said. "Look there." On the far side of the charred circle, right at the edge, a sliver of black foam lay in the green grass, right at the edge of the burned area. A tan, semi-circular *something* rested atop the foam.

"What is that?" Mallory asked, squinting. "Is it...?"

"The edge of a big toe; yes." Lewis nodded. "And a flip-flop. Just that much of whoever this was stood outside the circle, and it didn't even burn, much less evaporate." He shook his head in wonder. "What an incredibly localized event."

Mallory's stomach barrel-rolled into her throat. "I think I'm going to throw up," she decided.

"Do it into the creek!" Lewis said excitedly. "Let's see what it turns into!"

Mallory heaved and pushed her nausea down. "What's the deal, here? Someone was walking along, and all of a sudden—*poof*...he evaporated in a beam of light?"

"Light, yes, and heat. *Extreme* heat. Possibly in the tens of millions of degrees! Instantaneous incineration and evaporation. But so perfectly *localized*," he murmured in awe. He rubbed his chin as he contemplated the invisible column of energy. "We need to trigger it."

Mallory cocked her eyebrows. "Trigger it?"

"Yes...trigger it; the light, the heat. Given the perfection of the circles, the beam must come down *directly* from overhead."

His glasses had slipped to the end of his nose in his excitement, so he pushed them back up. "I hypothesize that when a being walks into one of these zones, the beam is triggered, and an unbelievably concentrated pillar of light and heat flashes down from above and obliterates everything in its path."

"You hypothesize?" Mallory asked. "We've been here for eight seconds, you already have a hypothesis?"

"A scientist *always* has a hypothesis," Lewis said proudly.

"A second ago, you thought it was caused by loud noises."

"New second; new hypothesis. We could learn so much, if we could only trigger the event…" He trailed off as he looked down at the burned circle. Then he looked up at Mallory. Then he looked down at the burned circle…then back up at Mallory again. "How fast can you run?" he asked.

"Uh-uh! No way." She crossed her arms defiantly. "You want to see the light so badly? *You* run through the kill zone."

"But I have to hold the thermometer," he explained.

"Men are all the same," she muttered with no small amount of irritation.

"You'll get to be part of science!" he insisted.

"No science for me, thanks," she said. "I'm full."

Lewis harrumphed. "Well, we need *something* to use as a trigger."

She glanced around the empty field and over at the creek. Her eyes lit up as she hit upon an idea. She turned and retreated toward the plasma. "Wait here."

"Where are you going?" Lewis called.

Mallory ignored him. She retraced her steps all the way back to the glowing green creek. She plucked a blade of grass from the bank and dipped it into the viscous plasma. The far end came back up as a writhing, hissing snake. She held the grass end of the abomination tightly between two fingers and gingerly carried it back to the scientist.

"Here," she said. "Here's your stupid trigger." Then she hurled it through the air, above the charred circle. As it broke the plane, a brilliant white flash seared the air. It was gone in an instant...and so was the half-snake.

Mallory looked down at Lewis. Lewis looked up at Mallory.

"Do it again," he said, pushing his glasses up his nose. "I wasn't ready."

CHAPTER 9

"EVERY SINGLE THING IN THIS TOWN is trying to kill me," Mallory lamented an hour later as they buckled themselves into the Winnebago.

"Once you make peace with that, it's really quite charming," Lewis said.

"How have you lived here for 12 years and not gone insane? Or dead?"

"How have I not gone dead?" he asked, raising an eyebrow.

"Shut up."

The scientist smiled and shrugged. "I just keep my head down and do my experiments. And safety first, always."

Mallory rested her head against the window. "I just want to get my car and go," she sighed. "Is that too much to ask?"

But Lewis waved this off as if it were nonsense. "Once you go back to real life, nothing will *ever* be exciting anymore! Everything you do from now on will be routine and boring and not-at-all baffling or mysterious compared to Anomaly Flats!"

"Routine and boring and not-at-all mysterious sounds like the perfect life."

Of course, that wasn't true. If it were, she wouldn't be in Anomaly Flats right now; she'd be sitting at her routine and boring desk in the routine and boring Wainwright Building in routine and boring St. Louis, responding to asinine emails and going blind from staring at spreadsheets and being verbally abused by whichever manager happened to be within shouting distance. She had rejected routine and boring and not-at-all-mysterious. That's what had gotten her and her little purple Jansport into this mess in the first place.

And she wouldn't go back for all the money in the world.

Though she certainly wouldn't mind actually getting *back* to the world. Lenore's people were expecting her later that night, but it'd be at least another 48 hours until Mallory made it out of the Flats and up to Canada—and that was barring any more trouble along the way. Lenore wasn't exactly painted as a patient person; Mallory desperately hoped she'd keep her promise and welcome Mallory with open, if somewhat annoyed, arms. "This isn't where I'm supposed to be," she sighed aloud, mostly to herself.

Lewis frowned over at her from the driver's seat. "Where *are* you supposed to be?" he asked.

Canada, she wanted to tell him. *A safe house. A place to lie low. A place where the past is dead and the future is waiting and bad decisions are wiped clean.* She wanted to tell him this, not necessarily because she wanted him to know, but because she needed to tell *someone.* She'd always been a loner, but for the first time in her life, she was truly—and, she now feared, irrevocably—on her own. But that was part of the deal. Take the backpack, and live the life. So instead of opening up to the nerdy but kind scientist, she just shook her head and asked, "Where are we headed to now?"

"To see something *very* curious," Lewis said happily, guiding the RV over the field and up onto the road.

"Oh, wonderful," she said, her voice oozing sarcasm. "I was just starting to wonder when we'd stop with all this *mildly* curious bullshit and start seeing something *very* curious."

Lewis smiled over at Mallory and gave her a little wink. "Perfect!"

They drove back toward town, then hooked north on a faded asphalt road that gave way to washed-out gravel a few miles in. The RV bumped and banged over the deep tire ruts, and even with her seatbelt, Mallory had to hold onto the handle above the window to keep from falling out of her chair. "Your Public Works Department sucks," she pointed out.

They drove into a thicket of trees that loomed high above a forest floor overgrown with weeds and bushes and God knew what other biological horrors. Just seeing the tangled mess of growth made Mallory's ankles itch with the phantom prickling of imaginary ticks crawling up her leg and burying their nonexistent heads beneath her skin.

Lewis pulled the Winnebago to the side of the road and turned off the ignition. "Well, here we are."

Mallory peered out the windshield, but saw nothing but trees. "Here we are *where*?"

Lewis grinned. He straightened his bow tie and said, "Come on. I'll show you."

"Are you going to lock it?" she asked as they climbed out of the Winnebago.

"Why would I lock it?" he replied, pulling out a small bag of research equipment.

"Because my backpack's in there."

"We're ten miles from the nearest house and three miles from a paved road. Who's going to break in?"

Mallory gazed around the densely wooded forest. Little light filtered in through the treetops, and the whole area was eerily quiet. It did seem rather remote. "I don't know. Bigfoot?"

"In Missouri, we call him Momo," Lewis informed her.

"I know that," she lied.

They left the RV and the gravel road behind and ventured out into the woods in search of the mysterious singularity. Mallory was about to point out that Lyme disease wasn't an anomaly at all, and that she'd go wait in the truck while he made the proud discovery of tick-administered nerve damage. But just as she opened her mouth, Lewis pushed aside a low-hanging collection of branches, and she saw what they had really come to examine: a fully functional traffic light sitting atop a shiny metal pole jutting up among the trees. The whole thing seemed to have sprouted up from a family of ferns, its yellow metal casing gleaming in the shaded forest.

The light was green.

"What the hell is a traffic light doing in the middle of the woods?" Mallory asked, bewildered.

"It just appeared three days ago. Fully functional," Lewis said, rubbing his hands together excitedly. "Isn't it *fascinating*?"

They crept through the brush to get a better look at the contraption, and as they approached, the light flickered to amber, then to red. Mallory froze. "Is it…telling us to stop?"

"Umm…it *might* be," Lewis admitted. Then he shrugged and waved her forward. "Come on."

"Whoa, whoa, whoa." Mallory grabbed his wrist and pulled him back. "Lewis. Seriously? When a demonic stoplight that mysteriously appears in the middle of the forest tells you not to go closer, you *don't go closer.*"

Lewis rolled his eyes. "It's not *demonic*, Mallory. It's from Ameren." He pointed to the base of the stoplight. The words AMEREN MISSOURI were stamped into the metal plating.

"Same thing," Mallory hissed. She was about to shoulder-tackle him into a tree to get him to stop walking when the light suddenly turned green.

"There," Lewis said, gesturing up toward the light. "Happy?"

"Generally, no," she mumbled.

They approached the traffic signal, which continued to cycle through its color scheme without seeming to give them any notice. Lewis set his bag on the ground and made a wide circle of the post. It was fixed to the earth with four large bolts, but the ground was soft and wet, and spongy underfoot. "That hardly seems stable," he said. He looked at Mallory. He gave her a good look up and down. "See if you can tip it over."

"What? No! *You* see if you can tip it over!"

"It's probably safe to touch," he pointed out. "Go on."

"Uh-uh. No way."

Lewis frowned. "I lost my last pair of leather gloves in the lava pits out on Route 109."

"So what?"

"So I have scientist's hands! They're *soft*," he cried, holding them up to show how smooth and pink and unused to manual labor they were. "They're not made for inter-dimensional contact."

Mallory put her hands on her hips. "And mine are?" she asked in a tone that clearly communicated that there was a right answer to this question, and an almost-infinite number of wrong ones.

But Lewis' intuition failed him. "It's not that. It's just that you're...sturdier than I am," he explained.

Mallory gasped. "I'm *sturdier*?"

"It's a compliment!" he insisted.

"*Sturdier?!*"

"You're bigger than me!"

"You're practically a midget!"

"I'm almost average!" he said defensively. "I'm just saying you're tall!"

"And *sturdy*!"

"It's a good thing!"

"You know what *I* think would be a good thing? If I punched your stupid face off."

"See?" he said. "That's a very sturdy way of thinking."

Mallory's vision exploded with little black stars, and she decided she was having an aneurism. *This is how I die*, she thought. *And I don't even care.* But after a few breaths, her eyesight cleared, and she was staring once again into the hapless, square-rimmed eyes of her dopey scientist companion. "Tell you what," she said. "You examine the demonic traffic light; I'm going to go be sturdy back in the truck."

Lewis frowned. "I could really use your help."

"Trust me. Removing myself from striking distance of your head *is* helping."

"All right," he sighed. "But I might be a while."

"I do not care."

"Okay. Here, take the keys."

"It's not locked," she reminded him.

"Yeah, but you'll need them if you want to listen to the radio. And also to get the hell out of the woods if I get eaten by a demonic traffic light."

"Good point." She swiped the keys from his hand and headed back toward the Winnebago.

"Oh, Mallory!" he called after her. She stopped, but she didn't turn around. "If you get out to stretch your legs, don't wander too far. And do *not* go up that ridge." She glanced to her right and saw that the woods rose to an uneven cliff high up the hill.

If there was one thing she hated more than putting herself in inter-dimensional danger, it was being told what to do. Especially by a nerd.

"Why not?"

"It's not safe."

"What is it?"

"*Not safe*," he repeated firmly.

"Now you're just making me want to go."

"Don't. I'm not joking. Promise me you won't go up to the ridge."

"But—"

"Mallory! *Promise* me!"

"Fine, fine," she said, irritated. "I promise I won't go up to the ridge."

As she headed back to the RV, she wondered what would be the fastest way to get to the top of the ridge.

X

Mallory was many things: a decent chef; a practiced eye-roller; a connoisseur of flavored martinis. But she was not an accomplished hiker.

An expert in the art of stealth was also not on the list.

As she panted her way up the hill, the underbrush snapped and crunched beneath her shoes like she had elephant feet. *Jesus, maybe I am sturdy*, she thought. With every rustle and crack, she stopped and held her breath, certain that Lewis would hear her plodding up toward the ridge. But he was wholly immersed in his stupid anomaly and didn't seem to hear. Besides, what was he going to do – restrain her? Sturdy or not, she could definitely trample the little scientist if push came to shove.

"Though someone should definitely try to stop you," she muttered to herself as she huffed up the hillside. "This is the stupidest thing you've done all day."

She wheezed and moaned her way up the hill, struggling hard even though it wasn't terribly steep. *The underbrush makes it impossible to walk*, she told herself as she trudged through downed branches and snarling vines, though in truth, it probably had more to do with the fact that she hadn't so much as laid eyes on a treadmill since she was 26. "Exercise is stupid," she spat.

A hissing pop sounded just to her left, and she screeched in surprise. She clamped a hand over her mouth as her brain fought itself over which threat to hide from first: the sudden sound, or the scientist's awareness. Fortunately, both threats resolved themselves almost instantly as the pop was followed by a loud static buzz that was cut with the female voice that had fizzled out of the loudspeaker back in town. Mallory was somehow not terribly surprised to see that one of the boulders sticking out of the mossy earth was actually a fake rock with a speaker built into it. Judging by the repeating squeal reverberating through the woods, the forest was full of hidden speakers. The all-enveloping hissing and popping masked Mallory's cry from the scientist's ears.

"*Attention, Anomaly Flats,*" the voice droned. "*A family of rabbits has escaped from the Anomaly Flats Zoo. The rabbits were in transit from the laboratories at Complexxus Industries, where they were undergoing specialized isotope injection testing. A gender-indeterminate spokesperson from Complexxus released the following statement: Quote, 'We urge the inhabitants of Anomaly Flats to remain calm. We are determined to find, imprison, and execute the escaped rabbits before Wednesday. The search team would like to remind us that we should be grateful that the rabbits did not escape on a Wednesday.'*

"'*The effects of the gentle, organic, non-violent, non-GMO, gluten-free tests Complexxus ran on the rabbits will not be known for another three to seven hours. The possible effects of the tests include, but are in no way limited to: severe pet dander; erratic behavior; foaming at the mouth; bleeding from the tips of the fur; hunger for human tissue; shocking and exponential levels of growth; flight; a complex mastery of the English language; time travel; and a penchant for baking complicated French pastries. If you come into contact with one of these rabbits, do what you do when you come into contact with any rabbit: Lie down and wait for the end, because rabbits are superior to humans in almost every conceivable way, and your death is assured. Complexxus Industries has worked hard to make it so.' End quote.*

"*The Walmart would like to remind you of its sale on canned tuna this week, three cans for $2.49. The Walmart would like to add that canned tuna is a natural rabbit deterrent, which we all know is not true. Attention, Anomaly Flats: If you go into the Walmart, you will be drawn into aisle 8. Do not go into the Walmart. Do not approach the escaped rabbits. Do not approach any rabbits at all.*"

The speaker squeaked off, leaving Mallory alone with her reeling thoughts, the thick brush of the woods, and a town filled with escaped, mutant, murderous rabbits. She promised herself that if she ever made it out of Anomaly Flats, she was never, ever, *ever* coming back to Missouri.

She peeked out from behind a tree and saw that Lewis hadn't skipped a beat in his examination of the traffic light. As she watched, he plucked a penlight from the chest pocket of his lab coat and clicked it on, shining the light directly into the glowing green bulb. He moved the light slowly from one side to the other, apparently giving the stoplight a vision test.

Mallory shook her head and continued her rugged climb to the top of the hill. She couldn't see the sun through the canopy of leaves above, and as she drew nearer the top of the ridge, the sky behind it began to take on an orange-ish glow. *No way is it sunset already,* she thought, checking her watch. This, of course, was pointless, because her watch had ceased its usefulness, and she didn't even know why she was still wearing it. Old habits die hard, she reasoned. She shook the broken watch anyway, and the hour hand spun wildly around, making six full turns of the dial in the span of two seconds. "Perfect," she murmured.

Watch or no watch, she knew it was nowhere near dusk.

A hard wind blew up on the far side of the ridge, and a storm of red sand whipped up behind the hill, spitting grit down on Mallory as it dusted the woods.

A forest butting up against a desert? she thought. *This place is so fucking weird.*

She reached the top of the ridge and found that the land fell away sharply after the forest rocks. She crouched above a sheer cliff that dropped straight down for at least 300 feet before opening up to a wide, desert plain. "Oh my God," she whispered. Her heart seized up in her chest, and a sickly whirlpool spun itself out of control in the pit of her stomach. Her head swam with the lightness of vertigo. If the swoon made her faint, she would pitch forward into the hellish landscape below. So she pulled herself back from the edge, gripping her fingers into the divots of the forest rocks.

The desert that stretched as far as the horizon was a deep, reddish orange. Mallory had never seen sand quite that color before. It was as if an entire empire of iron had rusted over, crumbled to dust, and coated the Midwestern plain with its red ashes. A fierce dust storm had brewed up in the center of the desert, over an outcropping of angry orange rocks that jutted up from the sands. It whipped the red-orange dust into furious dirt devils that blasted across the desert floor and spiraled up into a swirling mass of rust-red clouds above. Mallory shuttered her eyes against the blowing sand that shot over the ridge, but despite the onslaught and her dizzying fear of heights, she found she couldn't look away from the desolate landscape. The desert below was so raw; so uncivilized; so *primal*. The sun blazed down from above, pale, but still hot behind the roiling red clouds. Mallory couldn't help but notice that something looked off about that sun.

It was too small.

The wind down in the wide canyon whipped and whorled; the desert was devoid of any sound other than its frantic scream. This was a wild place, untamed, so undeniably natural and brutal that it mesmerized the woman hunkered down in the forest it bordered. She squinted in awe against the blowing sand. Her hand reached up, almost of its own will. Something about the nature of this strange plain made her want to reach out and touch the air, brush her fingers along the violent blast of sand, let this desert wind course over her skin. She reached her fingers forward, closer to the red-orange glow in the air…and closer… and closer…

"Mallory!" Lewis bounded up to her right and slapped her hand down. He was panting hard after sprinting up the ridge.

"Ow!" Mallory whined, shaking the sting out of her hand. "What was that for?"

Lewis doubled over, sucking air into his lungs with his hands on his knees. "What—did I—tell you?" he wheezed.

Mallory narrowed her eyes. "That I'm sturdy."

Lewis shook his head. "No—I said—don't—go up—the ridge."

"Because God forbid I get to the top and see the incredible view of a gorgeous desert," she sniped. "Holy shit, Lewis…you saved me from death by natural beauty. How can I ever repay you?"

"It's not—" Lewis panted. "It's—Mallory, that's—"

"Oh, for crying out loud, Lewis, *breathe*. It's what?"

Lewis straightened up and squeezed his eyes shut as he put his hands above his head and took deeper breaths. "It's Mars," he said.

Mallory stared blankly up at him. "It's what?"

"It's not a desert; it's Mars," he repeated. His breath was coming back to him, and he put his hands on his hips. His lab coat billowed in the blowing wind. "The planet Mars. I mean, not like the whole thing. Just two square miles of it."

Mallory's mouth fell open. Sand blew in and coated her tongue, but she didn't notice. She turned and looked out over the red plain. "That's…*Mars*?"

"Utopia Planitia," Lewis nodded, panting. "It starts—at this cliff and ends—way over there, just before—the bowling alley."

"There's two square miles of another *planet* between here and a *bowling alley*?"

"We take our cosmic bowling—very seriously."

Mallory shook her head slowly, taking in the bizarre majesty of the neighboring planet. "How did it…*get* here?"

Lewis shrugged. "I have no earthly idea. Heh…earthly." Mallory groaned. "But reach past the cliff here, and your hand goes into Mars' atmosphere. Goodbye, fingers."

Mallory instinctively crawled back a few feet from the edge of the ridge. "Lewis, how can that be *Mars*?"

Lewis shrugged. "How can anything be anything? It's Anomaly Flats…welcome to the weird. One of these days I'm going to make an extravehicular space suit from scratch and be the first human to explore it," he beamed.

"*You're* going to make a space suit?" Mallory asked doubtfully.

Lewis chose to ignore this particular question. "Until then, let's stay on this side of the ridge, huh?"

Mallory nodded. She slipped back down the hill into the surprising comfort of the tangled underbrush. She might get poison ivy, and she might get Lyme disease, but at least she wouldn't have her eyeballs sucked out of her skull and deposited somewhere on Mars, and that was something.

They were halfway down the hill before she realized she was shaking. She held her trembling hand up to her face and inspected it numbly. "Huh," she said.

Lewis frowned. He stopped and turned Mallory to face him. He pulled down at her eyelids with his thumbs and inspected her pupils. Then he put two fingers on the underside of her wrist. "Your pulse is racing, and your skin's going clammy. You're either in shock, or you're hungry. Possibly both. Sometimes people go into shock if they get hungry enough, though I'm not sure if shock can cause hunger. It's undocumented, as far as I know, but that doesn't mean there's no correlation. Which is probably neither here nor there."

"Probably not."

"Look, let's leave the traffic light for now, all right? Go get some lunch, boost your blood sugar a bit?" Mallory nodded. She felt like someone had snuck into her brain and placed pieces of gauze behind her eyes. Her brain felt detached, blocked, and her thoughts were fuzzy, if they were anything at all.

"Yeah," she said, trudging down the hill toward the Winnebago. "Lunch is good. No waffles, though."

"No waffles," Lewis agreed, taking her hand and helping her down the forest path. "Trudy may have a monopoly on breakfast, but there's plenty more for lunch."

"No Chick-fil-A, either," she added as she stumbled along.

Lewis smiled at that. "Not for lunch, no," he chuckled. "*Never* for lunch. But we'll go to Chick-fil-A eventually." He gave her a kind smile. "*Everyone* goes to Chick-fil-A eventually."

CHAPTER 10

"HOW'D IT GO WITH THE TRAFFIC LIGHT?" Mallory asked as they rumbled farther north. She gnawed on a granola bar Lewis had dug out from the glove compartment, trying not to break her teeth. It was a very old bar.

"It didn't go at all; I was interrupted," he said pointedly. Mallory made a sour face at him, but he didn't turn his head to see it. "I'll go back sometime when there are fewer distractions."

"I'm not a distraction," Mallory insisted. "I'm a delight." She gazed out at the forest, which seemed to stretch eternally in all directions. "How big is Anomaly Flats?" she asked.

"Oh, it depends," Lewis said as he struggled with the Winnebago's steering wheel. "Usually about 20 miles across, end-to-end. Bigger on Wednesdays."

Mallory raised an eyebrow. "How much bigger?"

Lewis shrugged. "I don't really know. No one's ever made it to the city limits on a Wednesday. They're too far away."

"What day is it today?"

Lewis reached down and turned on the radio. Their ears were assaulted by a storm of static. He fiddled with the buttons, and the radio cycled through a handful of stations; banjo music turned to a classical orchestra turned to a wailing sitar turned to a rasping voice spitting out evil-sounding epithets in Latin. One more turn of the dial, and a woman's voice crackled to life, the same voice that had been sounding over the town's speakers. "…inconsequential. This is the day, weather, and time broadcast. The day is: Friday. The weather is: As it should be. The time is: Inconsequential. This is the day, weather, and time—" Lewis shut off the radio.

"Compelling stuff," Mallory snorted. She took some comfort in the fact that the day of the week, if nothing else, was the same here. "You need a radio station to tell you what day it is?"

Lewis nodded. "The radio station makes all the important decisions," he said, as if that explained everything.

Mallory dug the heels of her hands into her eyes and rubbed. "This is the most lucid fever dream anyone's ever had," she decided.

"A fever dream?" Lewis asked with a shrewd little grin. He was clearly proud of himself for something, though Mallory had no idea what it might be.

As they rounded a corner, Mallory saw a gathering of Anomalians milling about in a gravel parking lot.

"Would a fever dream have food trucks?" he asked.

Half a dozen food trucks lined the far end of the gravel lot. Lewis pulled the RV off the road and turned into the gravel lot, narrowly avoiding three pedestrians. "Sorry!" he hollered through the closed window.

"My fever dream *would* have food trucks," Mallory said. "All of my dreams have food trucks, actually…fever or otherwise."

She tossed the petrified granola bar over her shoulder and got out of the cab. She stretched like a cat in the warm sun. Here, at last, was a part of Anomaly Flats she could get behind. *Food trucks,* she thought with a smile. *Mankind's finest invention.*

Of course, there was something a little off about these particular trucks. They were white, for one thing—pure, gleaming white, as if they'd each been freshly painted that morning, with no colorful logos, no oversized photos of food, no caricatures of short Mexicans in huge sombreros sinking their square teeth into overstuffed tacos. Just pure, sterile whiteness, except for their names, which were painted on in dull, black letters. And they weren't even fun names; there was no Neat-o Burrito or Thrilled Cheese or Moo-Moo Barbecue. Instead, all the trucks were marked with stenciled words that were more descriptors than names, and clinical ones at that. They read: PEELED SHRIMP, ENCASED MEATS, HARD-SHELL PORK PRODUCT TACOS, CHOCOLATE PUDDING FROM POWDER, RICE BOWLS WITH VARIOUS CANNED VEGETABLES, and SPECIAL.

"They need new marketing directors," Mallory decided.

Lewis shrugged. "They're government-sponsored trucks," he said, joining her on the gravel. "What do you expect?"

The Encased Meats and the Chocolate Pudding trucks seemed to be most popular among the assembled crowd, though every truck had at least one person in its line—every truck, that was, except for the Special truck. "What's the special?" Mallory asked.

"It changes every day. But don't do it, Mallory," Lewis warned. "Sure, sometimes it's lobster, and sometimes it's cheeseburgers. But I got the special once." His voice went quiet, and he cast his eyes down at his hands, which found themselves nervously rubbing the sides of his pants. "You don't want to do it. Okay? You don't want to take the chance."

"What was it? Napalm cups?" she snorted.

Lewis shook his head sadly. "I wish," he whispered.

Mallory's face dropped. Lewis wasn't joking. Something terrible had come out of that food truck; the drained, pallid look on his face was proof enough of that. There was no way she couldn't know now. "What was it, Lewis?" she asked, touching his shoulder lightly. The scientist flinched, and she drew her hand back. "What did they serve you?"

"It's not just that they *served* it," Lewis said quietly. "It's that I *ate* it. Mallory...I *had* to eat it. If you buy lunch from the Special truck, you have no choice but to eat it. Do you understand? They... they *force* you. I didn't *want* to eat it, but..." Tears streamed from his eyes, and his words choked off in his throat.

Mallory turned to face him directly and put both hands square-ly on his shoulders. She lowered her head so that he had no choice but to look her in the eye. "Oh my God…Lewis…*what was it?*"

Lewis tried to shrug out of her grip, but Mallory held firm. The tears stung his eyes red. He shook his head, and with all the courage he could muster, he whispered, "Pâté, Mallory. They made me eat pâté."

Mallory blinked. She didn't realize her fingers were digging into his shoulders until he whimpered a little in pain. "Are you kid-ding me?"

"It was horrible," Lewis insisted, wiping away a tear. "Duck liv-er, Mallory. *Duck liver.*"

Mallory released her grip on his shoulders. She took a deep breath and had to struggle like she'd never struggled before against the urge to punch Lewis in the mouth.

She succeeded, sort of.

She didn't punch his face. But she did slug his arm as hard as she could.

"Ow!" he whined. He rubbed at the pain as she turned and headed toward the Special truck.

"You are such a delicate little pansy," she said over her shoulder.

"Mallory, don't do it!" he called out after her. "It might be some-thing even worse this time! It might be haggis! Do you hear me, Mallory? *They might make you eat haggis!*"

A tall, strapping man in a reflective yellow work vest ap-proached the Special truck as Mallory made her way over. He had a dirty white hardhat tucked under his arm, and his thick leather boots were caked with mud. A small group of his fellow construc-tion workers stood what they seemed to consider a safe distance away from the line of trucks, hollering and hooting and egging him on. He grinned dumbly back at them and waved them off. As Mal-lory approached, his cheeks suddenly burned red, and he shifted his weight awkwardly, toeing at the gravel with his boots. "Your first time getting the special?" he asked bashfully.

"Yep. You?"

"Nah. I've had it a few times already. This is lucky number four...fingers crossed." He crossed the fingers on both his hands and held them up in the air. "Ha ha!" His laughter was undeniably nervous. He absently rubbed his brow with the back of his greasy, meaty arm as he laughed. Mallory noticed a long, white scar streaking across his forehead. She was about to ask what the specials had been on his previous visits when the service window on the side of the truck flew open with a loud *SLAM*, and a broad-shouldered man in a dark suit and dark sunglasses poked his head out. He wore an earpiece with a clear, coiled wire attached to it that disappeared into his collar. "One?" he asked, his voice cold.

The construction worker nodded and fished a ten-dollar bill from his pocket. The man in the suit put out his hand, and the man in the yellow vest laid the bill in his palm. "No change," the man in the suit said sharply. He pulled his hand back inside the truck and slammed the window shut.

"Great customer service," Mallory said.

"Ha ha!" the construction worker laughed nervously again. Sweat popped up along his brow as his eyes darted over to his buddies at the other end of the lot. They whooped and hollered encouragingly. The man wiped his sweaty palms on his yellow vest.

"What's wrong? You don't like pâté either?"

The man blanched. "Oh God...you think they're serving pâté today?" He looked like he might throw up, but he didn't get the chance. At that instant, the back doors of the food truck banged open, and a huge set of slimy, purple tentacles burst out of the truck. They waved menacingly in the air, as if sniffing out their prey, then they turned and shot out at the construction worker, fast as lightning. He screamed as one tentacle wrapped around his waist and another secured itself to his wrist. The creature began dragging him back toward the rear of the truck. The man screamed and begged for help, but his friends just looked on, shocked and dumbfounded, and a little sad. The man in the yellow vest looked at Mallory and pleaded for her to do something— *anything*. But a third tentacle shot out, clamped itself over his mouth, and lifted him into the air by his chin. The creature pulled the man into the back of the truck. The whole vehicle rocked violently from side to side, the tires lifting off the ground. The man's muffled screams were drowned out by a grotesque slurping and chomping and crunching of bones. Then the truck stopped moving, the unseen creature belched, and everything fell silent.

The man in the black suit slid the window of the food truck open. He poked his head out and looked at Mallory. "One?"

"Uhh...no, thanks. I've...changed my mind." Mallory turned on her heels and hurried back to Lewis and the RV. "What the *fuck* was that?" she hissed.

Lewis sighed and sucked at the corner of his bottom lip. "Some days, you eat the special, and some days, you *are* the special." Then he added, "It's still better than the pâté."

"Why didn't you say something?" Mallory snapped.

"I *did* say something! I said, 'Don't do it, Mallory, don't get the special!'"

"You didn't tell me I might *be* the special!"

"Every time I tell you not to do something, you do the opposite!" Lewis huffed. "So what's even the point?"

"The point is making sure your friends don't get eaten by a giant octopus! *That's one of the basic building blocks of life.*"

Lewis brightened around the eyes. "You think of me as a friend?" he asked, clearly pleased.

Mallory exhaled. She suddenly felt exhausted. "Look. Let's just get lunch, then you can take me back to the Roach Motel, where the tentacles are at least a more manageable size."

Lewis' smile fell. There was no disguising the hurt in his eyes. "Okay," he said. "If that's what you want." He rubbed his chin for a moment, as if he were on the verge of a very important decision. "I have just one more stop to make on the way. It's quick, and completely harmless, I swear. Then I'll bring you back to the hotel, and you won't ever have to see me again."

Mallory sighed. She grabbed Lewis' hand and gave it a good squeeze. "Look, Lewis, I just want to check back into the motel, go to my room, lock my seven locks, put up my barrier against demons, and wait it out until my car's ready and I can get the hell out of here. Okay? It's not you...mostly. It's this town. Really."

Lewis raised an eyebrow. "You mean it?"

Mallory shrugged. "Sure."

Lewis nodded. "Thank you for saying that. As far as lunch goes, I'd recommend the Rice Bowls with Various Canned Vegetables. Everything else is sort of greasy."

"Even the pudding?"

Lewis sniffed. "*Especially* the pudding."

CHAPTER 11

THE RV PULLED UP to their final stop for the day. Mallory was almost afraid to look out the windshield. When she did, she breathed a sigh of relief. "It looks peaceful," she smiled.

Lewis nodded. "It is peaceful. Peaceful, and calm, and basically non-threatening."

Mallory gave him a side-eye. "Basically?"

"Sure," he shrugged. "You know. Basically." He popped open the door of the RV and jumped down out of the cab. "There's not a whole lot that can go wrong here, I promise." He gestured grandly at the land before them with a wide sweep of his hand. "Welcome to Clone Lake."

The gentle lake waters stretched before them in a lazy curve that disappeared into the horizon on the north. Tall fir trees lined the eastern edge of the lake; the rest of the shore was lined by dark, wet sand that sloped gently up to a grassy ridge running alongside the water. Tall, willowy reeds sprouted along the shoreline, swaying lazily in the breeze. The water lapped quietly against the beach, and as Mallory shielded her eyes from the sun, she saw a graceful loon swoop down from one of the fir trees and skim along the surface of the lake, just barely hovering over, never quite touching the water.

"It's beautiful," she admitted with a smile. "A nice change in scenery. Thanks for bringing me here."

Lewis' cheeks blushed red. "You're welcome. I'm glad you like it."

He fished a small cooler and a handful of empty vials from the back of the Winnebago. He tucked the vials into his coat pockets and motioned for Mallory to follow. He walked over to where a small rowboat lay overturned on the shore. He struggled to set it right side up. "Do you want to come in the boat, or are you good on the beach?"

Mallory bit her bottom lip gently as she thought. "What sort of nightmare lives under the water?" she asked.

But Lewis shook his head. "Not a thing. Not even any fish! Promise. No tentacles, no teeth, no mouth, no eyes, nothing. Scout's honor." He held up three fingers, pointed toward the sky.

"And why is it called Clone Lake?" she asked suspiciously.

"Well, see how this is shaped sort of like a kidney?" he asked, pointing out the coastline that disappeared toward the north. "There's another lake in the next town that looks exactly the same. If you saw them on a satellite, you'd swear they were perfect clones. Hence Clone Lake."

"What's the other lake called?" Mallory asked.

"Evil Clone Lake."

"Funny."

Lewis shrugged. "I guess they figured a sense of humor is important when you live in a town with tentacle monsters hiding in food trucks."

"I bet."

Lewis struggled to push the little rowboat toward the water. "What do you say?" he asked, already breathing hard. "Want to come for a ride?"

Mallory edged warily toward the boat. "It's seaworthy?" she asked.

"Perfectly seaworthy; it *has* to be," he said, very seriously.

And here comes the catch, Mallory thought with a sigh. "Okay. And why's that?"

Lewis shrugged. "Otherwise, we'd sink."

"Oh." Mallory tilted her head. That made sense.

"Also—and this is just a small thing—the water is...unique. And it's best not to come into contact with it."

"I knew it!" Mallory cried, leveling an accusatory finger at his chest.

"But it's fine if you stay in the boat!" Lewis added quickly. "And it's not *dangerous,* it's just *unique!* You'll be perfectly safe, I promise! *I'll* be in the boat, and I wouldn't go into the boat if I didn't think it was safe."

"Oh, yeah, you've been a paragon of safety today," Mallory said, rolling her eyes.

Lewis looked hurt, but he held up his hands in defeat. "I understand," he said. "It's been a long day for you. I'll row out and get my samples, then we'll go back to the hotel. You stay here."

"Great," Mallory said, crossing her arms, "I will." Then a tree branch snapped somewhere off to her left, and she could've sworn she heard a wet snarl coming from something in the trees. "Wait, hold on...I'm coming!" she cried. She ran toward the boat and leapt into the stern just as Lewis pushed off the beach with an oar.

"Oh!" he gasped, startled. Water splashed up the sides of the boat, and he drew his arms inside in a panic. But the droplets fell harmlessly back into the lake, and Lewis smiled. "Welcome aboard."

"Thanks," Mallory grumbled, looking over her shoulder. She didn't see any creatures prowling the woods, but still. It was better to be safe than sorry.

Or saf*er*, at least.

"I'm not rowing, by the way," she added, noticing Lewis eyeing the other oar in the bottom of the boat. "I'm not sturdy."

"I wasn't going to suggest that you should," he said, pushing his glasses up his nose indignantly, though it was eminently clear to everyone in the boat that he certainly *had* been planning on suggesting it. He picked up the second oar and dipped both in the water, pulling them unsteadily away from shore.

"So level with me. What are you sampling for?"

Lewis hesitated. He was struggling against the oars, which were comically large in his small hands. After a few labored strokes, he said, "Uniqueness."

Mallory crossed her arms and glowered. "Right. I got that part. What *sort* of uniqueness? Life-altering, limb-mutating, radioactive uniqueness?"

"No, no! It's nothing dangerous, I *swear*."

Mallory snorted. "Sure. And I guess that's why there are no fish? Because it's not dangerous?"

"It *isn't* dangerous. Honestly. It won't hurt you a bit." He rowed a few more times in silence before adding, "Just...don't get any on you. Okay?"

Mallory shook her head and sighed. She hunkered down into the boat and closed her eyes. There was a light, pleasant breeze, and she grabbed her tangled hair and held it in a bunch on the top of her head, letting the cool air blow against the nape of her neck. With the warm sun and the easy wind and the gentle splash of the dipping oars, she could almost relax...if she didn't think too hard about the water. *This is what it'll be like in Saskatchewan,* she told herself. *Except it'll be colder. A lot colder.* Mallory hated the cold. She supposed she'd have to get used to wearing wool sweaters and down coats. Three down coats at once. *I hate you, Canada,* she thought.

But it would still be better than Missouri.

Lewis rowed them out toward the center of the lake. After a solid ten minutes of heaving and pulling and straining his poor scientist arms, he declared them a reasonable distance from the shore. He hauled the oars into the boat with a stern reminder to not touch the wet ends. Mallory smiled up into the air, her eyes still closed, and nodded. Here in the boat, she finally had the chance to rest a bit. For the first time in what felt like years, she was able to lie in the sun and not worry one bit about tentacles or spontaneous combustion or Mars or flies or goddamn waffles or police cars or any of the insanity that exploded its way into her life since leaving St. Louis and making a wrong turn into an inter-dimensional passageway. If pressed, she might even be willing to admit that she was edging her way toward a good mood. And that was a rare thing these days.

She opened one eye and spied Lewis pulling on thick, black rubber gloves that went up to his elbows. He picked up a small vial in one hand and leaned carefully over the edge of the boat. He dipped it slowly into the surface of the water, and when it was full, he lifted it and held it at arm's length, as if it might be caustic in spite of his insistence that it was fine. With the other hand, he grabbed the vial's lid and screwed it on, slowly, carefully, and methodically. He gingerly placed the sealed container into the little cooler and took a little breath of relief. Then he grabbed a second vial and started the process all over again.

Mallory smiled to herself. She didn't know if it was the sun, or the water, or the brain tumor that she was halfway certain had sprouted in the last 36 hours and given her severe hallucinations about a town from hell, but with Lewis teetering so precariously over the water, an opportunity presented itself that was just too wonderful to ignore. She'd been a hair's breath away from injury, maiming, and death by unspeakable means ever since she arrived in Anomaly Flats, but Lewis had skated breezily through all the perils without so much as a stutter in his step. She'd barely survived the last day and a half; he'd been living here just fine for twelve years. It didn't seem fair.

But now Mallory could even the scales a bit.

She bit her bottom lip mischievously and pulled herself up into a crouch. Lewis didn't notice her as he screwed the lid onto the second vial, lowered it into the cooler, and picked up a third vial. She crept forward, a wide grin spreading across her face, as he turned back to the lake. And when he leaned over to dip the vial in, she put both hands against his lower back and shoved him, screaming, over the side.

What? she thought, looking over the side and shrugging at her reflection in the water. *He said it wasn't dangerous.*

"Help!" Lewis yelled as he thrashed in the lake, bobbing under the surface and clawing his way up in a frantic spray of water. "*Help!*"

"Sorry," Mallory called out, laughing. "You're splashing a *lot*, and I'm not allowed to get the water on me."

"Mallory!" he sputtered, kicking and twisting and generally seeming to drown. "Get me out of this lake!"

Mallory frowned. She wasn't terribly adept at feeling guilt, and she wasn't actually sure if she would recognize it if she felt it…but she was fairly confident that she was feeling it now. The annoying part of her brain that tried to shame her for taking such reckless action cleared its throat knowingly. "Shut up, conscience," she said through gritted teeth. She grabbed one of the oars and held it out over the water. "Here…grab on."

But Lewis had sunk under the gentle waves.

"Lewis?" Mallory stood at the prow and leaned out over the water. Above the spot where he sank, a string of bubbles burbled up to the surface and popped into nothingness. "Lewis?" she asked again.

Oh my God, she thought. *I've killed him.*

She immediately began calculating the odds of successfully covering up his death by leaving the lake, taking her backpack, burning his RV to the ground, and skipping town on foot. They seemed pretty high, all things considered. If Anomaly Flats was good for nothing else, it *had* to be good for getting away with murder. But just as she was resolving herself to row back to shore and douse the Winnebago in gasoline, the surface of the lake frothed, and Lewis exploded up from beneath the waves.

And then he did it again.

Lewis surfaced, and then a second Lewis surfaced, and they both wailed and thrashed and cried out for help.

Two separate Lewises bobbed helplessly in the middle of the lake.

"What the shit?" Mallory whispered under her breath. Then, louder, she called, "Lewis?"

"Yes!" both Lewises screamed. They both swam for the boat, but they soon bumped into each other, and they each started frantically swatting at the other. They wrestled and yelped and cried—mostly, they cried—and tried to fight the other one off.

It was all too much to bear.

Mallory lifted the oar over her head and brought it slamming down onto the water with a loud *SLAP*. Both Lewises froze in midswat and turned to look at her. "What the *fuck* is happening here?" she demanded.

The Lewis on the left pointed at the Lewis on the right. The Lewis on the right pointed at the Lewis on the left. "He's a clone!" both Lewises cried in unison.

Mallory's knees became watery beneath her, and she sat down hard on the bench close to the front of the boat. "He's a clone," she snorted, more to herself than to either of the Lewises. "Of *course* he's a clone. Clone Lake doesn't hurt you; it just duplicates you." She stood up suddenly and screamed down at the Lewises, "*You told me it was called Clone Lake because there are two identical lakes!*"

"There are!" both Lewises cried. The one on the right swatted at the one on the left, and the one on the left swatted back at the one on the right.

"Mallory! It's me!" insisted the clone on the right, struggling to stay above water. "We met this morning, outside the Office of Tourism, and you were attacked by a swarm of flies!"

"No, *I'm* the original!" insisted the one on the left. "I took you to the food trucks, and you almost got mauled by the special! Remember?"

"Don't listen to him!" shrieked the Lewis on the right. "He has clones of my memories!"

"Spoken like a true clone!" screamed the Lewis on the left. They splashed at each other and both struggled toward the boat.

"If I were a clone, would I know that you smell like boysenberry and sweat?" the Lewis on the right screamed, trying desperately to make his case.

"If *I* were a clone, would I know that you snort like a hyena when you eat rice?" the Lewis on the left demanded.

"Keep it up," Mallory said with a glare. "See if I let *either* of you into this boat."

"Mallory, please!" both Lewises said at once. They each put one hand on the boat and started swatting at each other with the other hand. "Stop splashing me!" the Lewis on the left screamed. "*You* stop splashing *me*!" the Lewis on the right yelled back.

"Enough!" Mallory brought the oar back down onto the water, nearly taking off the fingers of both Lewises as it smacked down onto the surface. Both men grew quiet and looked up at her with pleading eyes as they treaded water. "Now, look: if one of you is a clone of the other, then you're both the same, right? Why don't I let *both* of you into the boat?"

"Oh, yes, good thinking!" cried the Lewis on the left. He reached up to grab the boat, but the other Lewis smacked his hand away.

"No!" shrieked the Lewis on the right. "He's not just a clone! He's an *evil* clone!"

"*You're* the evil clone!" the Lewis on the left shouted, and they began swatting at each other once more.

"Stop!" Mallory held the oar over her head, ready to strike. The Lewises subsided sheepishly. "Are *all* Clone Lake clones evil?"

"Yes!" cried the Lewis on the right.

"No!" cried the Lewis on the left. Then he looked over at the Lewis on the right. "Wait, yes!" he decided.

"So one of you is definitely evil?" she asked. The Lewises nodded. Mallory pointed the oar at the Lewis on the left. "And you were going to let both of you come up into the boat knowing that one of you is evil?"

"Well..." the Lewis on the left began, but he didn't seem to know what to say after that, so he just gave a sullen shrug.

"I'm gonna call 'not caring if an evil scientist gets into the boat with Mallory' the wrong choice." She swung the oar down at the Lewis on the left, and he shrieked and ducked under the water, avoiding a cranial injury by just a few inches. He came up sputtering a few feet away and began swimming frantically toward the shore, shrieking, "You'll be sorry! You'll *all* be sorry!" as he went.

Mallory lowered the oar to the remaining Lewis. He grabbed it gratefully as he struggled his way into the boat. He flopped down on the bench like a bloated fish, wheezing and shaking and clearing the water from his lungs. "Thanks," he managed to say between gasps.

"No problem." She fit both oars into the oarlocks and started rowing them toward the shore. Then she added, "Sorry about creating your evil clone."

"I *told* you not to touch the water," Lewis reminded her, panting.

"I didn't touch the water. I made *you* touch the water."

"The principle is the same."

"You said it wasn't dangerous."

"I said it won't hurt you. It's *that* kind of not dangerous."

"You should have been more specific," Mallory insisted, pulling at the oars.

Lewis gasped a heavy sigh. "I told you not to touch the water, and I was extremely careful not to get any water on me. What would you have liked me to say?"

"How about, 'Mallory, if you push me into the lake, you'll create my evil clone, so please don't'?"

"I didn't know you were going to *push me into the lake!*"

"Yeah. I'm as surprised as anyone," she admitted. "I just spontaneously decided that you really deserved it." She paused for a moment and rowed a few times, wondering if perhaps her remarks weren't terribly helpful. "Again…really sorry about that."

Lewis shook his head and sighed. There were plenty of responses he would have liked to give to that, but he decided to just stew quietly on his end of the boat instead.

After just two minutes, Mallory had managed to cover half the distance to the shoreline. "You're a really good rower," Lewis observed.

"I know, I know…I'm sturdy," she said, annoyed. "What do we do about him?" She nodded over at the evil clone, who was flopping his way toward the far beach.

"There's only one thing you *can* do with evil clones," Lewis said, sitting up and wringing the water out of his bow tie. "Destroy them."

Mallory started. "Whoa. Seriously? We're going to kill him?"

"I'm not sure he's a *him*. More of an *it*, I think. But that depends on your view of the human soul, and it brings up a lot of really intriguing and complex questions about the very nature of life. So, okay, we'll say 'him.'"

"You are so irritating sometimes," Mallory said, shaking her head.

"I've heard that before," Lewis sighed. "To answer your question, yes, we're going to kill him."

"Isn't that…you know…murder?"

Lewis shrugged. "It all depends on if you view the clone as a person or a thing. It goes right back into—"

"I know, I know, complex questions of the soul. Jesus, can't you just give me a straight answer like a normal person?"

Lewis cocked his head. "Is it your experience that most people give straight answers? I find that to almost never be the case."

Mallory closed her eyes and counted to three. "Never mind," she said. "I think I'm warming up to murder."

"Well, murder or not, the death of a clone is sanctioned in the Anomaly Flats town charter. It has to be, or else we'd be completely overrun by evil clones."

"How do you know you're *not* overrun by evil clones?" Mallory pointed out, bringing the boat to the shoreline. "What if the town is full of evil clones who killed their originals, just blending in and biding their time until they can rise up and murder all the non-clones in their sleep?"

Lewis blinked. "Great. Thanks for that," he said sourly. "Now I'll never sleep again."

The boat ran up on the beach, and Mallory and Lewis hopped out and dragged it up onto the shore. "So how do we do it?" Mallory asked with a frown. The idea of murdering someone didn't exactly sit well with her...even if the intended victim *was* an evil clone.

"Let's get back to the truck," Lewis said, still panting from his struggle. He put his hands on his hips and pulled in a few deep breaths. "I have some acids in there that should do the trick."

"Perfect. If we don't kill him, at least we can make him a Batman villain," Mallory said.

"Hey, we work with what we've got," he shrugged. He patted the pockets of his lab coat. "Do you have the keys?"

"Keys? Why would I have the keys?"

"Maybe I gave them to you."

"You did not give them to me. You had them."

"I'm not sure I—ah! Yes," he said triumphantly, hoisting a finger into the air. "I *did* have them. I left them in the truck."

Just then, the RV's engine roared to life, and gravel flew as the tires spun wildly. The RV lurched forward, onto the road, squealing the tires against the asphalt. The Lewis in the truck gave them the finger out the open window as the Winnebago disappeared over the hill.

Mallory turned to Lewis and shook her head. "Left the keys in the truck. Brilliant."

Lewis frowned. "Shoot."

They stared in silence after the RV.

Mallory gasped suddenly. "My bag!"

She took off after the fleeing clone on foot. "Wait!" Lewis hollered. He ran after her, which was no easy feat for a man who was terribly out of shape and who had just battled an evil clone in a deep lake. He more flopped than ran, gasping for air and wheeling his arms and loudly begging Mallory to slow down.

They reached the edge of the road, both of them panting and cursing. "What do we do?" Mallory demanded. "That son of a bitch has my bag! What do we *do*?"

"I don't know!" Lewis wailed.

The RV reappeared on the crest of a hill farther down the road, for the briefest moment, then disappeared again over the other side. "He's taunting me!" she screamed. She kicked the edge of the road and sent a spray of loose gravel flying. She stormed around in a circle, positive that it wouldn't help, but not sure what else to do. She gasped out loud and grabbed Lewis roughly by the lapels. "Look!" she cried. An old, blue, rusted-out Chevy truck was rumbling around the curve. "Hitch us a ride!"

"What do you *mean*, hitch us a ride?" Lewis whined. "That's Bill Stevison's truck. We don't want a ride with him…he's *strange*."

Mallory was having none of it. She shoved him out into the road.

"Ow! Geez, okay, okay!" He threw up his hands at the oncoming truck and screamed, "Bill, *stop*!" The sheer pitch of his voice shot daggers into Mallory's eardrums. Bill Stevison saw Lewis through the windshield, and his eyes grew as large as the Chevy's hubcaps. He hurriedly unbuckled his seatbelt, popped open the door, and, with a wild shriek, threw himself from the driver's seat and into the ditch that ran alongside the road. The truck veered off the road in the other direction, smashing straight into a massive fir tree. The Chevy shuddered, and steam hissed out from beneath the busted hood. Bill picked himself up out of the ditch, despite an obviously broken elbow, and scrambled away across the field, shrieking and crying and running for his life.

Mallory stared at Lewis. Lewis stared back. "I told you he was strange," he said.

They ran toward the truck, and they both made a dash for the passenger side. "What're you doing?" Mallory demanded. "You're driving!"

"I can't!" Lewis whined.

"You have to! I don't know the roads!" Mallory shouted.

"But these old trucks don't have power steering, and I can't turn the wheel!"

"What makes you think I can?!"

"Because you're—"

"*I am* not *sturdy, goddammit!*"

"You're weirdly strong!" he insisted.

"*I do yoga!*" She stormed around the front of the truck and hopped up into the driver's side.

Lewis pulled himself cautiously into the passenger seat and buckled his seat belt. "I hope you know how to drive a stick," he said miserably, glancing at the shifter jutting out from the gearbox.

"I was born and raised in Missouri," Mallory said, gritting her teeth, pressing the clutch, and jerking the shifter into reverse. "Of course I know how to drive a stick."

This proved to be a bit of hubris on Mallory's part. It took a few engine deaths before she could successfully maneuver the truck away from the tree and back out onto the road. The steering wheel had no give, so she pulled at it with both hands to direct the truck onto the asphalt. In under a minute, they were on their way, tearing down the backcountry road in pursuit of Lewis' evil clone.

"Where am I going?" Mallory asked, her body tense as she struggled with the steering wheel.

"Straight. This doesn't break off until it hits Cumberland, the main road through town. That's in about seven miles." He turned to Mallory with a grave look in his eyes. "There's no telling which way he'll turn. We have to catch up to him before then."

Mallory set her lips in a hard line. "Got it." She jammed the truck into fourth gear and pressed the gas pedal to the floor. "Buckle up."

"I *am* buckled up," Lewis said, confused.

Mallory rolled her eyes. "It was an expression, Lewis. It was for fucking effect. For crying out loud, watch a movie."

They sped along the road, Mallory gripping the wheel so hard her knuckles went white. The old Chevy lurched around the curves. At the crest of the next hill, the truck soared into the air for a split second and came crashing down on its axles. The tires swerved, and Mallory almost lost her grip on the wheel. She cried out, but with enough grunting and pulling, she managed to get the truck under control. She heaved down on the wheel as the road took a sharp curve to the left and just barely managed to keep it on the road as the passenger side squealed against the metal guard rail, sending a small spray of sparks up against the window.

"Getting there alive is preferable," Lewis said, squeezing his eyes shut and holding onto the dashboard for dear life.

"Picky, picky," Mallory mumbled.

After a few minutes, the old Winnebago came into view. "We're gaining!" Mallory said, surprised. "I am an amazing driver."

"The Winnie's old and slow," Lewis pointed out.

Mallory shook her head slowly. "Have I told you how wildly unsurprised I am that you're single?"

They approached the intersection with Cumberland. The evil clone blew right through the stop sign and veered the RV to the right without hitting the brakes. The Winnebago squealed and groaned and rose up on two wheels, and for a second, it looked like there was no hope for it but to tip over. But somehow, miraculously, the wheels touched down again, hard, rocking the RV violently.

"Shit," Mallory said through gritted teeth. "Hold on."

She gripped the top of the wheel with both hands and strained against it, struggling to pull the Chevy onto the new road. The wheel stuttered and shook in her hands. She grunted with the strain of it. The truck jammed to the right, and the centrifugal force pulled Lewis down the bench seat so he was suspended sideways by his seatbelt. The tires screeched on the asphalt, but thanks to the weight of the old truck, they stayed on the ground. Mallory jerked the wheel back to the left. The truck fishtailed, but it righted itself after a few heart-stopping skids, and they tore off down the road after the clone.

"Where's he going?" Mallory asked. Adrenaline pumped through her veins like rocket fuel, and her whole body shook. "Any idea?"

"How would I know that?" Lewis asked, though not unkindly.

"He's you, isn't he? Where would *you* go?"

But before Lewis could answer, something exploded against the windshield. Mallory swerved in surprise, barely keeping the truck on the road. "What the *hell*?"

Another little pop burst against the glass. Then another, and another. The clone was tossing little vials of brightly-colored liquid at them out the open driver's window.

"My acid collection! *Stop it, you monster!*" Lewis yelled, as if the clone could hear him.

"Why do you collect acid?!" Mallory demanded.

"Why *don't you*?" Lewis countered.

The little vials popped against the windshield, and a few of the acids began to eat through the glass. The windshield sizzled and melted away, and molten glass dripped down onto the dashboard. Wind whistled through the holes, and angry little droplets of acid flew inside the cab. "Don't let it touch you!" Lewis cried.

"Thanks for the tip, brainiac," Mallory mumbled.

She swerved to the right to avoid another acid bomb, then swerved back to the left. The assault continued as the RV careened down the road, wavering from one side to the other. "How big is this goddamn collection?" Mallory demanded, dodging a large beaker of green fluid.

"He's almost through it now," Lewis said sadly. "It took me ages to collect all those…"

"Let's hope he doesn't find your chainsaw collection next."

Lewis scrunched up his face in confusion. "I don't have a chain-saw collection."

"Seriously, Lewis? Which bottle has your sense of humor in it?"

The chase continued. The clone ran out of acid—or at least, he ran out of acid within arm's reach—and finally, the vials stopped flying. The Chevy's windshield was damaged, but not cripplingly so. Mallory urged the truck to move faster, and soon they were on the evil clone's bumper. "Should I run him off the road?" Mallory asked excitedly, though she had no idea how to actually run an RV off the road. But she was more than willing to try.

Lewis the Spoilsport shook his head. "If you run him off the road, there's a high probability of shattering most of the containers inside…mix some of those fluids, and we'll have an ecological catastrophe on our hands. No, he can't drive forever. Let's just follow him and see where he goes."

"This high-speed chase just got super-boring," Mallory complained.

Then the clone jerked the RV off the road and into a cornfield, and things got a little more exciting again.

"Hold on!" Mallory cried. She hauled at the wheel, and the Chevy peeled off the road and plunged into the cornfield after the Winnebago. The corn stalks were tall and brown and dry, well past the point of harvest. Ears of corn rotted away in their husks, oozing brown liquid through the leaves. The stalks folded and broke easily under the Chevy's bumper, and they slapped loudly against the truck as it mowed them down. They left a wide alley of flattened ruin behind them. "Somewhere, there's a farmer who is going to be *very* upset when he sees this," Mallory guessed. Lewis didn't respond. Mallory glanced over at him. He was huddled into a tight ball in his seat, his body pressed against the door, his hands covering his ears. "What're you doing?" she asked.

Lewis looked over at her, his eyes wide and wild with fear. "*Don't listen to it!*" he yelled. "*Shut your ears!*"

"Don't listen to what?" she asked. But even as she said the words, she began to hear whispers rising over the slapping of the cornstalk leaves on the truck. They seemed to drift in through the holes in the windshield, snaking their way lazily about the cab and slipping into her ear canals on a warm, welcome breath:

The best things in life are broken, the voices whispered.

The best way to scratch an itch is with a razor blade.

Tongues are an abomination.

There is an exquisite pleasure in scraping your veins clean with steel wool.

Children were made to set fire to.

Your blood would look much nicer on the outside of your skin.

A scream is worth a thousand dollars.

Loud screams are worth more.

Lungs were made to burst.

The sun will drip fire and set the Earth ablaze.

But Mallory didn't just *hear* these whispers; she *knew* them. They filled her, they penetrated her core, and they made *sense*. On some deep bedrock of intuition and awareness, she knew these whispers to be absolute truths. It was as if a thick veil had been lifted from her mind, and she was experiencing the true, clear, horrible nature of the world around her for the first time. "We were born to scrub the Earth clean," she said, relishing the truth of the words as they rolled off her tongue. "We are meant to scrub it clean of the blight of ourselves. That is our purpose."

She eased her foot off the gas. The truck slowed amid the corn, and more whispers flooded the cab. They were louder now, more insistent, more concrete. Mallory reached for the gearshift and snapped it easily from its base. The broken end, jagged with torn metal, gleamed in the sunlight that filtered in through the leaves. She pressed the sharp metal into her forehead and pushed until the gearshift punctured her skin, then her skull, then her brain, and come out the other end. *Yes,* she thought, as the jagged end of the stick bumped against the wall of the cab behind her. *This is better.*

Sharp stones are nature's surgical equipment, the voices urged.

Man was born to spawn maggots.

Flesh is tender.

Tender is delicious.

Mallory turned her head and gazed over at Lewis. His head had been replaced by a watermelon. It had a wide mouth and no eyes. "The speed of a blink is 42," Lewis the watermelon said. "Can I try your discouragement, please?"

Mallory nodded slowly. She thought she would like for Lewis to taste her discouragement. She thought she would like that very much. She opened it up to him. It sagged out of her heart and dripped greasy spits of sorrow onto the Chevy's upholstery. Lewis the watermelon leaned down and rolled his huge, oblong head around in the despair, letting it coat his rind and sink through the pores into his juicy pink flesh.

"I see the tree," Mallory said suddenly. She wanted Lewis to acknowledge that *he* saw the tree too. He had to see it. He *must* have been seeing it. Why wouldn't he say so? "Lewis," she droned, watching her fingers turn into daisies. "Lewis. Do you see the tree? Lewis?" She closed her eyes.

"Mallory," the watermelon said, coated in her despair. "Mallory."

His voice seemed far away now, as if it he were speaking from behind the sun. "Mallory."

Now urgently, and from the dark side of the moon: "Mallory!"

Now frantic, and choked with dirt, from six feet beneath the soil: "Mallory!"

And then, the voice came from somewhere new. Somewhere right next to her. It rang with a sharp clarity that pierced her brain and made the gearshift vibrate. "*MALLORY!*"

She gasped, and her eyes flew open. Her fingers were fingers again, and they were wrapped tightly around the steering wheel. The gearshift stood straight and tall on the floor, where it belonged, and Mallory's head was whole. The interior of the cab was free and clear of her viscous despair. The truck sat idling on the roadside; the cornfield waved starkly in the wind behind them.

"What…?" Mallory whispered, her voice trembling. She gazed at Lewis, regular, non-watermelon Lewis, with an ocean of troubled confusion.

"You're all right," he said, taking her hand in his. "Just take a minute. Take a breath." And then, because it seemed to be in his nature and, Mallory supposed, because he just couldn't help it, he had to add, "I told you not to listen."

Mallory turned in her seat and looked back at the cornfield. The brown, dead stalks dripped their rotted juices onto the hard, dry soil. The crinkled leaves waved in the air, bidding her a silent and mocking adieu. "What…happened?"

Lewis adjusted his glasses on his nose. "The Fields of Insanity happened."

Mallory's world was wrapped in gauze, and she struggled to peel away the layers. "The…what?"

"It's the corn," he explained, patting her hand. "It…has an effect on people. That's why no one eats it. That's why it's left on the stalk to rot. You can't listen to the corn, it does bad things to you. Do you understand? Don't ever listen to the corn, Mallory. And don't ever, *ever* eat it."

"The corn drives people insane?" She buried her face in her palms and tried to rub some sense into her brain. "Lewis, then why do you even grow it?"

"*I* don't grow it," he insisted, raising his hands defensively. "Farmer Buchheit grows it."

Mallory exhaled, annoyed. "Then why does *Farmer Buchheit* grow it?"

Lewis shrugged. "Because Farmer Buchheit's a real asshole."

Mallory shook her head and tried to regain some sense of herself. "Am I going to be okay?"

Lewis crumpled up the corner of his mouth. "Do you *feel* okay?"

"I feel like someone scooped out my brain and replaced it with a ball of hash browns."

Lewis squinted at her uncertainly. "You'll...*probably* be fine?" he guessed.

"How'd we make it through? I stopped the truck...how'd we make it out?"

Lewis shook his head. "You didn't stop the truck. You *gunned* the truck. It seems you have an incredibly powerful survival instinct. Which is good; that comes in handy around here."

"But I thought I stopped the truck..." Mallory drifted, looking down at the gearshift and remembering, quite vividly, the painless sensation of the jagged metal pushing through her gray matter. She shuddered from the chill of it, and her mind slowly began collecting itself. Then Mallory gasped. "The clone!"

"He didn't make it out unscathed." Lewis pointed out the windshield. On the other side of the dirt road, down a ways, the RV rested awkwardly on one busted tire. The clone stood outside of the truck, his hand against the side of the Winnebago for support. His legs wobbled as he steadied himself, and he thumped the heel of his free hand against his temple. "The driver's window tends to stick. It doesn't always roll back up once it's down. The voices must have been loud and clear." Lewis smiled. "That's what he gets for tossing my acid collection," he said smugly. "The value of those ruined vials alone is—"

"My bag!" Mallory interrupted. Across the street, the evil clone had pulled open the RV's side door and was digging Mallory's purple Jansport out of the back. He tossed it onto the ground and unzipped it. He peered down into the bag, then looked up at the RV. Then he looked back down at the bag. Then back up at the RV... then back down at the bag.

A wide grin spread across his face.

He did a quick rummage through the Winnebago, making a frantic grab for an armful of vials and beakers and lab equipment. He dumped the small load into the bag, zipped it up, and slung it over his shoulder. Then he sprinted away from the ruined vehicle and into the neighboring field.

"Son of a bitch!" Mallory screamed. She stomped down on the brake and clutch and turned the key in the ignition. The engine clicked, but didn't turn. "No, no, no, no," Mallory prayed as she tried a second time, then a third. "*No!*" She slammed her hands angrily against the wheel. "I'm gonna kill those motherfucking magnetics!"

"It's not the magnetic field. This truck is too old to have an alternator," Lewis pointed out.

"Shut up. Fix it."

Lewis tilted his head. "Fix it?"

"Fix it!"

"Did I not mention that I'm not a mechanic? I could swear this has come up before."

"Argh!" Mallory threw off her seatbelt, launched out the door, and took off on foot after the clone. "Give me back my goddamn bag!" she screamed.

Lewis gave a low whistle as he watched her go. "She sure likes that backpack," he said to the empty cab. Then he jumped out of the truck and ran to catch up.

Fortunately for Mallory, the clone had the same genes as her good-for-nothing scientist companion, and she could tell he was laboring under the weight of the bag. She was maybe only 100 yards behind, and gaining.

The original Lewis was faltering somewhere behind her. She was pretty sure she heard him collapse, wheezing, into the tall grass, but she didn't bother looking back. *Serves him right,* she thought.

Evil Lewis' pace slowed even more as he approached a makeshift plank bridge on the far end of the field that crossed a familiar-looking stream of neon green plasma. He unzipped the backpack as he neared the center of the bridge and dug frantically through its contents. He pulled out something that was too small for Mallory to see. Whatever it was, the clone crouched down and smeared it on the bridge, right in the middle. Then he stood, zipped up the bag, and ran across to the flat land on the other side of the creek.

Mallory pushed herself harder. The clone was closer now, only 50 yards, and she could catch him. She *knew* she could catch him. She could drive her sturdy legs faster, force her sturdy lungs to breathe, and choke the living shit out of that evil bastard with her sturdy fucking hands.

She sprinted up the bridge and was nearing the spot where the clone had paused when she heard Lewis' screaming voice behind her: "Mallory, *stop!*"

Stop? Was he insane? The only thing standing between her and that evil little twerp was half a bridge and a bit of grass. She couldn't stop. She could catch the clone, reclaim her bag, and plunge his little head into Plasma Creek so he turned into a walking dandelion that would ripen in a week and blow away in the wind to nothingness. That, she could do. But stop?

No.

She couldn't stop.

But then the bridge made a really good case for stopping by exploding right in the middle.

The force of the explosion lifted Mallory off her feet and tossed her through the air as if she were a pebble. She was so stunned at this sudden change in both events and trajectory that she didn't even think to scream until she crashed down on her shoulder and skidded for ten feet in the hard earth. Then she remembered to scream. A lot.

"Mallory! Are you okay?" Lewis asked, jogging up to her prostrate form, gasping for air. "Are you hurt anywhere?"

"I'm hurt *everywhere!*" Mallory screeched between strings of expletives. "I'm going to kill that little fucking clone. And then I think I'll kill you. And then I'll kill him again. *Harder.*"

Lewis stood up and put two fingers to his neck to check his pulse. "I told you to stop," he pointed out between breaths.

"You're gonna be so much less smug when I murder you," Mallory decided. She struggled to sit up.

"You should rest for a minute," Lewis said, though he reached down and helped her into a seat anyway. He inspected her carefully. "Are you burned? You don't look burned."

"Should I be burned?"

Lewis shrugged. "That depends on which explosive cream he used."

"Explosive *cream*?"

Lewis blushed. "It's my own invention," he said modestly.

"Congratulations, Oppenheimer; you're a monster." Lewis frowned. Mallory gave herself a once-over. She didn't *seem* burned. "I think I'm okay."

Lewis nodded his agreement. "He must have used the cold fusion cream," he murmured.

Mallory coughed. She wasn't exactly a physicist—and was not entirely sure she could even *spell* "physicist" if it came down to it—but she'd done well enough in science class to know there were at least two things distinctly wrong with Lewis' statement. One was that she was fairly sure that cold fusion *fused* things, which was the opposite of exploding them. But it was the second thing that really made her suspicious. "Doesn't cold fusion…not exist?"

Lewis nearly squealed with delight. "Not usually, no. But with the help of Anomaly Flats, I have unlocked the secret!" He beamed, and he clearly expected Mallory to share his excitement.

Instead, she just shrugged.

"Granted, it doesn't behave *quite* like it should," Lewis continued. "It's terribly unstable. It does more explosion than fusion, as you've seen. Actually, it hasn't done any actual fusion yet at all. I'm working out the kinks. But still! We were in theoretical territory until now. Who really knew *what* should happen when someone achieved cold fusion? Oh, Mallory, you should see the process! I'm a shoo-in for the Nobel Prize when I publish my notes to the scientific community. Just you wait! Won't it be wonderful?"

"Yeah, it's pretty wonderful that your clone used an explosive that you accidentally created to nearly blow my head off instead of using it for cold fusion."

Lewis frowned. "We'll discuss it later," he sighed. "When you're feeling better."

"Can we just get my bag back, please?"

"Um…" Lewis glanced nervously at the bridge, then back down at Mallory. "I think we may have to put this little chase on hiatus." Mallory struggled to her feet and looked at the bridge. The explosion had blown one end of it clear across the far side of the bank. The other end had plunged into Plasma Creek and had resurfaced as a baby panda that bobbed happily down the creek. As for Lewis' evil clone, he was busy disappearing over a ridge in the distance.

"What about the…whatchamacallits?" Mallory asked.

"Whichamacallits?" Lewis asked back.

"The thingies—the beams of light that make people burn. Why isn't he running into those?" The thought of him escaping certain disintegration made Mallory's heart sink, until she realized what would happen to her backpack if the clone were caught in one of the beams. She felt a little better about the lack of vaporization then.

"Ah! Those. We're too far north," Lewis said. "There haven't been any reports of that sort of thermonuclear activity in this part of the creek."

"Well, we can't lose him, bridge or no bridge. He's on foot, I can catch him." Mallory stepped up to the stream and considered the distance between the two banks. "And I can totally jump that," she decided.

"It's ten feet," Lewis pointed out uncertainly. "At the very least."

"So what? I can jump it. I'm positive."

"Mallory—" the scientist began.

"No! Listen to me, Lewis. That bastard clone has my backpack, and I need it back. Do you understand me? I don't just *want* it back; I *need* it back. Without that bag, this whole fucking misery has been for nothing, and that is *not* going to happen." She took a few steps back. She swung her arms and worked to loosen her legs. "I can do this," she reminded herself aloud, taking a deep breath. "Totally easy. I can do it." She braced herself to begin her sprint.

"You know, we *could* just grab him at dinner," Lewis said.

Mallory stopped and looked at Lewis. "Say what?"

"I said, you can either try to make an impossible leap and wind up plunging into a river of plasma that'll turn you into some sort of clump of rotting weeds, or you can wait a couple of hours and grab him when he goes to dinner tonight."

Mallory squinted, suspicious. "Where's he going to dinner to-night?"

"Chick-fil-A."

"And how do you know that?"

"Because it's Friday," he said with a little smile. "*Everyone* has Chick-fil-A for dinner on Friday."

Mallory screwed up her face in disgust. "Ew. What is that, some sort of weird, communal death-by-grease ritual?"

Lewis turned and started walking back to the broken-down ve-hicles. He couldn't fix the Chevy, but he knew how to change a tire. "Nope," he said, nodding for Mallory to follow. "Not a ritual. It's the law."

CHAPTER 12

"SO LET ME GET THIS STRAIGHT. You eat at Chick-fil-A on Friday nights, or else you go to jail?"

"Yep," Lewis said, putting the Winnebago into gear. "Tuesday lunches, too. If you take lunch anywhere else on Tuesdays, you go straight to the hole."

"The hole?"

"The hole."

"What's the hole?" Mallory asked, buckling her seatbelt.

"It's…pretty much what it sounds like," Lewis said sadly. Then he added, "But deeper."

"Is it even worth asking why?" Mallory sighed. She rested her forehead against the cool glass of the RV window.

"Because the Chick-fil-A is owned by the mayor. And she likes us to spend our money there."

"And surely an evil clone wouldn't dare get on the wrong side of the law," Mallory chided.

"You haven't seen our jail," he said. "Trust me. He'll be there."

As they drove back down Cumberland toward the downtown strip, Lewis laid out a plan. The dinner rush usually picked up around 6:00. He felt sure that the clone would either arrive extremely early or extremely late, in an attempt to avoid detection.

"Are you sure?" Mallory asked. "If it were me, I'd go in when it was slammed. Try to blend in with the crowd."

But Lewis was adamant. "Not a chance. He wouldn't risk bumping into me and causing a scene."

"But wouldn't he know that you would know that he would want to go early or late, and then *not* go early or late because he'd know you'd be there to catch him either early or late?" Mallory was starting to get the hang of clone-think. She wasn't sure that was a good thing.

"No," Lewis insisted, "because I know that *he* knows that *I* know that he'd want to go early or late, and he *knows* that I know that *he* knows that *I* know that he'd want to go early or late, so he's much more likely to reverse-double-cross himself by trying to double-cross-reverse me. You see?"

Mallory groaned. "Sure," she said. "So, what, we stake out a fast food joint for the next two or maybe seven hours and hope he shows?"

"There's a great spot right behind the used grease dumpster," Lewis beamed.

"Ew...they have a separate dumpster for it?" Her face paled at the thought of a dumpster filled with plastic bags full of used grease.

"Well, yeah. So you don't put grease in the spare-chicken-part dumpster," Lewis said, laughing a bit, because this was clearly the most obvious thing in the world. "Otherwise, the town mutants would get grease-flu when they swarmed the dumpster and fed on the spare chicken parts after dark."

They drove the rest of the way pretty much in silence.

X

"So. This is what chicken grease smells like."

Lewis made a surprised noise somewhere behind his nasal cavity. "Have you never smelled chicken grease before?" he asked.

Mallory sank down in her seat and pulled the collar of her t-shirt up over her nose. "Not in such...quantity," she said. The pungent smell stung at her eyes, and they glistened over with tears.

"But look at the vantage point," Lewis said, nodding toward the restaurant. They had an excellent view of both the side and back doors of the Chick-fil-A. They could see the employees in their chicken-stained red polos, wiping off tables and sweeping up floors and generally busying themselves in preparation for the mandatory dinner rush.

"Why are the employees all muscly bald man?" Mallory asked. Something stirred involuntarily in the depths of her stomach as she watched a sweaty lunk with fading blue tattoos shake a pan of dirty water down a drain. *Stop it, ovaries,* she silently cursed herself, embarrassed on behalf of her biological clock.

"Prison work program," Lewis said.

"They let prisoners work at Chick-fil-A?"

Lewis nodded. "They insist on it! It actually solves a few problems at once. The mayor is firmly against paying a living wage, and the prisoners would do literally anything to get out of the jail for a while. *Literally anything,* Mallory. Our jail is terrible."

"So I've heard."

Lewis gestured to the men working inside the restaurant. "This seemed like a decent solution for everyone."

"Are they violent?" she asked, working hard to keep a small hint of excitement out of her voice.

Lewis shrugged. "Some of them, sure."

Strangely, this did little to dilute her estrogen levels.

She gave her head a good shake and tried to focus. They had no clear view of the front of the building from this angle. "What if the clone goes in the front door?" she asked.

Lewis chuckled. "The front door? No one uses the front door. You get sliced in half by a giant saw blade if you go in that way."

Mallory coughed in surprise. "Seems like a strange way to run a business."

"It keeps the foyer clean," Lewis explained. "People tend track in a lot of mud."

A speaker just to their left squealed. Mallory jumped a mile. "Christ!" she said, putting a hand to her chest and catching her breath. "Does any place in this town *not* have a loudspeaker?"

Lewis looked at her strangely. "No," he said.

The now-familiar female voice crackled to life:

"Attention, Anomaly Flats: Next week, all water at the Anomaly Flats Island Adventure Water Park will be replaced by five metric tons of loose gravel as part of an ongoing experiment by a clandestine research group that you should never, ever inquire about. The water park will operate normally, at regular business hours, but with loose gravel instead of water. If you were planning on visiting Island Adventure Water Park next week, you should not change your plans. Anyone who has been planning on visiting Island Adventure Water Park but changes their mind because the water slides, lazy river, and wave pool will now be filled with loose gravel will be visited in the night by the clandestine research group and surgically removed."

The speaker squawked and screeched, and then cut out completely.

"They sure know how to keep up morale," Mallory grumbled.

"Yes," Lewis agreed. "Isn't it *fascinating*?"

A few early dinner patrons began filtering into the parking lot and sitting down to their chicken sandwiches and oversized Cokes, but they were older, much older, and the evil clone wasn't among them.

"So here's a question," she said, leaning back against the dumpster. The grease smell wasn't so pungent, now that her nostrils had gotten a good dose of it. "Since Evil Lewis is your clone, isn't he off the hook if *you* go in for dinner? I mean, they're going to be on the lookout for Lewis Barnish—"

"Burnish."

"—Burnish, sorry. But they're not going to be looking for *two* Lewis Barnishes, right?"

"Burnishes," he stressed.

"Get over it. You know what I'm saying, right? They're not going to be all, 'Oh, look, only one weird scientist came to dinner today, that's suspicious; shouldn't there be a second genetically-identical weird scientist that no one knows exists except for the weird scientist, the weird scientist's clone, and a super-hot tourist?'"

"Actually, they will. The mayor tracks everyone in town by heat signature from her fleet of drones. If they find his heat signature on the other side of town, he's dead."

"I thought you said he'd go to jail."

"You think my genetic duplicate would survive more than three hours in a prison? Especially *this* prison? Mallory, you haven't seen our jail..."

Mallory laughed. "I think your genetic duplicate would be lucky to survive more than three *minutes* in prison. *Any* prison."

"Well, that's...hurtful, mostly. But you see my point."

"But what if he risks it? What if he decides to take advantage of the rest of the town being empty to pull off some next-level evil clone shit?"

Lewis raised an eyebrow. "Next-level evil clone shit?"

Mallory shrugged with her palms. "You know. Sinister things. Like rig elections. Bomb buildings. Drown old people in ice water. Throw away their medicine. I don't know—what do the town's evil clones usually do?"

Lewis squinted one eye, poked his tongue out of the corner of his mouth, and tried to remember. "It's been a while since we've had one. I guess the last clone would have been Evil Lori Koppel. She set fire to the fire department and bulldozed the original bowling alley. Before that, Evil Mason Crosby poisoned the town's water supply, and before that, Evil Mary Twixby brainwashed all the children and led them on a death march over the Lava Cliffs into Sputtering Volcano. That's why everyone in town is sterilized now," he added. "Just in case."

"Wow," Mallory said, admittedly impressed in spite of the horror. "That's quite a mixed bag."

"It is," Lewis agreed. "You never really know what you're going to get. But don't worry. He'll come. He will. I know it. I *feel* it." He paused, and a heavy silence fell between them. "I would come."

Mallory started to respond, but movement in the corner of her eye caught her attention. A lone male walked up to the side door of the Chick-fil-A, wearing a pale blue bow tie, a green-and-yellow-checkered shirt, and a white lab coat over a pair of pressed khakis. "Lewis!" she exclaimed, grabbing him by the arm. "It's him!"

"Ow!" Lewis pulled his arm free and rubbed it tenderly. "Not so hard." He adjusted his glasses and squinted at the man approaching the restaurant. "Are you sure?" he asked.

"Are you kidding me? It's *you!*" Mallory leapt to her feet and started out from behind the dumpster, but Lewis grabbed her elbow and pulled her back.

"Wait!" he hissed. "I don't think it is."

"*What?*" Mallory hissed, exasperated. "He's wearing your *exact same outfit.*"

"Yeah, but look…that guy has a mustache." Sure enough, the man walking into the Chick-fil-A had a long, droopy mustache balanced precariously above his upper lip. "He's also wearing a bandana around his neck, and a sombrero."

"So what?" Mallory said, throwing her hands into the air. "The mustache is *clearly* fake."

Lewis frowned doubtfully up at her. "And the sombrero? You telling me that's fake, too?"

"It's a goddamn *costume*, Lewis!" she hissed.

"I don't think so," Lewis said, shaking his head. "I'd never wear a false mustache. It scares me too much. When I first arrived in Anomaly Flats, I grew out a beard. I thought, new life, new look! But facial hair changes you, Mallory. I believe that, in a very real sense. I grew that beard, and I literally didn't recognize myself in the mirror." He lifted his eyes, and they were clouded over by the pain of the memory. "It's a terrible thing to not recognize yourself."

Mallory clenched her fists. "Look, I'm going in there. He knows where my bag is, and I'm getting it back. Are you coming with me or not?"

Lewis frowned. "No, Mallory," he decided. "We can't risk giving up our hiding spot in case the *actual* clone is watching!" His grip on her elbow tightened. "We need to stay here."

Mallory crouched down and leaned in close to the scientist. "Listen, Barnish—"

"It's Bur—"

"I DON'T CARE WHAT IT IS! You're going to let go of my arm right now, for two reasons: One, because that's the evil clone, and I'm going to go stop him; and two, because I haven't peed once all goddamn day, and if you don't let me go into that restaurant, I'm going to let my bladder explode all over your face. Got it?"

Lewis let go of her elbow and scooted farther away, as if something from inside of Mallory might drip onto his shoes. "Geez, you could have just said you had to go…"

"I. JUST. DID." Mallory turned and marched over to the Chick-fil-A. She pushed open the door and was greeted by the harsh, sickly-sweet smell of fried things and cheap cheese. The restaurant looked like every other Chick-fil-A she'd ever been in, except that this one didn't have computerized cash registers, of course. Instead, the counter was lined with four old-fashioned registers that ding-ed and clanged and popped little currency flags up and down like prairie dogs. The poorly-disguised evil clone was standing at one of these registers, placing his order with a bemused and sweaty man behind the counter, so Mallory figured she had some time. She hurried to the bathroom, which was remarkably clean for an establishment with a janitorial staff composed entirely of male criminals.

On her way back out, she crept slowly down the little hallway and peeked her head around the corner. *Shit*, she thought. The clone was no longer at the counter. She did a quick scan of the restaurant, but he was nowhere to be seen. From her post near the door, she could see out the windows of the restaurant...and the clone wasn't in the parking lot, either.

Shit, shit, shit.

"Well," said a sharply familiar voice in her ear. "Look who came to dinner."

Mallory whirled around and threw her closed fist instinctively at the Evil Lewis's face. He caught her at the wrist and yanked her in close, so that the lid of his sombrero crushed against her forehead and the hairs of the ridiculously oversized mustache tickled her chin. "Looking for me?" he asked.

"I want my bag back, you little twerp," Mallory seethed. She pulled her hand back, but the evil clone's grip was strong, much stronger than the real Lewis'. Even so, Mallory's anger was undeterred. "*Now.*"

Evil Lewis made a grand show of pretending to consider this option. "Nah. I think I'll keep it," he decided with a wicked grin. "It's just filled with such *wonderful* things..."

Mallory stepped in even closer and grabbed the clone by the lapels of his lab coat. He gave a little yelp of surprise. "Listen to me, you little nerd: I *made* you, and I can *end* you. Tell me where my bag is right this second, or I swear to God, I will rip your face off your skull and use it as a dust rag."

Evil Lewis giggled. "First of all, a strip of face would be horribly ineffective as a dust rag. I mean, just think about it."

"Oh my God...you even *dweeb* like Lewis," she said, disgusted.

"And second of all, I'd proceed very gently if I were you." With a huge, deranged grin plastered across his face, he slowly grabbed hold of one flap of the lab coat and lifted it gingerly. Beneath it, he wore a vest made of dynamite sticks bound together by electrical tape. The dynamite was wired to a small detonator that he held up in the other hand. "We wouldn't want there to be any accidents."

Mallory's heart froze. She loosened her grip on his lapel, and he squirmed out of her clutches.

"That's the smartest thing you've done all day." He closed his lab coat and un-crumpled his sombrero. From around the corner, a burly male voice called, "Order 52!" Evil Lewis licked his lips. "That's me," he said. He gave her a wink. "Chow time." Then he skirted around the stunned Mallory and made his way to the counter, tucking the detonator into his coat pocket. He picked up his grease-soaked bag and tipped his huge hat to the man behind the counter. On his way toward the door, he stopped at the hallway and smiled up at Mallory. "Don't even think about following me," he said, his voice taking on a hard edge that belied the dumb grin on his face, "or I'll blow the bag to kingdom come."

"You wouldn't," Mallory challenged, summoning up at least a semblance of stubbornness. But she felt pretty certain that he very much would.

"Try me." Then he walked to the exit, squeezed the giant sombrero through the doors, sauntered out into the parking lot, and disappeared around the corner.

That, Mallory decided, *did not go well.*

CHAPTER 13

"THIS IS BAD, Mallory," Lewis frowned, plunging his nugget into a cup of honey mustard. "This is really, really bad."

"Yeah…my sandwich isn't so great either," she said, peeling back the bun on her spicy chicken. Two sad, defeated pickle disks stared back up at her.

Lewis jammed the nugget into his mouth and chewed. "I don't mean the food," he said crossly.

"I know, Lewis," she said with a heavy sigh. "It was a joke." She felt a weariness that could have been made of concrete for all its weight. Everything that had happened since she'd arrived at Anomaly Flats—and even the events *before* she arrived, ever since she'd woken up in St. Louis the previous morning for what she knew would be the last time—it all made her tired, physically, mentally, emotionally, spiritually, and every other –ally in the book. And now, to have lost her backpack? That was to lose *everything*. She liked to think she was a fighter by nature, but now she felt the undeniable and uncontrollable urge to slide off her chair, curl up into a ball beneath the table, and die right there in the Chick-fil-A. She nibbled at the edge of her spicy chicken. "Actually, this is really pretty good," she admitted. And that was the last straw. It sent her into tears. "I hate my life," she sniffled into her napkin.

Lewis stared down at his hands. Emotions made him uncomfortable. So they ate in silence as the Chick-fil-A filled with the citizens of Anomaly Flats.

Maude Roach arrived, looking prim and sour and generally mean. She gave Mallory a hard stare, but did not say hello. The tourism director came in not long after, a trio of agitated flies buzzing in tight circles around her head. She didn't need to open her mouth to order; the restaurant employees had her sack of food ready and waiting. At some point, they'd probably learned the hard way that a swarm of flies didn't exactly make for successful health inspections.

Trudy shuffled in, too, carrying two waffles wrapped in a napkin. She didn't look terribly pleased to be there. When her order came up, she removed the flimsy bun from her sandwich and placed the chicken patty and its trimmings between the two waffles. This seemed to brighten her up some. She saw Mallory watching her and passed her a little wink.

More and more folks filtered in, until the tables were all taken and there was barely any standing room left. The line went out the door and around the corner. Finally, Lewis crammed the last chicken nugget into his mouth and wiped his hands on his lab coat. "We should get going," he said, snapping Mallory back to reality. "Give up the table for someone else." Several impatient diners edged eagerly toward them, shooting each other threatening, violent looks.

"All right," Mallory agreed.

She finished off her fries and stood. The second she was up, a small woman with bony hips slammed into her, knocking her out of the way and skidding into her seat. "Mine!" the woman snapped at every person in earshot.

"Geez, these people..."

As they squeezed past the line of people and out the door, Mallory noticed Rufus the mechanic standing in the queue. He hadn't changed out of his sweaty, greasy coveralls, but he'd added some oil smudges to both cheeks and to his forehead. His mouth hung open, of course, and his saliva dribbled out and spattered on the shoulder of the suit jacket of the man standing in front of him. Neither man seemed to mind.

"How's the car?" Mallory pleaded, grabbing the mechanic's sleeve as she passed. "Is it fixed? Please tell me it's fixed."

Rufus turned to her and titled his head a bit, as if trying to remember how he knew this particularly disheveled woman.

Mallory's heart sank. "It's not fixed, is it?"

Something in the man's brain clicked then, though his expression kept it mostly to itself. "Impala," he said.

Mallory waited for more, but there *was* no more. "Yes, Impala," she said impatiently. "The alternator. Any chance you built it fast?"

"The alternator," Rufus agreed, letting his saliva spill onto the increasingly dirty Chick-fil-A linoleum. "'Bout half done."

Mallory sighed. It wasn't exactly great news, but it wasn't bad news, either. "Probably done tomorrow," he added, and that brightened her up a bit.

"I know you're doing the best you can, but…the faster the better." She patted his arm and let herself get caught up in the eddy of diners pushing their way out of the restaurant.

"I'll fix the dent in the door," he called out as she was swept away.

She gave him a thumbs up without turning her head. "So. What do we do now?" she asked Lewis as they stalked back toward the Winnebago.

Lewis sighed. Between the drawn look of his cheeks and the two dark pouches that were growing larger and larger under his eyes, he looked about as exhausted as Mallory felt. She wondered if she had pouches under her eyes, too. "Well, he's up to something big, there's no doubt about that. He made a dynamite vest *and* put together an impenetrable disguise. I think he's showing us that he has something complex in the works."

Mallory wanted to point out that the disguise was nowhere near impenetrable, but thought better of it. Now probably wasn't the time. "You don't think he just picked up the vest somewhere? Doesn't this weird-ass town have a Bombs 'R' Us or something?"

Lewis shook his head. "No. I mean, we *did*. Obviously. But the night manager's smoking habit sort of took care of that. And that was years ago. Now we have to make our own bombs."

Mallory squinted at him, sizing him up for a joke. "Why do I think you're being serious?" she asked.

"Why would you not?" he asked, honestly confused. "Anyway, it's not just that he built a dynamite vest; it's that he built a dynamite vest when he had any number of threatening devices and serums to carry around. I mean, the cold fusion cream is one of my *least* explosive inventions. But he went ahead and made a dynamite vest anyway. I mean, where did he even *get* dynamite? The TNT trees pretty much all withered away last summer."

Mallory's head lolled back on her shoulders. "TNT trees. *Obviously.*"

Lewis nodded. "The TNT trees are how the townspeople were able to blast out the quarry a few decades back. Until they hit that underground civilization and had to stop. After that, the dynamite was mostly used for parties. And for fishing. But the trees all got some sort of root disease last year. They got all weak and brittle. The TNT snapped off the branches, and, well...now the old TNT tree grove is the new barren crater."

Mallory looked at Lewis. She blinked. She blinked again.

Lewis gave her a tired little smile. "Okay, I made that up."

"Well, holy shit, Lewis. You *do* have a sense of humor," Mallory said, patting him on the shoulder. "It's a painfully lame sense of humor, but...hey. Points for trying."

"The fact remains that I don't know where he would have gotten the dynamite, though. He went to pretty great lengths to make that vest. There's a bit of theatre there that scares me, Mallory. If he put that together in a couple of hours just to go to dinner, what do you think he'll do with a few days under his belt? A week?" Lewis pulled off his glasses and wiped them nervously on the hem of his lab coat. "I fear we're in grave danger."

"Well, I've got news for Evil Lewis: I don't *have* a week. I need to be out of here *tomorrow*. We need to get my bag back."

"And stop him from wreaking destruction on the town," Lewis added.

"Well," Mallory said, rolling her head and cracking her neck, "mostly the bag. Saving the town is great and all, but it's sort of Priority B."

Lewis frowned. "This is my home, Mallory. It's a *lot* of people's home. We can't just let him destroy it."

"Sure, right, I know," she said. "It's fine, it's whatever. I'm just saying, on the to-do list, it's like, one: bag, two: town."

Lewis planted his fists on his hips. "Nice attitude from the woman who created the evil clone in the first place," he challenged.

"My attitude is my strongest trait," Mallory insisted. "Everyone says so."

Lewis set his lips into a hard line. "Hmph," he said.

Mallory sighed. "Look. We find the clone, we find my bag. We find my bag, we can use it to bludgeon the clone to death. Happy?"

Lewis considered this. "It's not a very *elegant* solution…"

"Oh my God, Lewis, I'm going to bludgeon *you* with it. The point is, we'll stop the clone. I'll help you stop Evil Lewis. Okay?"

"Okay." Lewis stuck out his hand for Mallory to shake. Mallory just looked at it. Shaking represented a commitment, and commitment made her feel queasy. "Okay," he said again, more tensely.

"Oh, fine." Mallory gripped his hand hard enough for some of his small scientist bones to pop. "Okay."

"Great," Lewis grunted, pulling his hand back and putting it into his coat pocket so Mallory wouldn't see how red and mangled it was from her grip. But she did see it, and it brought her joy. "Then it's settled."

"It is," Mallory agreed. "We're going to save the freaking day. Just one question: Evil Lewis is gone, and we don't know where to find him, and we don't know what he's planning. So. What do we do now?"

Lewis took a deep breath. "I think there's only one thing we *can* do now," he said, exhaling slowly and shaking his head. "We need to go visit the oracle."

CHAPTER 14

"**YOU HAVE AN ORACLE?**" Mallory asked. She hated to admit it, but she was impressed. Having an oracle in town was the psychic equivalent of living next door to Mick Jagger. "Like, a vapor-breathing, future-seeing, riddle-rambling, Delphi-style oracle?"

Lewis' eyebrows lifted themselves and knitted together in surprise. "Yes, actually. Something very much like that."

"Look, don't sound so surprised. It's insulting," Mallory said, slumping down in her seat and putting her feet up on the Winnebago's dashboard. "You're not the only one who can read a book, Lewis."

"Sorry," he said, focusing back on the road. "You just don't strike me as the Greek history type."

"Women can learn about all *sorts* of things these days," she said, her voice heavy with sarcasm. "History, biology, math, even chemistry. We're not just for kitchens anymore. It's a brave new world out there."

"Okay, okay, I'm sorry. Yes, a real oracle. She should be able to tell us what my clone is planning."

As they drove on, Mallory tilted her head against the window and fixed her gaze on the western horizon. The sun was setting now, and the sky was streaked with reds and oranges and purples and deep, dark blues. Something shivered inside her chest. She wouldn't miss much about Missouri, but she sure would miss the sunsets.

The sky directly above the road was already dark, and the constellations were just beginning to twinkle to life. "Look at that," Mallory said, a slow, lazy smile spreading easily across her face. "There's so much beauty in the stars."

"*Don't look at them!*" Lewis screeched. He slammed on the brakes, and the RV skidded to a stop on the shoulder of the road, throwing loose gravel into the field that ran alongside it.

Mallory flew forward, and her seatbelt caught her hard in the chest. "Fuck!" she cried.

"Don't look at the stars!" Lewis screamed. He threw his hand over her eyes and poked his index finger directly into her pupil in the process.

Mallory cried out and swatted at his offending hand, and he reached over and covered her eyes with his other hand. "Lewis!" she shouted, slapping at both of his arms. "Stop it!"

"Close your eyes!" he insisted, struggling against her assault. "Don't look at them!"

"Okay, okay! Christ!" Mallory straightened up in her seat and readjusted her belt. "What is the *matter* with you?"

"I'm sorry," Lewis said, breathing heavily and trying to regain his composure. "I'm sorry. It's just…dangerous to stargaze around here."

"No shit. You get a scientist's finger jammed in your eye when you do," Mallory said irritably.

Lewis turned to face her. "Look. The sky here is…different. Different than the sky in most places. Not the daytime sky, I mean. That's the same. Or close to the same. It has a little more blue on the ultraviolet scale than this part of the globe should have, and—"

Mallory cleared her throat, annoyed, signaling for him to get on with it.

Lewis coughed. "Right. It's basically the same sky, except at *night,* it's a *different* sky. As the sun sets, the sky over Anomaly Flats is slowly replaced by a…well…I guess you'd call it a…a void."

Mallory crossed her arms and eyed the scientist. "A void?"

Lewis nodded. "An all-consuming void. Basically, as soon as night starts falling, the sky starts trying to swallow you up. Not really physically. Though *sometimes* physically. More like…mentally. And psychically. The stars you see when you look up there—Mallory, *don't look up there!*"

"I'm sorry!" she cried, shading her eyes as best she could. "It's a habit! You said the stars up there, so I looked up there…leave me alone!"

Lewis covered his mouth as he exhaled sharply. "The stars that you *would* see up there if you *did* look, which you should very much *not* do, *ever*, aren't really stars at all. They're…well, I guess you'd call them projections."

"Projections?"

"The void is projecting those images onto itself to trick you into looking up. Once you look, it starts showing you *new* projections—*shinier* stars, spinning constellations, swirling galaxies—and all of a sudden, you're falling into them, and you're surrounded by darkness and pinpoints of light, and you're swimming through the galaxy, and your whole spirit is suddenly gone, sucked away by the void. That sky up there," he said, pointing up through the roof of the cabin, "wants to feed on you."

So many thoughts and questions occurred to Mallory at once, but one managed to elbow its way to the surface above all the others. And it was somewhat an odd question, given all the other, much better questions she could have asked, but out it came just the same: "What does it do during the *day*time?"

Lewis shrugged. "What am I, an astronomer?" He put the Winnebago into gear, but he didn't pull away from the shoulder quite yet. "Here's the point: Remember when you said that every single thing in this town was trying to kill you?" Mallory nodded. "You were right." He cleared his throat awkwardly as Mallory's face drained a little of its color. "We're going to get up to some pretty dangerous stuff here, with the evil clone and all, so I think you should be prepared. The void, the creek, the clone, the flies, the weird, glowing light out in the woods behind the Del Taco…they're all…I mean, yeah, every single thing is pretty much trying to kill you. So just… be ready. I guess…I guess that's the lesson here."

They sat in silence for a few moments.

"We should probably go see the oracle now," he said.

Mallory coughed. "Is *she* going to try to kill me?"

"It wouldn't be the first time." Then he checked his mirrors, pulled back onto the road, and drove them to the oracle of Anomaly Flats.

X

"The oracle lives in a roller rink. Of course she does."

Lewis pulled the RV into the dark, deserted parking lot and rumbled to a stop beneath the only working light. The other three had all been either burned out or knocked out. There was so much glass in so many various colors on the asphalt, it was hard to tell how much of it might have started life as a light fixture.

"Well, it's a bit more accurate to say she *is* the roller rink," Lewis said, peering into the gulf of darkness between themselves and the cinder block building in the center of the lot. The roller rink had once been painted in sunrise colors, yellows and oranges fading up into pinks and purples, but so much of the paint had peeled away, revealing little spots of bare gray blocks beneath, and the building looked old, tired, and stricken with a particularly ashen brand of chicken pox. He turned off the engine but left the headlights on. They illuminated the front door and showed a path that was mostly clear of glass and debris. "It's sort of a…symbiotic relationship."

"What the hell does that mean?" Mallory murmured, not entirely sure she was interested in the answer.

"The oracle is a person, but she's also *more* than a person." He flipped off the headlights and popped open his door. "Just try not to touch anything, okay?"

They crunched their way toward the entrance, little pieces of glass and plastic popping underfoot. "Not a very happening spot for a Friday night," Mallory observed.

"No one really comes here anymore," Lewis confirmed. "The skating was fun, but every time you made a lap, the oracle would chatter on about how this skater was going to die, or how that skater was about to get cancer, and it sort of dampened the mood."

"I bet," Mallory snorted. She looked up at the unassuming, long-neglected building. "So she's the real deal, huh?"

"Oh, yes," Lewis said, nodding vigorously. "She's never been wrong. Not once."

"Does she get her Chick-fil-A delivered?"

Lewis cleared his throat. "She…doesn't care for fast food."

"But I thought everyone—" Mallory began.

Lewis stopped her with a wave of his hands. "She and the mayor had their disagreements about it. The mayor sent a security team after the oracle, and the oracle prophesied that the mayor would die at the oracle's own hands by drowning in a dumpster full of chicken grease."

Mallory blinked. "Oh."

"Yeah," said Lewis. "That pretty much ended that. She's allowed to keep to herself now. In fact, it's encouraged." He reached for the door handle, then he paused and added, "I wouldn't bring it up."

"Uh-huh."

Mallory wasn't sure what she expected the inside of the roller rink to look like. But as they stepped into the strangely-lit space, there was no denying that the oracle's home was exactly as it should have been.

They entered into a small anteroom with posters from the 1980s advertising a drug-free life in startling neon colors. The fluorescent lighting was dim, since only two of the four tubes worked, and even those flickered like they were gasping for air. On the far side of the room, a Plexiglas window separated the foyer from a ticketing counter. There was a little, round speaker set into the center of the window, and a Post-It taped up beneath it from the inside read "GO ON IN."

Lewis glanced at Mallory. "I guess we go on in."

"Go on, then," Mallory said, ushering him toward the pair of swinging doors that led to the main room of the rink. "In."

There was no way she was going first.

Lewis nodded stoically, as if he considered it his sacred duty to go through first and act as a human shield for whatever unnatural horrors the oracle might have in store for them. He paused before the doors, took a deep breath, and tightened his bow tie. Then he pushed through the entryway, and Mallory followed close behind.

The first thing Mallory noticed was the carpet. It was the kind one might expect to find on the floor of a 1970s rape van. It was threadbare, and pea green, and it had all the wrong sorts of stains in the wrong sorts of places, and it was not at all pasted to the floor like a good carpet should be. Instead, it was tacked to the walls, where it could safely muffle sound, while also providing skaters with an opportunity to cringe with disgust any time they accidentally put a hand on it for support.

The rink was surrounded by a four-foot wall, both sides of which were covered in the same awful green carpeting as the rest of the walls…and hidden somewhere behind it all was a historic set of speakers pumping out loud disco. A thin congregation of colored lights spun lazily from racks bolted into the ceiling, covering the whole roller rink in sickly rainbow spots, made dull and watery by the harsh glare of fluorescent lights overhead.

Across the tile floor and off to the left stood a snack counter that Mallory was gratified to see somehow advertised both Coke and Bud Light in the same flickering neon sign. The thin, twisted pretzel racks stood naked in the air, and the giant popcorn machine on the back shelf was dark and powered down, but not quite empty: half-popped kernels lay strewn about the bottom tray, and some had managed to escape over the edge and onto the counter. The ICEE machine chugged proudly along, though, mixing-mixing-mixing its red and blue drinks under the beaming smile of a cartoon polar bear in a blue knit sweater.

To Mallory's right ran the skate rental counter. Legions of skates stood quietly in the cubbies stacked on the back wall, all the way to the ceiling. Most of them were uninspiring brown leather with dirty, streaked orange wheels, but every now and again, hidden within the army of drab brown, were pairs of vanity skates. Here was a white pair with pink wheels and pink laces; there was a black pair with lime green wheels and dirty white laces. And up there, way up in the top row, sat the king of all roller rink skates: a pair of gold-painted leather with clear wheels and bright, sparkly red laces.

"Hoity-toity," Mallory muttered under her breath.

Beyond the rental counter stood a line of quarter-operated lockers. They were sky blue, mostly, which stood out in stark contrast to the pea green wall cover, though the paint was so nicked and dented, the lockers could have given any Jackson Pollack a run for its money. The rest of the sizeable room, of course, was dedicated to the skating surface itself. Three cutouts let skaters onto and off of the polished wooden floor...or, at least, they would have, if there had been any skaters to *go* onto or off of the floor.

As it stood, though, Mallory and Lewis were the only human beings in the room.

"Where's your fortune teller?" Mallory asked, looking doubtfully around the rink.

"I told you," Lewis said, his voice quiet and careful. "She's all around us."

Just then, the fluorescent lights went out, plunging the entire building into near darkness. The only light came from the manic, colored party lights that spun their brightly colored spots across the floors and up the walls in dizzying patterns. Then Mallory heard a sound she hadn't heard since grade school.

Even so, it was unmistakable.

It was the sound of roller skate wheels skimming over a wooden floor.

"Welcome, Scientist Lewis," called a bright, mellow female voice from the oval rink. It glided around the room, following closely on the heels of the sound of the skates. Mallory just barely caught quick glimpses of her as she sailed through the swirling mass of bright circles. "And welcome to you, Stranger with Unkempt Hair."

"Hey!" Mallory said. She reached up and smoothed down her hair as best she could. "I didn't shower today," she grumbled, though she immediately realized that this explanation didn't really help defend an attack on her personal hygiene all that much.

"It is wild and natural," the soothing voice sang. "You are most welcome here. And your name is…Juanita. Yes? Welcome, Juanita!"

"Juanita?" Mallory soured. She elbowed Lewis in the side. "Juanita?"

"You look like a Juanita," the voice confirmed as it skated laps around the rink.

"She's not portending yet," Lewis explained in a whisper. "When she portends, she's always right. Always. She just has to… you know…warm up first."

The skates skidded to a halt on the other side of the wall where Mallory and Lewis stood. The fluorescent lights flickered back to life. The woman standing before them was tall and willowy, strong and beautiful. She had long, honey-brown hair held down by a wide cloth headband with an intricate pattern of interlocking elephants printed on it. Her eyes were green and bright, and her pale skin was dotted with freckles. She wore a pair of brown hemp capris and a sleeveless white linen blouse that allowed her powerful arms to move freely. She smiled at Mallory in the newly restored light, looked her up and down, and said, "You look much more like a Juanita with the lights on."

Mallory, who was wholly uncertain how to respond to such a remark, simply said, "Thanks."

"Scientist Lewis," the oracle gushed, taking one of his hands on both of hers. "How wonderful to see you. How have you been?"

"Troubled," Lewis admitted.

But as he said it, the oracle closed her eyes, shook her head, and said, "Shh-shh-shh-shh-shh. You do not have to say it. I can see it in your eyes. You have been troubled."

Mallory scoffed. "This is our best hope for saving the town?"

"Is the town in danger?" the oracle asked with a dreamy smile.

Lewis nodded. "I think so. That's why we're here, we need your help."

"Ah." The oracle's face fell, and she released Lewis' hand. She pushed back from the wall and skated slowly away, her legs weaving in and out gracefully, propelling her backward. "I had hoped you were here for Disco Night," she sighed.

"Maybe next time. We need a prophecy."

The oracle brightened a bit. "Yes, of course! How wonderful. It's been ages since anyone's come to call." She skated around the rink, her legs pumping powerfully, her arms swaying with the motion. "People stopped coming because I kept telling them how they would die," she called out, explaining to Mallory from across the rink. She made the turn and spun to a stop near her guests once more. She smiled sweetly and placed her hands on Mallory's shoulders. "Would you like to know how you'll die?" she asked.

"Uh..." Mallory stared doubtfully at the oracle. Then she looked over at Lewis. "I think I'll wait outside," she decided. She turned back toward the doors, but the oracle snatched her hand and held it tightly.

"Wait! You must have an ICEE first!" She leaned in and whispered with a wink, "They're free."

"Well, holy shit…if they're *free*," she said. But the oracle smiled pleasantly, and Mallory realized just how exhausted she was. Her misadventures had taken their toll, both physically and mentally, and she decided that a nearly-lethal injection of cold sugar might actually help a bit.

"Wonderful," the oracle decided. "And you, Lewis. You should *not* have an ICEE, because you are a very small person, and the sugar might overpower you to a dangerous degree."

"That's fine," Lewis said, waving her off. "Listen, I really do enjoy our visits—you know I do—but—"

"Of course!" the oracle gasped. "The prophecy! Wait here, scientist, I'll fetch the vapors." She skated over to one of the other cutouts and hopped up from the rink onto the old tile floor. She glided over to the row of sort-of-blue lockers, popped one open, and began rummaging around inside.

Meanwhile, Mallory was having a hell of a time figuring out how to work an ICEE machine. She held a cup beneath the spout on the blue side and pulled the little white lever, but nothing came out. She tried the red side and failed there, too. She smacked the side of the machine, which chugged along happily, mixing up the slushy inside and generally ignoring Mallory's attempts to fill her cup. The Wait – Do Not Pour light was off, and the Ready light was on, but still, she couldn't figure out how to make the ICEE flow. "I have a master's degree," she hissed at the stupid thing. "Now pour me a fucking Slurpee!" She threw her cup at the ICEE maker. It bounced off harmlessly and clattered to the ground. Mallory scowled. "Fine." She reached around to the back and pulled the ICEE mixer's plug out of the wall. The machine lost power, and the arms stopped their incessant mixing. Mallory smiled ruefully. "I win."

I wonder if I have anger issues, she thought idly as she walked away from the snack counter.

The oracle turned from the locker, holding a cup of water in one hand and a small mesh bag that seemed to be full of rocks in the other. She skated breezily back onto the wooden floor and skimmed over to the center of the rink. She set down her items and pulled up a hidden latch on one of the boards. The wood came up, and the oracle placed the plank gently to the side. She picked up the little mesh satchel, untied it, and dumped its contents into the open space between the floorboards. They *were* rocks, or something quite like them; shiny, black, grape-sized stones poured from the bag and disappeared beneath the floor. Then the oracle took the cup and spilled the water down into the channel. It hissed and spat as it splashed down onto the rocks, as if they were hot coals, and a dense smoke billowed up and began to spread across the rink. Smiling, and satisfied, the oracle stood up, wiped her hands on her blouse, and swizzled her way around the rink.

The dense white cloud grew thicker, and it wafted out to the further edges of the rink. The acrid smell of frankincense stung Mallory's nose, and her eyes began to water. Lewis seemed to be having a similar reaction; he sneezed four times and rubbed vigorously at his quickly-reddening nose. But the oracle spread her arms wide as she skated around and around through the growing mist, breathing deeply, letting the vapor fill her lungs. She closed her eyes, and Mallory thought for sure she'd plow face-first into the far wall, but she navigated the oval perfectly, with practiced, fluid glides.

"What is it you seek?" the oracle called out airily as she zipped past her visitors. "Speak, Scientist Lewis, and know what the future holds." As she took the curve, she gasped and said, with no small measure of delight, "Lewis! I didn't know you had an evil clone!"

Lewis nudged Mallory. "See?" he murmured. He cleared his throat and spoke louder. "That's what we came to inquire about. What atrocities does he have planned for Anomaly Flats?"

The disco music continued to bump its way through the old speakers, and the oracle bobbed her head to the rhythm. "The well of his hatred is deep. He is small in stature, but fierce and powerful in spirit." Mallory couldn't tell for sure in the dim lighting, but she thought she saw Lewis' spine straighten with pride at the sound of that...which she found a little perverse, if she were being honest with herself. The oracle continued, her voice growing hollow and cold: "He is a creature of great danger who seeks to plunge us into darkness. Mark my word, Scientist Lewis, and hear me well; I see only a glimpse of what is to be, but not how it will resolve." The oracle skated to a stop at the wall and grabbed Lewis' hands, this time both of them. She opened her eyes, and her bright green irises had been replaced by a milky whiteness so that her pupils were pinpoints of ink against pearls. "At sundown tomorrow," the oracle whispered, her voice sharp and full of urgency, "the clone will endeavor to open the door." The fluorescent lights went dark once more, and the oracle released Lewis' hands and pushed herself back into the cloudy darkness of the roller rink. "He will endeavor to open the door," she repeated with a hiss.

"Wait!" Lewis pleaded, leaning out over the wall. "What door? *Which* door?!"

The swarm of rainbow lights dappled the vapor mist, but the fog was so thick, it swallowed the woman completely. From within the cloud of swirling light echoed the final words of the oracle.

"Inside the Walmart. Aisle 8."

CHAPTER 15

"YOUR EVIL CLONE is going to Walmart?" Mallory asked suspiciously as they pulled away from the roller rink. "He's going to destroy the world with discount savings?"

"The Anomaly Flats Supercenter is much more than just great values and low prices," Lewis said seriously, navigating onto a dark and twisting road that wound back through the woods. "It's also a place of unspeakable evil."

"Whoa…I know they don't pay all that well, but are we really calling minimum wage unspeakably evil?" Mallory asked.

Lewis shook his head. "No, not that," he said. Then he thought a minute. "Well…yes. That, too. But the evil inside the Walmart goes far, *far* beyond substandard wages."

"Ah," Mallory said. "Off-brand cheese."

Lewis peeled his eyes from the road and shot Mallory an angry, searching look. "Is this a joke to you?" he asked.

Mallory shrugged. "Almost anything can be a joke if you get the delivery down."

Lewis returned his eyes to the road and maneuvered the RV to the shoulder. He pulled the world's most awkward U-turn, nearly bashing the Winnebago into several trees in the process, and headed back in the direction from which they'd just come, away from town. "Where are we going?" Mallory asked.

"I'm taking you back to my place," he said, turning down a narrow road that ran along the border of the woods and a barren field.

"You know that I'm *definitely* not sleeping with you," Mallory pointed out. Lewis' hands jerked involuntarily, and the RV swerved off the road and into the grass. He overcorrected, and the Winnie screeched back and forth on the pavement before settling down on a straight path.

Lewis cleared his throat. "I'm not—I don't—" he began.

"Calm down," Mallory said, rolling her eyes, "it's a joke." She thought for a second, then added, "I mean, it's *not* a joke. I'm not sleeping with you. But you know. You know what I mean."

They drove along quietly for a few minutes, each trying desperately not to think about what the other person might be thinking about. Finally, Mallory broke the silence: "Wait, why *are* we going back to your place?"

"It's very important that you understand what we're up against," he said. "There's something I want you to hear."

X

Lewis' house turned out to be an old barn that crouched at the northern edge of Farmer Buchheit's property. "I thought you said Farmer Buchheit was an asshole," Mallory said.

"He is," Lewis said, pulling open the front door. "You should see what he charges for this place."

By Mallory's estimation, anything over $10 a month was too much. The barn's scant renovations amounted to the addition of a gas stove against one wall, a small icebox next to it, and a mattress that was slung down onto the floor of the hayloft overhead. The only light came from three bare bulbs suspended from the ceiling and one solo bulb fastened to the wall near the door. The sink was nothing more than a pig trough bolted to the wall and fed with a garden hose, and the shower appeared to be a bucket with holes punched in the bottom. Lewis had amassed a small collection of plywood boards, and by balancing them on various stools and crates, he'd created a series of tables. Most of them were covered with laboratory equipment. One was covered in dirty dishes. "How do you do science in here?" Mallory demanded.

Lewis blushed, clearly ashamed to be showing his little home to another person, especially to a person who was a reasonably-attractive-if-wild-haired woman. Mallory would have bet the bank that she was the first pair of X chromosomes to ever step through these barn doors. "I do most of my work in the RV," he said quietly, brushing some of the dust away from the floorboards with the toe of his shoe. "The lighting's better in there. And the electricity's more reliable."

"But...where's the bathroom?" Mallory asked, wholly unable to keep the horror out of her voice.

"There's an outhouse."

"An *outhouse*? Christ, are we in *Arkansas*?"

"Yes, an outhouse. It's only a quarter-mile walk out the back."

"Seriously? And this no-plumbing cowshed is your *home*? Who the hell is your realtor?!"

"You don't like it," he said, crestfallen. He tugged at the lapels of his lab coat and hugged the white cloth tightly around himself.

"I mean..." Mallory paused and tried to summon up some words of encouragement. "It's...it's really fine, Lewis. It's just really *fine*. Yeah. You know? Someone could *definitely* live here. Totally."

Yep, she thought. *Nailed it.*

Lewis' face grew even darker red. Mallory hoped it wouldn't explode...it would make a horrible mess, and she didn't know how to get blood out of things. "No one really pays me for my experiments," he said, skirting around the house, stacking up dishes and tidying up as best he could. "I make a little money, you know, from odd jobs and things, but this is, ah...well, this is what I can afford. You know?"

Mallory shook her head and held up her hands. "I'm sorry, Lewis. Really. I didn't mean that. Don't listen to me. It's nice. Really. It is." She picked up some of the dishes and set them in the pig trough. She turned on the hose and sprayed them down. Water splashed everywhere, and a piece of something hard and brown that had been dried onto one of the plates flew into her eye. She tried not to gag. "It's cozy. Very...rustic."

Lewis frowned and cleared off the rest of the table, dumping papers and beakers and plates into a heap in the corner. "Don't worry about all that," he said, nodding at the pig trough. He shimmied up the ladder to the loft, disappeared up there for a few moments, and then reemerged holding a little black rectangle. "This is what I wanted to show you."

Mallory squinted up at the thing in his hand. "Is that a tape recorder?" she asked, disgusted. "You know they make, like, iPhones, right?"

Lewis stepped carefully down the ladder and motioned for Mallory to join him at the table. "Magnetic fields," he reminded her. "Have a seat." He placed the recorder on the flimsy plywood surface and perched on a stool at the head of the table.

Mallory joined him, balancing precariously on a stool of her own. She felt the thin wood shift under her weight, and she silently cursed Chick-fil-A. *One bag of waffle fries, and now I'm fat.* She wondered if there was a yoga studio in town. Probably not. And if there was, she reasoned, it was probably run by vampires.

"The threat posed by my clone is...significant," Lewis began, fiddling nervously with the recorder. "I knew he was evil, obviously, but *this* evil? The Walmart...aisle 8...Mallory, it's not just bad. It's potentially world-ending."

Mallory looked at him skeptically. "You mean, like, your own personal world? Or literally the whole world?"

Lewis set his mouth in a grim line. "Both, I'm afraid. The destruction will start with us here in Anomaly Flats, and spread quickly, wiping out the whole of planet Earth."

"Huh." Mallory couldn't argue; that *did* sound significant. The very idea that an abomination of *her creation* could bring about the end of the world…well, it didn't exactly seem *feasible*, but it *did* seem significant. It also made her kind of proud, in a macabre sort of way. A strange question occurred to her then: "Hey, what about Mars?"

"Mallory…" Lewis began, sounding unbelievably tired.

"No, I'm serious! It's a whole other planet, but it's *also* part of Anomaly Flats. Do you think Mars will get destroyed too?"

Lewis sighed heavily. "I honestly don't know," he said. "And I'm hoping not to find out."

Mallory shook her head and, in doing so, nearly toppled off the flimsy stool. "This is ludicrous," she said, grapping the table for support. "I'm as socially anti-Walmart as the next upper-middle-class white person, but the destruction of the entire planet? Maybe *two* planets? Come on. Sam Walton wasn't Hitler." She thought for a moment, then added, "But some of the greeters *are* pretty awful. I've met a few front-door retirees who have attitudes like A-bombs."

"It's not the Walmart itself that's the problem," Lewis said. "It's what's *inside* the Walmart. In aisle 8. It's this." He nodded down at the tape recorder. It sat there, matte black and unassuming. Lewis picked it up and hovered his finger over the play button. "About ten years ago, one of our citizens went into the Walmart. They were having a special on canned beets that day. Two for thirty-nine cents. It was an incredible deal. He just couldn't resist."

"Who could?" Mallory mumbled sarcastically. Lewis ignored her.

"We told him not to go in. We begged him. We *pleaded*. But a man's love for beets can be stronger than reason," he said seriously. Mallory tried hard to stifle a laugh, but she didn't do a very good job. Once again, Lewis ignored her. "He came out…changed."

Now *that* piqued Mallory's attention. "Changed? Changed how?" she asked, leaning gingerly forward.

"Listen for yourself. This interview took place about an hour after he was deposited outside the Walmart."

"Deposited?" Mallory asked, raising an eyebrow.

Lewis nodded gravely. "We're not sure who—or what—escorted him out. But he was ejected rather forcefully. He skidded along the parking lot for almost ten feet. He had to have three different skin grafts." Lewis clicked the play button, and the microphone whirred to life. The speaker popped, and a scratched, faded version of Lewis' own voice came through: "This is Dr. Lewis Burnish. The date is September 25, 1993, 10:37 pm."

"1993?" Mallory asked, confused. "I thought you said ten years ago..." But Lewis shushed her with a wave of his hand, and the Lewis on the recorder continued:

"Post-trauma interview with Subject R, who entered the Walmart at approximately 8:45 pm and was ejected roughly 45 minutes later, at approximately 9:30 pm. Subject has severe lacerations extending from his neck to his ankles, caused by rough and prolonged scraping with asphalt. He also appears to be physically and mentally altered. His posture has slackened, and all hair seems to have been removed from his body. Not shaved; literally *removed*. Prior to this trauma, Subject R was articulate and roundly considered to be of high intelligence. His profession was medical surgeon at Anomaly General. I say 'was' because the subject no longer appears capable of performing complex medical procedures, or even simple ones. This is untested; however, his speech is slow, and he is having trouble connecting ideas. His movements and reactions are delayed. There is a five-inch scar running horizontally across his scalp along the frontal lobe. I don't know if this existed prior to his experience inside the Walmart or not, but it appears to be a recently-healed incision. We will begin the interview now.

"Do you consent to the recording of our discussion here today?" the Lewis on the recorder asked someone on the other side of the microphone.

There was a long pause, then a second male voice said, "Yes." He slurred his *s* a bit, so that it almost sounded like he ended the word with a slurp.

"Why did you go into the Walmart?"

Another long pause as the recorder hissed and popped. "Cheap beets," Subject R finally said.

"And how often do you eat beets?" Lewis asked.

A third voice piped up from somewhere in the background, a female voice. "How is that relevant?" the voice snapped.

"I'm curious!" Lewis hissed back. "Who would risk Walmart for beets? Beets taste like dirt!"

"Some days I eat beets," Subject R answered, seemingly heedless of the sniping back-and-forth going on around him. "Some days…not."

"It's just weird," Lewis continued quietly, harping at the unseen woman who hovered in the background. "I'm trying to establish that it's weird."

"Just get on with it," the woman hissed back.

Mallory gave Lewis a questioning look. The scientist shrugged. "I stand by it. It's weird."

"Who's the woman?" Mallory hissed. She didn't know why she was whispering. It wasn't like she was going to interrupt the conversation in the recorder.

"The mayor," Lewis replied.

"*That's* the mayor?" Mallory asked. She thought for a second. "I like her," she decided.

Lewis shook his head and motioned back down toward the microphone. His digital voice continued.

"Let the record show that Dr. Lewis Burnish advised Subject R against entering the Walmart, as did several other friends and acquaintances, but the subject went in anyway and is solely responsible for the effects of his decision."

"I hardly think this is the time or the place—" the mayor cried, and tape-recorded Lewis acknowledged this with a quiet, agitated, "All right, all right! Now, then. Subject R. Tell us what happened when you entered the Walmart."

The directive was followed by several long moments of silence. The other man seemed to be moaning, maybe in fear, or maybe in frustration, as if he were having trouble remembering the scene, or reliving it, or both. Finally, he said, "Bright. Lights...bright lights... on the ceiling. Made the produce look...real pretty. But it wasn't pretty. It was...horrible. All the produce was horrible."

"Yes, good. Go on," recorded Lewis urged. "What else?"

"There was a...monster. At the door. A...mummy. Old, and... white. Chalk. Skeleton mummy. I could see...all his bones. I... pressed myself against the wall...closed my eyes and...went past. The skeleton mummy reached out...said, 'Hello'...almost grabbed me...but I got away."

"That was the greeter," Lewis explained. "You were smart to keep your distance. What next?"

"I saw the peppers...and the broccoli...and the raw beets. I... wanted to...the beets...I wanted to buy them...not go to aisle 8, but...raw beets...were not on sale."

"So you went past the produce section?"

Here, Subject R began to sniffle a little, and Mallory thought she could hear a gentle, muffled sob. "Yes," the voice sniffled.

"What's wrong? What is it?" the mayor asked gently.

"In the produce...by the cilantro...I was...I was..."

"Yes?" the mayor urged. "You were what?"

"I was...I was..."

"It's okay," Lewis said. "This is a safe space."

"What happened?" the mayor asked.

There was more sniffling from the subject. "I was...misted."

"Misted?" Lewis and the mayor asked in unison, both sounding equally confused.

"The sprayer," Subject R sobbed. "It misted me."

Lewis cleared his throat, and the mayor gave an unmistakable sigh. "Let's...get back on track here, okay?" Lewis asked.

"I don't like water," the subject explained through his tears.

"Okay. So you made it through the produce section. Then what?"

"I...I went through the...through the...through the...make-up," he finally said, sounding unsure.

"Cosmetics," Lewis said helpfully. "You went through cosmetics."

"I saw a woman...in a blue vest...I asked her where to find... canned beets."

"What did this woman look like?" the mayor interrupted.

Subject R made some low, guttural noises as he struggled to remember. "Red hair," he spat out, grasping for memories. "Curly. Nice. Cheap Trick tattoo on her arm."

"My God," the mayor breathed. "That was Sandy Sullivan. My former deputy assistant! We lost her to a Walmart job fair *years* ago."

"Sounds like she's still in there," Lewis said. "Go on, what did she say?"

"She...she...pointed toward aisle 8. I went."

"You went to aisle 8?"

"Yes."

"What was it like?"

There was more sniffling on the other end of the recorder. "It was...cold. Colder and colder. Aisle 2 was...warm. Aisle 4 got... colder. Aisle 8 was...like ice. So cold. So cold."

"Listen to me," Lewis said. "This is important. Okay?" There was some sort of muffled response from the subject. "Did you get a jacket from menswear?"

"Lewis," the mayor snapped.

"What?"

"Who gives a shit if he got a jacket from menswear?"

"Science cares!"

There was a loud slam of hands against wood. When the mayor spoke again, her voice was louder, closer to the microphone: "What did you see in aisle 8?"

Subject R's teeth chattered with the memory of the sub-zero temperatures. Speaking through the clattering took great effort. "C-C-C-Canned goods," he finally managed. "So many...so many c-c-canned goods."

"Good," said the mayor. "That's very good. What else did you see?"

"F-F-Fog. Mist. From the shelves. So thick...couldn't see the Sun D-D-Drop."

"According to the schematics, the soda is kept on the far wall after the end of the aisle," Lewis explained to the mayor. "Okay, so. Cans, cold, and mist. This is all very good. Keep going. What else?"

"The beets. There was red."

"The beets? The beets were red?" Lewis asked. There was a quiet shuffling sound, and then Lewis said, "The subject shook his head no."

"Were the *cans* red?" the mayor asked.

"Red...*b-b-behind* the cans," Subject R said. "Light...bright..."

"There was a red light coming from behind the cans," Lewis said. Mallory could hear him scribbling notes on a pad of paper. "Good, good. Did you notice anything else?"

"B-B-Bugs. S-So many b-b-bugs. Bugs everywhere. Crawling on the cans. Dropping...Dropping from the ceiling. C-C-Crawling on my...skin. C-Crawling out...of the beets."

"Ew," Mallory said, disgusted. "No wonder they were on sale." Lewis shushed her again and nodded at the recorder. His own recorded voice spoke next.

"What sort of bugs?"

"Centipedes...mostly. Beetles...and centipedes."

"Good, good." There was more scribbling. "What did you do? Did you kill any of the bugs?"

"No. Too many. Too...cold. I...grabbed a can. Of beets." The subject began sobbing uncontrollably. "His voice," the man choked out through his tears. "Filled me with...his voice."

"Whose voice?" the mayor demanded. "What did it say?"

"It said...it said...'Free me.'"

"Where was the voice coming from?" Lewis asked. "It came from behind the beets?"

"C-C-Came from...*everywhere*. Came from...aisle 8."

"Do you know who it was?" Lewis asked. "Do you know who the voice belonged to?" A moment of silence, then, "The subject is nodding his head. Who was it? Who told you to free him?"

"It was...it was...an ancient...evil."

There was a pause on the other end of the microphone, a shuffling of papers, and an uneasy clearing of throats. "An...ancient evil?" Lewis asked.

"It...wanted to be...free," Subject R said, sounding resolute through his tears.

"How the *fuck* did an ancient evil get trapped behind the canned beets?" the mayor demanded, slapping her hands on the table.

"Marcy—" Lewis began.

"No! This is my town, and I want to know how an ancient evil got trapped behind the goddamn canned beets!"

"Not...just beets," Subject R said. "Canned corn...canned green beans...canned corn beef hash...all...of aisle 8."

"*This is unacceptable*!" the mayor screamed.

Recorded Lewis shushed her, then returned his focus to Subject R. "What happened next? After you touched the can of beets and the voice filled your head. What happened then?"

"I...dropped the beets. They...they were so cheap." The subject lapsed into a fit of sobbing once more. "They were so cheap, but I...I left them behind."

"Good," Lewis said, his voice soothing. "Good. That was a good thing to do. We can get you canned beets at the Aldi."

"Not as cheap," the man pointed out through his sniffles.

"But still very inexpensive. And the town will pay the difference." The mayor began to object, but something—probably Lewis—silenced her. "What happened after you put down the beets?"

"I...tried to walk...but the bugs...attacked by the bugs. They... chewed me from...the inside...out. Hollowed me out...crawled in through my mouth and...chewed me away."

"Oh, that's disgusting," the mayor soured.

"Then what?" Lewis said, ignoring her.

"Tried...to run. But the floor...went down. Sucked me down. The evil said...'Free me...I'll make you richer than...Queen of England.' But...I don't...like foreigners. I...told him so. Then everything went...red. Pain in my head. Then black. Then I woke up... here. In this room."

"Is there anything else? Can you remember anything else at all?"

Subject R paused. Then he said, "The devil lives in aisle 8."

Lewis clicked off the recorder and set it on the plywood table. "*That's* what we're up against, Mallory. *That's* what makes the clone so dangerous. If we don't stop him, he's going to release the ancient evil that lives behind the canned goods in aisle 8. And yes, I know how absurd that sounds, but it's the truth, and it's not a joke. If he succeeds, it will mean the unspeakable destruction of Anomaly Flats. And almost certainly beyond."

"What unspeakable destruction?" Mallory asked. This whole thing, the very notion that an evil creature was locked up in the canned foods aisle of the Walmart, was beyond insane. But so was a creek filled with plasma, and so was a bed and breakfast that encouraged you lock the door with a chalk spell, and so was a cornfield that whispered you into insanity—and those were all plenty real, here in this place. Was an ancient evil any less likely? Mallory discovered she could actually wrap her head around it a bit, if she didn't try too hard. "What would this evil thing do?"

Lewis gave her a grim frown. "Let me show you." He hopped off his stool and retrieved a thin, blue binder from a pile of books and papers near the back corner of the barn. Then he flopped it down on the table and slid it in front of Mallory. "I have to warn you, it's... not easy to look at."

"What is it?" she asked, flipping open the cover. She gasped when she saw the image on the first page...then she scrunched up her face and brought her nose closer to the page, inspecting it closely with a sort of macabre pleasure. "What the hell *is* this?"

"They're woodcuttings. Or mimeographs of woodcuttings, to be exact."

The picture before Mallory showed a line of men, naked and in obvious anguish. Each man was bound by the wrists to a log that was suspended horizontally a few feet over the ground. They appeared to be perched atop long iron stakes stuck into the ground. As Mallory looked closer, she realized the men weren't perched; they were *impaled*. They had been lowered down onto the iron poles from above.

"But...what is *this*?" Mallory repeated. She pointed down at the line of naked men, in case that helped clarify the question.

The scientist shifted uneasily on his stool. "That...ah...well... that is a group of men being impaled. Through the—" He cleared his throat uncomfortably and shifted again. "Through the rectum."

"And what is this?" Mallory asked, pointing at the base of one of the poles. She was experiencing a grotesque wonder like nothing she'd ever known before. This woodcutting was thrilling and horrible and the living embodiment of everything she'd ever wanted to do to her own gallery of asshole exes. "What's this down here?"

"That...ah...appears to be fire. The flames, you see, they, ah... they heat up the metal rods and...well...cauterize the...anus." Lewis' face burned a brighter shade of red than hot iron could ever hope to achieve. He untied his bow tie and loosened the collar of his shirt. Little beads of sweat bubbled up on his brow, and he wiped them away nervously.

"But...*why*?" Mallory asked, her eyes wide with wonder.

The scientist pointed to a dark figure standing alone near the top of the image. The resolution was terrible, but she could see clearly enough that the figure had only a smooth, white surface where his eyes, ears, and nose should be. "This is the ancient evil. As best we can tell, he has impaled these men for…" He cleared his throat once more. "…sport."

"Where's his face?" Mallory demanded.

"I don't know why he's pictured that way. But it's the same on all the pages." He scooted his stool closer to Mallory's and began to leaf through the pages. There was a tableau of women being stewed alive in a large cauldron with feral badgers being dropped into the boiling soup; a depiction of several men wearing their own torso skin loosely around their waists like skirts; a scene with young children with feathers streaming out of their mouths marching along a river of fire holding decapitated heads atop little pikes. And on every page, the darkly-dressed figure looked on from afar, his face a smooth, white, impassive surface.

"How many of these things are there?" Mallory asked, amazed, flipping through the binder.

"Seventeen. They were unearthed by an archeologist working in Anomaly Flats in the '60s. He found them inside a petrified bison carcass he dug up from the parking lot of the old Blockbuster south of town. It was pretty widely known that the Blockbuster was built on top of the ancient Anomalians' sacrificial killing fields—"

"On top of *what*?" Mallory cried.

"—but this was something different," Lewis said, ignoring her outburst. "The archeologist had found plenty of elk and raccoon and small bird skeletons, all with the traditional sacrificial intestines wrapped around their necks, but he'd never found a fully preserved carcass before, and *never* a bison. And certainly never a bison with a series of complex and horrible woodcuttings foretelling the grotesque and agonizing end of Anomaly Flats stuffed down its throat." He took a breath. "They're in the town archives now. In case you want a better look."

Mallory found that she *did* want a better look; she'd never seen anything so grotesque in real life. But she sensed that her fascination with these torturous wood carvings might be looked upon as socially unacceptable, or at the very least socially concerning, so she said, "No, I think this is fine." She flipped the page and examined a mimeograph of deer with their own heads replaced with the detached heads of humans. The men-deer were leaping through a field and munching on dandelions. "How do you know this is *the* ancient evil? And not just some William Blake knockoff?" Lewis gave her a surprised look, and Mallory rolled her eyes. "I've been to a museum, Lewis."

"Of course. I'm sorry. I didn't mean—just…look. Here." He pointed to a block of text that ran along the bottom border of the mimeograph. It was printed in a language Mallory didn't recognize, much less understand.

"What does it say?" she asked.

"It's Coptic." Lewis cleared his throat a little and said, "Should I assume you learned how to read it in a museum?"

"Oh, shut up."

Lewis allowed himself a little, self-satisfied smile. "The Coptic language is sort of a mix of the Greek alphabet and the Egyptian Demotic. It came to prominence sometime after the first century C.E. It doesn't translate perfectly, but this bit here says, roughly, 'Welcome to Anomaly Flats: City of Evil.' And there's a year here, too: 2098."

Mallory furrowed her eyebrows as hard as she possibly could as she looked at another one. "Welcome to Anomaly Flats," she said, her tone flat and dry. "City of Evil. 2098."

Lewis nodded. "Roughly."

Mallory looked down at the paper. She looked back up at Lewis. She looked back down at the paper. Then she looked back up at Lewis. "Welcome to Anomaly Flats, City of Evil, 2098."

"Yes."

Mallory held her hands up in confusion. "Are these *postcards*?"

Lewis shrugged. "More or less. Someone—or some*thing*—not only predicted an evil future for Anomaly Flats, but started *marketing* for it! Isn't that fascinating?"

"You know, you keep saying things are fascinating when they're really just terrifying and horrific," Mallory pointed out.

"Horrific things are almost always fascinating," Lewis insisted. "And look here!" He stubbed his finger against the page, just below the man without a face. Mallory leaned down and squinted hard. There were small letters below him, too. "This appears to be a formal title. It translates into 'Celestial Anathema,' or 'Abomination of the Heavens.' He's given the same title on every carving."

"So this guy—this thing—he's...what? A demon?"

"Or maybe even the great fallen one himself!" Lewis beamed, sounding entirely too excited, given the circumstances. "Not that that's a good thing," he said, catching himself. "But you have to admit, it *is* fas—"

"I know, I know. It's fascinating." Mallory flipped through the binder. "You know, the year 2098 isn't *that* far away. In the big picture."

"No, it's not," Lewis agreed. "We don't know who made the carvings, so it's hard to say why that particular year was chosen; if it's a prophecy, or a guess, or arbitrary, or what. Regardless, this is the future under the reign of the ancient evil. Ultimately, the year is unimportant."

Mallory screwed up her face in disgusted fascination as she turned the pages. Each engraving was more disturbing than the last. "This...I mean, this is pretty gross, Lewis."

Lewis nodded his agreement. He pulled the binder back, closed it, and slid it across to the far end of the table. "I know. I wouldn't have shown it to you, except I think it's vital that you understand the gravity of the danger we're in. We *have* to stop my clone, Mallory. We *have* to."

Mallory sighed and rested her head in her hands. "I just want to get my bag and go to Canada," she murmured.

Lewis raised an eyebrow. "What's in Canada?" he asked.

"Lonely, muscular men in Mountie hats who are just aching for American women, if there's any justice in the world." She rubbed her eyes and shook some life into her brain. "This all seems very... strange. And awful. And maybe like you're drawing a few too many conclusions based on these carvings."

"How so?"

"Subject R said there was an ancient evil. You have these pictures that you think represent an evil. So, great. But who's to say they're *actually* related?"

"Subject R is, I'm afraid. I played you the second portion of the tape just now. Let me play you the beginning." He picked up the recorder and rewound the tape until the machine clicked. "This is what we heard immediately after the subject was thrown from the Walmart; this is what he said to us as we approached." He clicked the play button, and the speakers crackled to life once more. Mallory heard the same male voice from earlier, but now it was speaking gibberish. The sounds hurled out of his mouth as if he were spitting venom, snarling and growling and hissing as he spoke. It was the voice of a man perfectly enraged.

"What's he saying?" Mallory whispered.

Lewis exhaled deeply. "I'm not entirely sure," he said. "It's Coptic. And I can translate it on paper okay, but I can't speak it." He clicked off the recorder and set it back down on the table. "The subject doesn't remember any of that. And even before, when he *was* a surgeon, he certainly was not fluent in a language that's been dead for centuries. The ancient evil touched him...even spoke for him, I'm guessing, for a little while, anyway. Then it left him broken beyond repair. A brilliant surgeon turned into a slow, mumbling halfwit who can't even remember how to swallow."

Mallory's ears perked up. Her breath caught in her throat. "No…" she whispered, faltering.

Lewis gave a slow nod. "Subject R. One of the most intelligent minds Anomaly Flats had ever seen. He still lives here, all these years later. He's not a surgeon anymore, but he does still get to work with his hands."

"Rufus," Mallory said. "The mechanic."

She didn't need to see Lewis' nod to know that she was right. "Laid low by a sale on beets. That's how the Walmart tries to lure us in…with especially good savings on our favorite canned goods. It worked with Rufus. It's almost worked with several others."

Mallory closed her eyes and shook her head. "Wait, so… *Walmart* is doing this? On purpose?"

Lewis shrugged. "My guess is, Walmart just wants to get rid of the ancient evil and will keep offering steep discounts until they can get someone to let it out of the canned goods aisle."

"When all they had to do is wait for some idiot to come along and make an evil clone," Mallory sighed.

Lewis took her hand in both of his own and gave it a good squeeze. "You see? This is why we need to stop him."

"And how do we do that, exactly?"

"I was hoping you'd ask," Lewis said, giving her a wry little smile. "Believe it or not, I have a plan."

CHAPTER 16

"THAT'S YOUR PLAN? Get to Walmart first and shoot the clone?"

"What's wrong with it?" Lewis asked, his face falling.

"I wouldn't call it a *plan*," Mallory said. "More like a 'plan.'" She used air quotes to make sure the not-really-a-plan-ness of it came through. "Something really obvious that someone with no plan whatsoever just decides to do one day."

"It's elegant in its simplicity," Lewis said, trying not to let his hurt feelings show.

"It's stupid in its stupidity," Mallory countered.

"A plan doesn't have to involve code names and secret weapons and hand-drawn maps and needlessly complex pulley systems to be a good plan!" Lewis insisted.

"No, but there should be some sort of *planning* involved. And what the hell sort of plan has a needlessly complex pulley system?"

"I'm sorry it doesn't strike the perfect balance between sparkling ingenuity and detailed machinations. But it *will* work." Lewis crossed his arms and set his face into a stern scowl.

Mallory rolled her eyes. "Fine. You're right. It's fine. It's simple, and it'll work. It's a great plan."

Lewis nodded primly. "Thank you." Then he added, "There's also a back-up plan."

"What is it, lie down and hope he trips over us?"

"Mallory!"

"I'm sorry...I'm sorry. Okay. What is the back-up plan, and why is it not the primary plan, and do we actually need a back-up plan if the most crucial element of the primary plan is 'get there a few minutes early'?"

Lewis clamped his mouth shut and took several big, labored breaths. His face was splotchy and strained with emotion. "I don't anticipate needing a back-up plan. But *if* we fail—not that I think we will, given the *elegant simplicity* of our primary plan—and *if* the clone sets the ancient evil free, we'll need a plan to stop it from escaping aisle 8. We need to be prepared to kill it."

"The back-up plan is a plan to kill an ancient, all-powerful demon?" Mallory asked. Lewis nodded. Mallory rubbed her hands together. "Now we're talking. Lay it on me, Hannibal Smith." Lewis gave her a questioning look. "What? Hannibal Smith. 'I love it when a plan comes together'? *The A-Team*?" The scientist only shrugged. "Jesus, Lewis, turn on TV Land once in a while."

"We don't really get television out here," he said simply. He hopped off the stool and rummaged through a different pile of books and papers, stacked up beneath the hayloft. "Now where is that...?" he mumbled to himself.

"How does one even kill an ancient evil?" Mallory called. "Smother it with love?"

Lewis found what he was looking for in the pile and held it above his head triumphantly. "Nope! You kill an ancient evil with this." He jogged back to the table and slapped the piece of paper down in front of Mallory. It was a crude drawing of some sort of long, thin metal tool.

"A crowbar?" Mallory asked, confused. "You kill an ancient evil with a crowbar?"

"A crow—? What? No, it's a spear," Lewis said, stabbing his finger at the drawing. "Look. There's the tip, there, and the rest of this is...you know...spear. The shaft."

"But it's split at the end," Mallory pointed out, tracing the back end of the tool with her finger. "And it curves. It's definitely a crowbar."

"It's a spear!" Lewis insisted. "And a spear of great power, I might add."

"Crowbar," Mallory said, crossing her arms.

"It's not a great drawing," Lewis explained, getting a little huffy.

"I think it's a very good drawing," Mallory said. "Of a crowbar."

Lewis sighed with frustration. "Fine. It's a crowbar. A crowbar that's actually a spear of great power. It's called the Spear of Rad, and it might just be the only thing that can destroy the ancient evil."

Mallory raised an eyebrow suspiciously. "The Spear of Rad?"

Lewis shrugged. "It was discovered in the '80s."

"What does it do, play David Bowie's greatest hits while riding a BMX?"

"Ha, ha," Lewis said dryly. "It's actually *very* powerful."

"Let me guess. You dug it up outside a RadioShack."

"Close. Circuit City."

Mallory leaned back and rolled her eyes. "Of course."

"As far as anyone can tell, the spear seems to have arrived as a comet, encased in ice. It crashed into the Earth several centuries ago."

Mallory crossed her arms. Her skepticism was palpable. "So this comet crashes into town, and instead of destroying all life and sending Anomaly Flats the way of the dinosaurs, it just sort of sits there quietly and melts?"

"It did leave a crater. But yes."

"And you're *sure* that's what happened."

"Fairly certain. See these markings on the shaft?" he asked, tapping the drawing of the spear. "Definitely an alien language."

"Oh, definitely," Mallory agreed, nodding. "And now we're going to use this to kill an ancient evil."

"If we have to," Lewis said grimly.

"One question: Why don't we just use, like, a knife?"

Lewis laughed out loud. The sound surprised Mallory so much, she had to grab the bottom of her seat just to keep from sliding off it. "You can't kill an all-powerful ancient evil with something as crude and unremarkable as a *knife*, Mallory. Everybody knows that." He chuckled as he took off his glasses and wiped them on his coat. "You have to use an archaic weapon with great, mystical powers."

"Oh, of *course*," she said, setting a new record for the most eye rolls in a 24-hour period. "And the Spear of Rad is that archaic weapon with great, mystical powers, and it can kill the ancient evil."

"It is, and it can," Lewis said. Mallory had to admit, he *did* sound impressively confident.

"How can you be sure?" she asked.

"Because it says so in the manual."

Mallory stared at the scientist. It took a few tries to get her mouth to work. "The manual?"

"Yes," Lewis nodded.

Mallory paused. "Okay, so…wait. The Spear of Rad, a great, mystical weapon that arrived in a comet from an alien world, came with a *manual*?"

"Written in English and everything! Isn't it *fasc*—"

"Yeah, yeah, I know, I know," Mallory said, waving him off. "It's fascinating." She wondered, not for the first time, if she were having the world's longest, most drawn-out embolism.

"According to the manual," Lewis continued, admiring the little drawing, "the spear can vanquish demons, archdemons, reapers, wraiths, shape shifters, succubae, incubi, and ancient evils. The manual also gives detailed instructions on proper care for the spear and an address to contact about returns and exchanges, though it's in a nebula I daresay we won't be able to reach with manmade spacecraft for at least another millennium or two."

"How stupidly bizarre," Mallory muttered. "Okay, so we get to Walmart early tomorrow and shoot the evil clone dead. In case that fails, because we forget how to tell time or how bullets work, we use this conveniently-super-powered crowbar to destroy the ancient evil as he emerges through the canned goods. Yes?"

But Lewis frowned. "Technically, yes, that is the plan. Though I wouldn't call it convenient. Obtaining the spear is going to be… tricky."

Mallory sighed. Of course it was going to be tricky. "How tricky?"

Lewis rubbed the palm of his right hand nervously. "When the Spear of Rad was discovered, the mayor wanted it housed in the town museum, where it could be both admired by the public and guarded by the highly-trained special forces team that for whatever reason volunteers as museum docents on the weekdays. But the woman who found the spear…she opted to keep it in her…private collection."

Mallory was confused. She wasn't terribly political, but she had a working knowledge of how the government operated. "If the town mayor and SEAL Team Six wanted the spear, why didn't they just, like, *take* it?"

Lewis inhaled sharply through his teeth. "Well…you see, Colleen's not exactly the type of person you just go *take* things from."

"But *we're* going to go take it," Mallory said, for personal clarification.

"We're…going to try."

"You don't sound very confident."

"I'm *not* very confident."

"What's the worst that could happen? She says no?"

"Yes. The worst that could happen is that she could say no," Lewis said, swallowing hard.

"So what?"

"So Colleen likes to say no with her shotgun collection."

Mallory started. "She has a *collection* of shotguns?"

"Thirty of them, at least."

Mallory dismissed this with a wave of her hand. "Doesn't matter. She could have a hundred shotguns, she can only shoot one at a time, right? As long as we stay spread out, she can only take out one of us before the other runs away, and I'm pretty sure she'll shoot you first. She's known you for years; I've only known you for a day, and I'd definitely shoot you before me."

"Actually…I wouldn't be so sure."

"You think she'd shoot me first?" Mallory asked, trying not to sound offended.

"No. I mean there's a reasonably good chance she could fire her entire collection of guns at once."

Mallory snorted. "How is *that* possible?"

"She's resourceful."

"Well, shit, with a pep talk like that, how can we go wrong?" Mallory scowled. She slapped the table with the palms of her hands, and the plywood wobbled and bounced and threatened to collapse completely. Mallory didn't care. "Let's do it. Let's go get that Spear of Rad and stab a primeval demon to death, or else get riddled with holes trying."

Lewis tapped his teeth together nervously. His eyes darted out toward one of the windows, and he considered the full darkness of the world outside. "I think we'll hold off until tomorrow."

"Why? No time like the present, right? Seize the day, up and at 'em, eyes on the prize, all that shit."

"It's too dark," Lewis insisted.

"It's just dark enough," Mallory countered. "If we're going to get shot at by an army's worth of bullets, I'd rather not see them coming."

But Lewis held firm. "Trust me. You don't want to approach Colleen's place at night. We wouldn't make it past the gate. We'll get some sleep, then head over in the morning. If she doesn't shoot us and stuff us on sight, we might actually have a chance at the spear. Then we can worry about the clone and aisle 8."

"You know, it sure sounds like we're putting ourselves in an awful lot of danger just so we can go somewhere else and put ourselves in an awful lot of danger," Mallory pointed out.

Lewis smiled grimly. "Welcome to Anomaly Flats." He stood up from his stool and stretched. His back popped, and he winced. "Come on. We should get you back."

"Back where?" Mallory said miserably. "The Hellmouth Bed and Breakfast?" She planted her forehead on the plywood and muttered, "I can't handle any more tentacles."

Lewis straightened up a bit. He cleared his throat nervously. "Well, ah…you're…ah…you're welcome to…stay here tonight," he offered.

"I'm not sleeping with you," she reminded him, her voice muffled by the tabletop. Lewis blushed so hard, he couldn't speak. Instead, he coughed out a series of syllables so clogged and haphazard that they made Mallory roll her head over so she could get a look at the scientist and determine whether or not he was actually choking to death on his embarrassment. His face looked like it had been dipped in cranberry juice, and his mouth was opening and closing at an alarming rate, but he was taking shallow gasps of air, so she decided he'd probably live. "Good lord, Lewis. You have *got* to get laid," Mallory said, pushing herself up to a full seat. "Not by me, obviously. But, you know. By someone." She hopped off the stool and looked around the miserable-looking barn. "Which way to the guest room?" she asked.

Lewis managed to catch his breath. He pulled off his lab coat, balled it up, and fanned himself with it. "No guest room," he said, shaking his head. His face slowly drained back to a non-lethal shade of pink. "You can sleep in the bed, up in the loft. I'll take the couch."

Mallory looked doubtfully around the room. "*What* couch?" He nodded at a pile of blankets that sat before the corner of the barn that, judging by the scorch marks, Lewis liked to use as a fireplace. "Looks…comfortable."

"The outhouse is out that way," Lewis said, nodding toward the back of the barn over his shoulder, "if you want to use it before bed."

Mallory made a sour face. "A quarter-mile walk in the dark? In this place? I think I'll hold it."

"Come on, I'll walk with you. It's not *that* dark. The lava pits do a pretty good job of lighting the way." Lewis reached into a milk crate near the hayloft ladder and pulled out an old revolver. He loaded the chambers, cocked the hammer, and pointed the gun straight ahead as he opened the back door and stepped into the darkness beyond. "We'll almost certainly be fine."

CHAPTER 17

MALLORY AWOKE THE NEXT MORNING to a familiar, sickeningly sweet aroma wafting through the stale barn air. "Oh my God," she mumbled before even opening her eyes. "That had better not be waffles."

"I got waffles!" Lewis called happily from below. He ducked just in time to avoid getting clobbered in the face by Mallory's thrown shoe. "What? You don't like waffles? Are you a monster?" He opened up the brown paper sack and pulled out a little plastic container full of thick, brown liquid. "There's field mouse syrup, too."

Mallory sighed as she threw off the covers and shook her fingers through her hair. "I *did* like waffles, before waffles were the only thing on the menu," she said, stretching and yawning and trying to coax her limbs out of apathy. She sniffed at her shirt; it didn't smell all that bad for being her only clothing option for three days straight now. It didn't smell all that *great,* but it didn't smell all that bad. She wouldn't be attracting flies, at least. Not like Marcy, anyway...

She shivered as she thought of the cloud of flies swarming out of the tourism director's mouth and decided maybe she should just go back to bed and lie there until she died.

"I'm an eggs and bacon man myself," Lewis admitted, pulling the Styrofoam containers out of the bag and placing them on the table. He stopped and thought a moment, and a certain sadness settled over his shoulders. "Of course, that was before the chicken incident," he said quietly.

"*What* chicken incident? Tell me the truth about those god-damn chickens!" Mallory demanded, half-climbing, half-falling down from the hayloft. The mystery of it all was driving her mad. Lewis was ready to respond, but just then, a speaker bolted to the wall just beneath the hayloft eaves squawked to a painful, screeching sort of life. Mallory threw her hands over her ears and said, "You have a speaker in your *house*?"

Lewis tilted his head and gave her a quizzical look. "There's a speaker in *every* house," he said, as if it were the most obvious and natural thing.

"*Attention, Anomaly Flats,*" the voice from the speaker said. "*The truce between Anomaly Flats and the subterranean nation that exists beneath the overpass has been violated. I repeat: The three-year truce between Anomaly Flats and the subterranean nation that exists beneath the overpass has been violated. One of the mole-women was seen lounging in the wildflower patch adjacent to the overpass, which is a clear and aggressive violation of the treaty. The mayor is attempting a diplomatic resolution by flushing a warning bucket of boiling hot sulfuric acid into the mole-peoples' water table, as is Anomaly Flats' diplomatic tradition. The Mayor's Office would like to remind everyone that poisoning the water is only the first step in a long, diplomatic approach to peace, and warns that citizens should not expect a swift conclusion. Additional diplomatic steps include, but are not limited to, colorful threats, unusually bright flash bombs, showers of inorganic waste materials, and care packages of highly explosive materials hidden inside of raw potatoes. Residents are reminded to place all of their inorganic waste materials and unused potatoes in the yellow bags that the town government has already placed in the crawlspace in their attics in an effort to aid the diplomatic process.*

"*Attention, Anomaly Flats: The Anomaly Bijou movie theater would like to remind you that Mandatory Monday is just two days away. All citizens are required to purchase tickets to one of three showings of* Howard the Duck. *Ticket discounts will not be given— especially not to the elderly. Enjoy the movie! You have to. It's the law.*"

"She really brightens the day, doesn't she?" Mallory said after the speaker clicked off. She twisted her back, and it gave a loud pop. "Aging is bullshit," she decided.

Lewis pulled out a stool for her at the table. "Trudy's waffles may be the best thing for that," he said, pushing his glasses up his nose. He wasn't wearing his lab coat this morning, but Mallory saw that a fresh, clean coat hung on a peg near the front door, ready to be thrown on at a moment's notice. He wore a pink-and-green plaid shirt and a purple bow tie with pink polka dots. His outfit looked pressed and tidy, and made Mallory's three-day old t-shirt and jeans ensemble that much crummier by comparison. She sniffed the air near her shoulder, just for reassurance, and was almost positive she detected a hint of swamp mud this time.

"Why's that?" she asked, climbing onto the stool with a sigh. "The secret ingredient is arsenic, and it puts you out of your misery at an unnaturally early age?"

"Not at all," Lewis said, shaking his head and taking his own seat at the end of the table. "It's just that there's a very good possibility that eating Nite-Owl waffles gives your body the preternatural ability to defy a standard timeline."

Mallory stared at the little nerd on the other stool. "Which means?"

"The waffles *may* cause your body to automatically slow, or even selectively reverse, time."

"Oh, come on," Mallory snorted, popping open one of the Styrofoam containers. She prodded the waffles inside with her finger. They were crispy and fluffy, and they smelled like wonder. But a DeLorean, they were not. "You're telling me this waffle is a time machine?"

"I'm still studying them, but the evidence is compelling."

Mallory picked up her fork and stabbed at the golden brown delight. "Can they take me back to before I came to Anomaly Flats?"

Lewis shrugged. "Who knows?" He opened his own container and set to work cutting up his waffles. "I haven't seen any effects on that level, but I can confidently say that my wrinkles have been smoothing over ever since I started eating them. And my bad elbow is just a regular elbow now. It's not a trip to the past, but it's something."

"It's something, all right," Mallory murmured. She took a bite of waffle and closed her eyes as the flavor melted across her tongue. Whatever else the waffles might be, they were undeniably delicious. Completely, frustratingly, and undeniably delicious.

"Eat up," Lewis said through a mouthful of food. "You're going to need your strength today. And also," he said, swallowing a lump of waffles down, "it might be your last meal."

X

Colleen Branch lived in a house in the middle of nowhere— and considering it was situated in a nearly-impossible-to-find town in the middle of a state like Missouri, that was really saying something. Mallory reflected on this as they drove farther and farther along a long-neglected dirt road that constantly curved to the right. They drove through fields and hills and forests and, at one especially confusing point, a small ocean, and still, the road continued, disappearing around a curve ever to the right. "How long have we been driving?" Mallory demanded after what felt like half her life bouncing around through washed-out ruts and wayward stones.

"We're almost there."

"We've been through three different woods," she pointed out.

"Just one more."

"And a few dozen fields."

"I know."

"And part of an ocean."

"It was a very small ocean," he said.

"Lewis, where are we going?"

"Mallory, we are going to the boonies."

Mallory snorted. "This whole *state* is the boonies."

"We're going to the boonies of the boonies," Lewis clarified.

"No shit," Mallory muttered, staring out the window at the sprawling woods outside. "Am I drunk, or have we been curving to the right this entire time?"

"I don't believe anyone's ever reported a sensation of inebriation from Trudy's waffles," Lewis said. He glanced at Mallory, his eyes bright with interest. "Do you *feel* drunk?"

Mallory rolled her eyes. "It's an *expression*, Lewis."

"Oh." Lewis focused back on the road, unable to hide his disappointment. Discovering new symptoms, Mallory guessed, was something of an enjoyable pastime for him. "Yes, we've been curving to the right this entire time."

"Then call me crazy, but shouldn't we have eventually made a circle? Or, like, a million of them? Shouldn't we have met our own road a bajillion times by now?"

"You would think so, wouldn't you?" Lewis asked with a smile. "The road to Colleen's farm is…unique. It's sort of like a reverse nautilus. Or a regular nautilus, I guess, depending on which end of the nautilus you start from."

"We're spiraling into smaller and smaller circles?"

"Not smaller and smaller so much as deeper and deeper."

Mallory ducked her head and peered out the windshield. "What are you talking about? The land is totally flat here."

"Not deeper and deeper *geographically*; deeper and deeper *metaphysically*. This road is something of a three-dimensional representation of a five-dimensional downward spiral that leads to a new elevation of a separate dimensional aspect." Mallory sighed and laid her forehead down against the dashboard. The world hurt a little bit less when she closed her eyes. "Try not to think about it too much," Lewis advised. "It's largely uncharted territory, since Colleen gets so few visitors. And besides…we're here."

Mallory lifted her head from the dashboard and saw a wood rail fence winding its way through the trees and across the road. A wide metal gate spanned the road between fence posts and forced Lewis to slow the RV to a rumbling halt. The gate wasn't locked, at least not in a traditional sense; a bungee cord wrapped in the split rubber of an old garden hose snaked through the bars of the gate and looped around the nearest fence post. It wasn't exactly a major deterrent. But what *was* a major deterrent was the collection of old, weather-battered signs that had been tied to the gate with barbed wire.

NO SOLICITORS.

DO NOT ENTER.

NO UNAUTHORIZED VISITORS.

SECURITY SYSTEM PROVIDED BY THE SECOND AMEND-MENT.

DEAD MEN ONLY BEYOND THIS POINT.

BEWARE OF CROTCHETY OLD BITCH.

NO TRESPASSING: VIOLATORS WILL BE SHOT, STABBED, BEATEN, SKINNED, GUTTED, ROASTED, EATEN, DIGESTED, AND FLUSHED.

"She seems sweet," Mallory offered dryly.

"She's...different." Lewis unbuckled his seatbelt and popped open the door. He stuck both arms out and held up his hands so they were in plain view from the far side of the fence. "Stay here," he murmured. Then he tumbled awkwardly out of the Winnebago and began a slow, cautious creep toward the gate.

"Colleen?" he called, his voice sinking into the thick brush that lined the dirt road and disappearing among the trees. "I'd like to talk for a few minutes, if that's okay?"

His plea was followed by several long moments of silence. Then a small, oblong object bounced onto the road just inside the gate and bumped and skittered along the hard-packed dirt. Mallory squinted through the windshield and screamed when she realized that it was an olive green grenade.

Lewis threw himself into the ditch that ran alongside the road and tucked his head under his arms just as the grenade exploded.

Mallory screamed again, and then she screamed a third time, just for good measure, because for the love of God, a *bomb* had just gone off thirty feet away.

But the explosion was smaller than she'd expected. It was more sound than fury, though it did leave a small crater in the dirt road. There were some small bits of shrapnel that peppered the trees, and a few bits of casing chipped against the RV, but there didn't appear to be much major damage to the vehicle, to the fence, or to the little scientist crouched down in the drainage ditch.

A good and decent person, Mallory knew, would have sprinted out to check on Lewis, to make sure he was still in one piece and do some amateur field surgery if necessary. But *her* first instinct was to stay relatively protected in a giant shield of metal and glass rather than go galloping across a road that was susceptible to grenades.

So she ran with it.

She hunkered down lower in her seat and called, "Lewis? Are you okay?" through the open driver's side door. But either he didn't hear her...or he was dead after all, because he didn't so much as twitch. Mallory eyed the keys to the RV, which Lewis had left in the ignition. It took almost no time at all to realize that, yes, she would most certainly leave a man behind.

Suddenly, a second grenade plunked its way down the road and exploded just a few feet away from the crater left by the first. Mallory cried out and ducked down behind the dashboard. This explosion was bigger, and it shook the Winnebago on its tires. More shrapnel and dirt rained down on the RV. "Fuck this," she murmured, sliding into the driver's seat. "Sorry, Lewis."

But just as she reached for the keys, Lewis raised his hands a bit in the ditch and stood up on trembling legs. He shook the dirt off himself and called out, in a voice as steady as he could manage, "Colleen, we just need to talk!"

Mallory stayed her hand. She'd wait and see how this played out.

Lewis crawled out of the drainage ditch and, despite the fact that it was now the target of what Mallory considered a vicious and unrelenting onslaught, cautiously approached the gate. "Anomaly Flats is in danger!" he hollered up the road. "Real danger! And I think you can help!"

A spray of shotgun pellets sprayed the dirt near Lewis' feet. Mallory didn't hear the actual gunfire until almost two full seconds later. Something in the back of her brain tried to signal to her how strange that was, but the rest of her brain was too busy expressing a desperate desire to get the hell out of Dodge to really pay attention.

Lewis leapt back, but he didn't retreat. "Colleen, I'm coming up! I am unarmed, and I don't mean any harm!" He gingerly lifted the bungee cord loop from the fence post and let it hang limply from the gate. "I have a friend with me, and—"

More lead shot sprayed the air, whizzing off into the trees and exploding against the bark of a tree not far to Lewis' right.

"She's a *friend*!" Lewis repeated, sounding frenzied. "She can be trusted! I promise!" He paused and tensed, waiting for another warning shot.

But it didn't come.

He exhaled slowly and pushed open the gate. It swung on rusty hinges that hadn't been put to great use in the past few decades. "I've opened the gate," he called out. He began slowly backing up toward the RV. "We're going to come up now, okay?" A lone rifle slug ricocheted across the dirt, but it felt like a half-hearted shot. "Okay," Lewis said, smiling with relief. "Okay."

He eased his way back to the Winnebago, still not turning his back on the gate. He reached out and fumbled for the door as he backed into it, then skirted around and leapt into the RV. He mopped the sweat from his brow and exhaled hugely. "That went better than expected," he said.

"I am *amazed* that you're not dead," Mallory admitted.

Lewis shrugged. "The trick is to know where to stand," he said. He fired up the RV, and they rumbled slowly through the open gate.

Mallory peered up through the windshield, but all she could see in the distance was the ever-curving road and more trees. "Where's the house?" she asked, confused.

"It's another ten minutes or so. About five miles up the road."

Mallory scanned the woods. "But...where was she shooting from?"

"Her front porch, I imagine," Lewis said.

Mallory scowled. "Are you telling me this crazy old bitch can lob a grenade for five miles?!"

"I know what that sign said, but she's not actually old," Lewis said. "And I have to say, I know you're the one with a shared female experience, but I really think the word 'bitch' is—"

"Not the point!" Mallory cried. "What are you driving me into, Lewis?"

Lewis tick-tocked his head back and forth a few times, trying to decide how best to proceed. Finally, he said, "Colleen's farm is really quite special."

Mallory snorted. "Is it a catapult farm?"

"In principle, you're not too far off," Lewis said. "Distance is relative in this part of Anomaly Flats."

"How fascinating," Mallory said dryly.

Lewis couldn't help but beam. "It *is* fascinating," he agreed. "If only someone else had claimed the property instead of the Branch clan." A Claymore mine exploded to their right, as if to punctuate his point, uprooting a small tree and blasting a casing full of metal shot harmlessly into the woods. "That was a little over the top," Lewis murmured to himself.

"Are you going to tell me what sort of farm this is or not?" Mallory demanded. "Enough cryptic bullshit. What sort of farm makes distance fucking relative?"

"That kind," Lewis said tensely, nodding up the road. An old, weathered cabin came into view around the curve. Its once-brown planks had been stripped by decades of wind and sun and were now a dusty, exhausted gray. The cedar-shingle roof slouched in the middle and drooped over the edges of the house like petrified gelatin. A splintery rail ran along the front of the house, and half the steps leading up to the porch had broken through. A pair of tough, leathery feet were propped up on the railing. They belonged to a middle-aged woman in a pair of dirt-stained denim overalls and a dirty mesh trucker hat that said SKOAL across the front. She held a long-barrel shotgun in one hand and a small silver pail in the other. The gun was pointed toward the sky; the pail was tipped up to her lips. She drank deeply from it, and rivulets of liquid dribbled down her chin.

"It's not your typical farm," Lewis continued, his voice quieting. "You can't grow fruits or vegetables up here; the soil won't support it. There's only one thing that *will* grow: wild po—"

He was interrupted by a shotgun blast from the front porch. The metal shot peppered the driver's side of the RV, which probably should have struck Mallory as odd, since the woman had barely moved, and the shotgun was still pointing straight up in the air. Tendrils of smoke floated up lazily from its 30-inch barrel and disappeared above the porch. But she was far too busy ducking and screaming to be concerned with the particulars of physics.

"I should have left you to die at the gate!" Mallory cried from her crouched spot on the floorboards.

"You were going to leave me to die?" Lewis gasped, his face drawn.

"It crossed my mind," she said, wondering what exactly it would take for him to realize that the only person's survival she was wholly invested in was her own. The way things were going, she'd have the opportunity to prove it to him very, very soon.

"Thanks a lot." He put his hands out the window of the RV so the woman on the porch could see that they were empty. "I'm coming out, Colleen. *Don't shoot.*" Colleen pulled the trigger again, just to show him where he stood. She fired to the left, and the shot popped into a tree to the right. This time Mallory *did* notice the discrepancy, and she found it exceedingly confounding.

Lewis cautiously opened the door and slipped out onto the mud and weeds that served as Colleen's driveway. He walked slowly toward the cabin with his hands raised as Colleen reloaded the shotgun. "Morning, Lewis," she said, her voice calm and pleasant, and even a little chipper. "How's the science business?" She clicked the barrel back into place and balanced it across her lap.

"It's actually a little pernicious right now," he said, stopping about halfway between the RV and Colleen's porch.

"Pernicious?" Colleen snorted. She picked up the tin pail and took another drink. "You studying for the ACT?"

Lewis tensed. He desperately hoped he hadn't offended her with his language. "It means—"

"It means the powers of Anomaly Flats are conspiring against us all for the umpteen millionth time," Colleen interrupted him. She swirled the drink in her pail and muttered into it. "I took the ACT once." She set the pail down on the porch. Then she picked up the shotgun and eased the barrel onto the railing so that it wasn't pointed at Lewis...but it wasn't far off, either. "What do you want?"

"We need to talk to you. It's *extremely* important. I wouldn't have come all the way out here if it weren't."

Colleen nodded toward the Winnebago. "Who's the new kid?"

"Her name's Mallory. She's...passing through."

Colleen spat a huge glob of phlegm onto the floorboards. "I remember a time when *you* were just passing through. How long are you gonna stay in the Flats?"

"For the rest of my life, which will be cut unnaturally short if you can't help us," the scientist said miserably. "Can I put my hands down?"

Colleen nodded. Lewis sighed with relief and lowered his aching arms. "What's the life-threatening disaster *this* time? Mutant bears? Flesh-eating bacteria? An army of undead mules?"

"Worse," Lewis frowned. "Much, much worse."

Colleen smirked and considered first the scientist, then the woman in the RV. Finally, she propped the shotgun against the porch railing and said, "All right. You've got ten minutes before my hospitality hits its limit."

Lewis exhaled and waved Mallory over. She clamored out of the truck and stepped her way nervously up to the porch. "Am I getting shot?" she asked.

"Time will tell," Colleen said. "First, Lewis is gonna run inside and fetch the gin. I never talk shop without gin."

X

Mallory leaned against the porch rail while Lewis paced in front of the rocking chair, explaining their predicament. Colleen rocked slowly and thoughtfully as she slurped from her newly replenished bucket. As Lewis began explaining their meeting with the oracle, Colleen held up the bucket to Mallory and said, "Drink?"

Lewis, clearly unhappy about being interrupted, put his hands on his hips and said sourly, "It's a little early for us, thanks."

But Mallory leaned forward and peered down into the pail. Somewhere between high school and undergrad, she'd learned that it was never too early for the right kind of drink. "What is it?" she asked suspiciously.

"Gin bucket," Colleen answered.

Mallory wrinkled her nose. "What's a gin bucket?"

"It's a bucket. Full of gin."

Mallory bent down and sniffed the pail. "And what else?" she asked.

"This and that," Colleen said with a gleam in her eye. "A can of lime juice concentrate, some Fresca, a little bit of orange juice. But mostly gin." She inhaled deeply of the bucket's citrus-and-juniper aroma and sighed with a smile. "Better kick than coffee," she promised.

"I usually take my gin with an olive," Mallory said hesitantly, considering the concoction. "But hell, it's almost 10, right? And when in the hillbilly backwoods of Rome…" She took the bucket and drank down a swallow. It was cold, and sweet, and it tingled against all the right spots. "Oh my God," she said slowly, letting the magic of the gin bucket caress her soul. "This is my new favorite thing." She took another huge gulp.

Colleen snatched the bucket back. "Don't wear out your welcome," she said testily, cradling the pail against her chest.

"*Anyway*," Lewis said, his eyes bugging out of their sockets a bit, "if we can get back to the mortal disaster at hand, I'm trying to tell you that my clone is planning to release the ancient evil that lives in the Walmart *tonight.*"

Colleen turned her sharp eyes on the scientist. Mallory already felt a little like a fuzzy pinwheel from the gin bucket, but it didn't appear to be dulling the other woman one bit. "I see," she said. "You're here for the spear."

Lewis wrung his hands nervously. "I promise I'll bring it right back."

Colleen set the gin bucket down on the floorboards, and Mallory briefly debated making a grab for it. Then she remembered the shotgun, and the grenades, and the Claymore, and decided perhaps it'd be best to wait for another invitation. "Lewis," Colleen said, leaning forward in the chair, "it's a mystery to me how you could've forgotten what happened when you borrowed the Amulet of the Distempered Wolf Priestess and promised to bring *that* right back."

"That was *very* different," Lewis insisted, raising his hands defensively and taking a step backward. "The chances of that particular band of cannibal gypsies having possession of the laser diamond from the treasure of Shmubla Shman were *infinitesimally* small. Never in a million years could I have—"

"And I trust you remember what happened the last time the sheriff's own police came out here and tried to relieve me of my AKs," Colleen interrupted.

"Yes, of *course* I do," Lewis said. "I was down at the Dive that night, I saw the National Guard go by. *And* the Red Cross. But listen—"

But Colleen cut him off again: "So you *know* I don't like it when folks try to take my things. And you *know* I've got no reason to trust you when you say you'll bring it back. So then you also *know* that when you ask me to borrow the Spear of Rad and tell me you'll bring it right back, I'm liable to blow your jaw off just for asking."

"I—I *do* know all of that—" Lewis began.

"Good," Colleen said, with an iron tang of finality. "So long as we're clear." She sat back in the rocking chair and pulled the shotgun up onto her lap. She cradled it like a baby lamb as she rocked slowly back and forth. "You know you'd save yourself a big heap of trouble by just getting to the Walmart early and shooting him when he gets there, right?"

Lewis began pacing once more. "I know. I *know*! Showing up early and shooting him *is* the plan." Mallory snorted at the mention of the word "plan." Lewis shot her a cutting look. Mallory stuck her tongue out at him. "But I'd feel a whole lot better if we had the spear as a back-up plan."

"All you gotta do is get there early. You want a back-up plan? I'll lend you a spare wristwatch." She picked up the gin bucket and glanced over at Mallory as she gave it a few thoughtful swirls. "What about you?" she asked.

"What *about* me?"

"What's your part in all this?"

Mallory sighed. "I just want my car and my bag and to get out of this town." And then she added, "And maybe some more gin bucket."

But Colleen didn't offer her the pail. Her eyes flashed, and her stare became hard. "Just blowing through, are you?" she asked.

Mallory shrugged her shoulders sadly. "I'm trying."

"Yeah...just blowing through," Colleen repeated. "Like an F5 tornado."

Mallory's skin pricked up along the back of her neck. She suddenly didn't care for the way this conversation was turning. "Yeah, I guess," she mumbled, pushing herself off the railing. She gave Lewis a look. "Maybe we should go," she said, taking a step toward the busted stairs.

"You can take the spear," Colleen said, and Mallory froze in her tracks.

Lewis exhaled with relief. "Thank you!"

"On two conditions. One, you bring it back. *Actually* bring it back."

Lewis rubbed his jaw. "If we succeed, I promise to bring it back. If we fail, I'm not sure if it'll make it out in one piece, but you also won't be around long to care."

Colleen's eyes bore into the little scientist. "Bring it back," she said.

"Even if it's—"

"Bring it. Back."

Lewis sighed. "All right. What's the second condition?"

Colleen smiled and turned to look at Mallory. "She goes in to get it."

"'She' as in *me?*" Mallory asked, surprised. "Goes in where?"

"Colleen—" Lewis began, but she silenced him with a glance.

"Either she goes in, or it doesn't come out."

"Goes in *where?*" Mallory demanded. Why was it so goddamn impossible to follow a conversation in this town?

And *why* wouldn't Colleen give her another sip of gin bucket?!

"Into my museum," Colleen said, snorting happily into her bucket. "You'll find it out around back."

X

"I feel like this is some sort of trick," Mallory said quietly, crossing her arms and eyeing the Spear of Rad nervously. "I mean, it's just…*sitting* there. In the middle of the yard. Do I just walk up and take it? What's the catch?"

Lewis plucked his glasses from his nose and wiped them nervously on his lab coat. "Remember when I told you this farm was unique?"

"It's landmines, isn't it?" Mallory asked miserably. "She grows landmines."

"Not…exactly."

"Then what?"

Lewis turned and looked at her with somber eyes. "Portals," he said. "It's a portal farm."

Mallory glanced dubiously at Colleen's backyard. It spread for a few hundred feet in every direction, and was bordered by tall sycamores on every side. Scattered throughout the yard were the various pieces of the eccentric woman's "collection": a platoon of small toy army men made out of solid gold; a cardboard crown with multicolored jewels pasted onto the points; several ornately-framed velvet paintings of llamas; a large granite slab with a six-pointed star and a series of esoteric runes carved into the face; a crackling branch of energy that appeared to be a lightning bolt in stasis; clay pots and vases from seemingly every era in history; several unusually sized tin cans; and, of course, the Spear of Rad, occupying a place of honor in the center of the yard, lying upon a dry, cracked, concrete birdbath.

"What do you mean by portals?" she asked. "All I see is a bunch of crap."

"A portal is a gateway of sorts that—" Lewis began.

Mallory held up a hand to cut him off. "I know *what* a portal is, Lewis. What do you mean she *grows* them?"

"I mean just that: she grows them. Out of the ground. Like tomatoes." He held out his fist, palm up, opened his fingers, and raised his arm to simulate either agricultural growth or a severe aneurysm. Mallory decided it was probably the former. "They sprout up all over this part of the land naturally. They're almost impossible to detect; they're perfectly transparent. If you step into one, you come out somewhere completely different. Some of the portals lead to other spots on the property; that's how Colleen's able to sit on her porch and lob grenades five miles away. Others lead to different locations altogether. Outside of Anomaly Flats. And beyond."

Mallory didn't like the hollow way he said "beyond." It sent a chill across her shoulders.

She surveyed the field. It seemed like a perfectly normal lawn that was hosting the world's weirdest yard sale. There wasn't even a hint of anything besides grass and weeds growing out of the earth. "Why can't you see whatever's on the other side?" she murmured.

"That's a different varietal," Lewis said, shaking his head. "She grows those too, out on the eastern slope."

Mallory crossed her arms as she gazed across at the Spear of Rad. "So let me get this straight: the spear is *right there*, but there are God knows how many invisible portals between here and there, and stepping through them sends you to somewhere else entirely."

"That's about it," Lewis said with a shrug.

"Is anything easy in this goddamn town?"

"Nothing I've seen so far."

"Well?" Colleen hollered from the back porch, swirling the gin bucket. "You going in or not?"

Mallory frowned. "I don't suppose you have a map," she said.

Colleen snorted and spat. "Are you kidding? Some of them portals lead to places I wouldn't send my worst enemies. And I *hate* my worst enemies. Of course there's a map."

Mallory's stomach churned. She guessed there wasn't a whole lot that a woman who lobbed hand grenades at friends might not wish on her enemies. "Well, can I borrow it, or…?"

Colleen took a sip of her cocktail. "No," she said, wiping her lips. Then she tapped her temple. "It's all up here."

"Wonderful," Mallory grumbled. She turned back to Lewis. "All right, I'm sorry about what I said about your 'show up and wait' plan not being a real plan. It *is* a plan. It's a *great* plan. It's so great, we don't even need a back-up. Let's just go there now and wait. That gives us, like, eight hours to go inside and practice shooting things. We'll get really good at it."

Lewis set his mouth into a hard line and frowned a bit at the edges. "You don't have to do this if you don't want to. We can go back to town and hope for the best. But I'd feel much better about our chances if we had the spear. And I think I can help guide you through."

"How's that?" Mallory scoffed. "With the magic of science?" She arced one hand through the air like a sparkling rainbow that dripped with fairy dust. It was a very nuanced hand gesture, and she wasn't sure Lewis picked up on that.

"No…with the magic of sticks," he said. He bent down and picked up a few from the grass and handed them to Mallory.

"I didn't peg you for a druid," she said dryly.

"Just hold one out straight in front of you while you walk. If you hit a portal, the stick will disappear into it, and you'll know you need to change your course."

Mallory hefted the sticks. "That's actually a surprisingly decent plan," she admitted. Colleen cleared her throat impatiently from the back porch. "Okay, okay," Mallory said irritably, "I'm going." She gave Lewis a minor death stare. "This spear better be worth it."

"It will be," he assured her. "I promise."

Mallory waved him off and turned to face the portal field. She tucked three of the scrawny twigs in her back pocket and held the fourth in front of her with both hands. "Here goes nothing," she muttered. Then she took a step toward the Spear of Rad.

"I'll give you a freebie," Colleen called out from the porch, clearly enjoying herself. "Don't go that way."

"Why not?" Mallory asked without turning around. She was sick of that woman already, throwing Mallory into this little spatial minefield for her own sick enjoyment without even offering her a single second sip from the gin bucket.

"The portal just ahead of you leads to the lair of a mutant raccoon that lives down by Plasma Creek." Colleen took a slow pull from her pail. "But do whatever you want."

Mallory exhaled irritably. She thought about going straight ahead anyway, just for the sake of spite. But as a girl, she'd had a life-scarring experience with a presumably non-mutant raccoon at Girl Scout camp, and she wasn't terribly eager to intrude upon a mutated version. So she begrudgingly turned to her right and crept slowly forward.

After a few feet, the tip of the stick disappeared. It just vanished. Mallory pushed the stick forward a bit farther, and it disappeared almost all the way up to her knuckles.

Six inches of gnarled tree finger, swallowed up by an invisible portal.

"Hoooly shit," she whispered. "This is weird as hell."

She pulled back on the stick, and it reappeared, bit by bit. She gingerly touched the end between her forefinger and thumb; it felt cold. *Really* cold.

Okay, she thought. *Let's not go in there.*

She turned a little back toward the left and, using the stick as a diving rod, managed to keep the Spear of Rad more or less straight ahead as she threaded the gap between the portal to Coldtown and the portal to Mutantville. She pressed on slowly through the grass and tiptoed alongside the pile of solid gold Army men. Each one was probably worth a car payment at least, and she considered putting a few in her pockets...but then she thought about Colleen's penchant for violent weapon usage and decided that being sans-gold was somewhat preferable to being dead. So she skirted the pile of Army men rather than stealing them.

The tip of the stick disappeared again. Mallory stopped abruptly. She prodded the stick deeper into the portal, and something caught her eye off to the left. She glanced over and saw the last six inches of her stick hovering four and a half feet above the ground, about twenty yards away. She pulled her end back toward her chest; the hovering stick drew back and shrank in size. She pushed her end back into the portal; the hovering stick grew longer.

"This is incredible," she murmured.

She glanced back over her shoulder and looked to see if Lewis was as astounded as she was. The expression on his face was something much more like alarmed nervousness. He paced the ground in front of the back porch furiously, his arms crossed tightly at the chest, his mouth fidgeting. Colleen loomed over him from the porch, plunking a few fresh ice cubes into her gin bucket and grinning down at the entertainment that was Mallory's confusion and endangerment.

Mallory turned back to her stick. Then she pushed her left hand into the portal.

She felt a tight, fizzling crackle along her skin as her fingers disappeared…and then reappeared in mid-air off to her left. So she pushed her whole hand into the portal, up to the wrist. Her arm appeared to end in a clean stump. Mallory waved at herself from across the yard.

Farm Portals was instantly her new favorite game.

"Lewis, look at this!" she shouted gleefully. She pushed her whole arm into the portal up to the shoulder and gave him a thumbs up from the other side of the yard.

"Mallory…" he warned, sounding tired.

"What?" She reached her second arm into the portal and gave an awkward, exaggerated shrug that was all hands and elbows.

"Can you please just—"

"Lewis!" she cried, interrupting him. "My arms are closer to the spear than the rest of me!" A devilish grin crossed her face.

Lewis held up both hands in protest and shook his head violently. "No, no, no," he said. "Absolutely not!"

"Should I do it?" she asked playfully.

"Mallory…"

"I'm going to do it!"

"Mallory!"

"Okay, okay…geez," she said, pulling her arms back with a pout. "I won't go through the portal." She took a step backward and considered the empty space before her. Then she lowered her head, gave the scientist a grin, and leapt directly through the portal.

She was through in an instant. But it was an instant she'd never forget. In the space of a nanosecond, her entire body seemed to squeeze itself into a hard lump, like coal squeezed into a diamond, and then expand again into a full Mallory shape. Every cell felt as if it had been run through a laundry wringer and then reinvigorated with a straight injection of coffee concentrate.

"I need a portal farm," she decided aloud. "Do these things grow in Canada?"

"Mallory…"

"For that matter, do any of these *go* to Canada?"

"Mallory! The spear?" Lewis said, spoiling everything like he always did.

"Yeah, yeah, yeah. I'm working on it." She shook her head irritably and walked toward the birdbath, moving more quickly now that she knew how fun it could be to traipse through an invisible portal. She still held the stick out ahead of her, but she bounced along with a bit more carefree abandon. After just a few steps, the tip of the stick disappeared again, and Mallory looked excitedly around the yard, trying to find where it had surfaced. But the branch was nowhere in sight. "Where do you think *that* one went?" she asked, waving her hand through the air just this side of the portal. "Should I go in and see?"

"Mallory, please!" Lewis begged. He had begun nibbling at his cuticles.

Even from her considerable distance, Mallory could see the little droplets of sweat beading down from his hairline.

Mallory laughed and rolled her eyes. "Oh, Lewis, it's—" But before she could finish her sentence, something on the other side of the portal pulled hard on the stick and yanked it out of her hands. She cried out and fell to the ground, scrambling back from the portal until she felt the now-familiar tingle in her fingertips. She looked back and saw that her hand had disappeared into another portal behind her. She yelped and yanked her hands back, then leapt to her feet and stepped frantically in a tight little circle. She suddenly felt horribly claustrophobic in the middle of this open yard. "What the *fuck* was that?" she yelled up at the cabin.

Colleen grinned. "Probably don't want to know." She sat down on a long, low bench that ran along the cabin wall and began cleaning a series of pistols that she'd brought out onto the patio. "But here's a hint: it has a shit-ton of teeth."

Mallory glanced anxiously in the general direction of the invisible portal, doing her best to keep her distance from an intangible object she could not see. "It can't...*come through*. Can it?"

Colleen pulled an oily rag through the empty barrel of a Glock. "Happens all the time," she said. She nodded at the ground at Mallory's feet.

Mallory looked down and recoiled in horror when she saw the mess of oversized hoof prints stamped into the hard dirt beneath her. "I don't suppose this is also a horse farm," she said nervously.

Colleen blew across the top of the gun's barrel. "Nope."

"Lewis!" Mallory cried, focusing all her attention at the general space where the portal stood and tensing every muscle in her body. "I don't want to do this anymore."

Lewis ran his hands through his hair, leaving it sticking up in every direction. "I'm not sure the way back is any safer than the way forward," he said.

"Of course not," Mallory grumbled. The game of Farm Portals was suddenly not so fun anymore. "I'd better get to stab *something* with this fucking spear." She pulled a second stick out of her back pocket and held it out like a magic wand. She skirted around the general area that contained the stick-eating hoof-monster portal and resumed her snail-slow, creeping pace toward the Spear of Rad. After eight feet of walking, the tip of the new stick disappeared, and Mallory instantly yanked it back. It had only been on the other side of the portal for two seconds at the most, but even so, that edge of the stick was glowing orange and dripped like lava onto the grass.

She was almost positive that sticks were supposed to burn and not melt.

Mallory screamed and dropped the stick. It smoldered in the grass for a few seconds before cooling without starting a raging backwoods forest fire. "*Will you just tell me where to go?*" she yelled over her shoulder at the gun-happy hermit on the porch.

Colleen only shook her head. "My spear, my rules. Take it or leave it."

Mallory growled—actually *growled*—as she whipped the third stick from her back pocket. She held it straight out in front of her and moved more slowly than ever, winding her way through the portal field and inching toward the birdbath in a frustratingly roundabout way. Each time the tip of the stick disappeared, she yanked it back and leapt away in the opposite direction. This method proved reasonably reliable until she found herself leaping backward through a portal that stretched up directly behind her. For a split second, the ground didn't appear beneath her like it should have, and she flailed her feet. She heard Lewis start to call out, but by the time his voice had a chance to take shape, she'd already passed through the portal and had slammed down onto her back in this new and terrible place.

The impact crushed her sternum against her lungs; she wheezed as the air crumpled out of her chest. It was dark in this new place, almost pitch black but for the torches that lined the earthen walls and cast their unreliable, flickering glow about the chamber. She grunted as she struggled up, turned, and sat. The fall had disoriented her; she had no idea which way she'd tumbled through, or where the portal was. She heaved herself up to her hands and knees and tried to ignore the stitch in her chest as she patted forward, searching for the invisible doorway back to Colleen's yard. The dirt floor was cold and moist beneath her hands, and she grimaced as she felt the wetness soak into the knees of her jeans. She was grumbling something or other about the vengeance she vowed to take on the gun-crazy alcoholic on the other side of the portal when she heard a slow rattle of chains from the darkness behind her.

She spun around to face the noise, but the torchlight didn't reach into the vast gulf between her and the far end of the chamber; there was nothing but complete, suffocating darkness and the increasingly loud jangle of chains that groaned and scuffed as they were dragged across the floor. She scooted as quickly as she could in the opposite direction, praying that she'd tumble through the portal...but instead, she bumped up against a wall, and the thing dragging the chains got closer, and closer.

She willed her legs to work, but she was gelatin from the waist down. She screamed for help, from Lewis, from Colleen—from *anybody*...but the sound of her own shrieks only sank into the dirt walls of the chamber. She pulled her knees up to her chest, into the orange light of the flames where the darkness couldn't touch them, though she didn't know what this could possibly accomplish. The chains dragged even closer, and a shadow began to emerge from the unwavering blackness. The shadow slunk forward and became a man, a hulking monster clad all in black.

He wore an executioner's hood over his head.

Mallory screamed and scrambled away against the wall, clawing her way between pools of torchlight. The man in the hood followed, lumbering across the stone floor in his heavy boots and dragging something with both hands. He stepped into the light, and Mallory's scream caught in her throat...the thing he dragged was a massive axe, its sharp, gleaming head the size of an end table, its handle nothing less than a small tree. It must have been excruciatingly heavy, because as the executioner dragged it with his two ham-hock hands, it dug a deep trench in the ground below.

His wrists were bound by shackles; each cuff dragged several feet of heavy, grease-black chain links that had been hewn from whatever fixture had once held them, and he dragged them freely through the dungeon. He heaved the axe up with a loud grunt and hoisted it above his head, preparing to bring it slicing down on his prey.

Suddenly, Mallory found her feet.

She scrambled up and dove to the right just as the executioner brought the axe crashing down at the spot. The dull thud of metal on mud shook through her bones as she tumbled forward even further, into the darkness.

The monster followed. He crept forward, and the shadows swallowed them both. Mallory kicked herself to her feet and slipped backward on the wet earth. She tried to control her breathing, because surely the man in the hood could hear her. She clamped her hands over her mouth and stopped moving. She willed the darkness to cloak her and keep her safe. Suddenly, the air was still; the chains did not rattle, and the man's clunky footsteps stopped. Mallory prayed that he would turn and lumber back into whatever cave he'd slunk out of. Just as she was about to make a beeline for where she thought the portal was, she felt a strong gust of wind blow past her chest. It took a few seconds for her brain to recognize what had happened.

The man had swung his axe at her throat and had only missed by inches.

Her scream found its voice once more, and she plunged deeper into the darkness. The beast behind her clomped after her, and she heard the axe head drag through the dirt again. Mallory threw her arms out and ran forward, screaming and crying and cursing at the darkness. She heard the gentle whoosh of the axe begin its wide arc, and she dove forward as the blade buried itself into her spine.

Except there was no pain. Mallory had never been sliced in half from the spine outward before, so she wasn't exactly an expert, but she had assumed that a somewhat severe level of pain would have accompanied that particular experience. She opened her eyes, and her eyelashes brushed against blades of grass.

She was back in Colleen's yard.

She gasped for breath and jolted to her knees. She clawed at the ground and scrabbled forward until her fingers disappeared into another portal. She pulled them back out, flipped onto her back, searching wild-eyed for the creature...but he hadn't followed her through the portal. "*Lewis! Get me out of here!*" she screeched.

"Mallory!" Lewis cried, clenching and unclenching his fists, pacing helplessly on the edge of the field. "Where did you go?"

"Get me the fuck *out* of here!" she repeated. Up on the porch behind him, Colleen laughed uproariously.

"I don't know the safe path! Tell me what you saw!"

"A huge fucking monster with a huge fucking axe!" she screamed. "Black hood, dark tunnel, and a *huge fucking axe!*"

"Oh!" Lewis exhaled in relief. His shoulders relaxed, and he actually laughed. "Thank goodness!"

"*Thank goodness*?" Mallory screamed, not taking her eyes from the general area of the portal into hell. "*Thank goodness* that I fell face-first into a medieval torture chamber?!"

Lewis was still laughing. "No, no," he said, waving his hands through the air. "That wasn't a medieval torture chamber. It was the Check Into Cash, over on Dollop Street."

Mallory froze. She twisted her neck slowly until she was staring directly at the scientist. "The Check Into Cash?"

"Yes! The man in the black hood...that was just Merle. He runs the place. I'll grant you, he *does* dress strangely. The hood is...I don't know, some weird personal thing. But he wasn't trying to kill you; he was trying to sign you up for an unreasonably high-interest loan."

"By chopping me to pieces with an axe?!" Mallory screamed.

"A blood signature is part of the contract. It's pretty standard for those kinds of places, I think."

"How do you even *have* a Check Into Cash? This town has never seen a computer!"

Lewis shrugged. "I never said it was a thriving enterprise."

"I told you she'd be fine," Colleen said, snapping her revolver back together and admiring its luster.

"I'll show you fine," Mallory grumbled. She'd never been more furious or terrified in her life. She searched the ground and laid her eyes on a baseball-sized rock. She picked it up and hurled it toward the woman on the porch as hard as she could. It sailed through the air, heading straight for its target...but then it disappeared, swallowed up by a portal. Colleen leered down on the scene from her perch. Mallory was about to throw a world-champion barrage of curse words her way when the very same stone came hurtling out of a portal behind her and smacked right into her own shoulder blade. "Ow!"

"Mallory..." Lewis began.

"Don't 'Mallory' me!" she snipped, working out her shoulder. "I want out of this fucking farm! I'm done!"

"Mallory..."

"I'm *done!*"

"But *Mallory*," he insisted.

"*What?!*"

Lewis pointed just over her left shoulder. "You're right there."

Mallory whirled around. There, at waist-level, lay the Spear of Rad.

"Oh."

The weapon was smaller up close than it had seemed from afar. It was made of iron, and she could clearly see a set of strange runes stamped into the shaft, though she couldn't make heads or tails of them. A strange sort of bluish-red rust had crusted over much of the spear, but the arrow point at the tip was clean and sharp; it gleamed in the mid-morning sun. The other end curved upward and split like a snake's tongue.

It was definitely a glorified crowbar.

Mallory raised her hand and reached out toward the spear. Then she stopped and glanced back toward the dungeon portal. "What about the Gimp?" she asked.

"He won't follow you," Lewis assured her. "He has a business to run."

"Happy to shoot him if he does," Colleen added. She popped a series of bullets into the pistol's magazine and slid it into place. "I hate predatory lenders."

"Great." Mallory turned uneasily back to the birdbath. The spear rested atop it, seemingly innocuous. She raised her hand once again and started hovering it closer to the weapon. "Do I just…grab it?"

Colleen shook her head. "Nope. You'll want to replace it with a bag of sand that weighs exactly the same. Otherwise, the fountain sinks into the earth, and the whole backyard turns into one big booby trap."

Mallory stayed her hand. She glanced over her shoulder. "Seriously?"

"Of course not. That shit would cost a fortune."

Mallory shook her head and turned back to the spear. "All right," she said aloud, taking a few deep breaths. "Here goes nothing." She reached for the iron shaft…and when she was just a few inches away, her hand disappeared. "Oh, for crying out loud," she said. "You *encased it in portals*?!"

Colleen nodded proudly. "Safer that way."

Mallory's fingers had slid back into existence just behind the spear, about a foot above the curved, forked end. She set her eyes on the disembodied hand, determined; her tongue poked itself out of the corner of her mouth as she focused on the angle. She twisted her arm upward, and the hand above the spear turned downward. She reached her arm up, and her hand reached down. It sank closer and closer to the spear, and just as she was about to seize the curved iron fork, her fingers disappeared again and reappeared on the far side of the birdbath, just out of reach of the center of the shaft.

"Oh, come on!"

She pushed her arm in up to the elbow. The hand to her left disappeared completely as the disembodied wrist pushed deeper into the second portal, and her fingers stretched out across the way and grasped for the spear. She twisted her arm down; the wrist on the left turned up, and the fingers curved down. *Christ*, she thought, *it's like guiding a forklift through a mirror.* She twisted and turned, and her fingers responded in their own distinct physical reality. She pushed her arm in just a bit further and gave a little snort of triumph as her fingers brushed the cold, rough iron. She grasped the shaft and spun it around on the birdbath so that it pointed straight away from her hand, and straight toward her own waist. Then she heaved it up, drew it straight back, and the spear and her arm came together through the two portals, retreating through the air of three spaces at once.

And just like that, Mallory held the all-powerful, extraterrestrial iron Spear of Rad.

"Okay, you're right," Lewis said, squinting at the weapon in Mallory's hand. "It *does* look like a crowbar."

CHAPTER 18

"**WELL?**" Mallory said, balancing the Spear of Rad across her lap. "Happy now?"

Lewis glanced over at her as he navigated down the slightly curving road. "I'm feeling better about our chances, yes," he admitted.

"Then why do you still sound so damn depressed?"

"Because *better* chances don't necessarily mean *good* chances. We're dealing with an ancient evil here. They tend to have a few tricks up their sleeves. Plus," he added, "she didn't keep the manual."

"Some ray of sunshine you are," Mallory muttered. She bent over and examined the weapon in her lap. It was heavy, but small, and it wasn't as unwieldy as she'd expected an all-powerful demon weapon to be. "Any idea what this says?" she asked, running her fingers along the runes stamped into the rusty iron.

"Sponsored by Dish Network," Lewis said without looking.

Mallory wrinkled her eyebrows. "Get out of here," she said.

"Honestly. That's what it says."

"How is that even possible?"

"Dish Network sponsors all sorts of things."

"Including ancient alien crowbars?"

Lewis just shrugged. "Apparently."

Mallory shook her head. "This place is *so* weird." She hefted the spear a few times and picked at the rust that had crusted over the curved end of the spear. Then she shrugged and tossed it into the back of the RV. It crashed against a crate and shattered the beakers inside. "Whoops…"

Lewis sighed. "It's fine. I have more."

Mallory nodded. "I figured you did." She propped her foot up on the dashboard as they rumbled through the uninspiring countryside. "So what'll Jane of the Jungle do if you don't get the spear back to her?"

Lewis bit his lip nervously. "Probably use me for some sort of target practice."

"She sure loves her Second Amendment," she said.

Lewis nodded. "It's one of her favorites."

"Okay, look, I'm just going to say it," Mallory said, slapping her knee. "She terrifies me."

Lewis smiled a bit. "Exactly why she's a good person to have on your side."

Mallory was about to ask exactly what it was that psychopaths brought to the table when suddenly there was a low hum from overhead. She craned her neck and looked up through the window, but she didn't see anything. Whatever it was that was making the sound, it was directly overhead. "What is that?" she asked.

"Drone," Lewis said.

A long, thin, white aircraft zoomed ahead of the RV from above and skidded to an unceremonious stop in the road. Lewis slammed his foot on the brake, and the Winnebago shuddered to a halt, just two feet before grinding the drone into the gravel. Mallory threw out her hands and braced against the dashboard, but Lewis braked calmly, as if sudden stops were the most natural and expected thing in the world. And really, they probably were. "Are you expecting a message?" he asked.

"A message?"

Lewis nodded. "Drones do four things in Anomaly Flats; monitor activity from above, shoot lasers, drop bombs, and deliver messages. This one landed, and we're not dead."

"So it's a messenger drone."

As she said it, a small hatch opened on the top of the plane, and a scroll ejected from somewhere inside. It flew in a lazy arc and bounced lightly in the road, rolling in the wind and tumbling down into the drainage ditch on the south. Then the hatch closed, the drone fired up, and it zoomed down the road and back up into the air, disappearing above the trees.

"Well, it's effective," Mallory admitted.

Lewis unbuckled and jogged out after the message. He returned with the scroll and handed it over to Mallory. "It's for you."

She frowned as she took the message. It was sealed with a blue sticker that had FEMALE IMPOSTER printed on it in white. "Nice," she muttered. She peeled back the sticker and unfurled the little scroll. She read the message aloud. "Interloper: Your vehicle repairs are complete. Retrieve your vehicle and redistribute yourself appropriately beyond our borders." It was signed by the Anomaly Flats Information Dissemination Department.

"Hey, that's great news!" Lewis said cheerily.

"Music to every interloper's ears," Mallory replied, rolling her eyes.

"People don't...love outsiders here," he said, as diplomatically as he could.

"I've noticed. Your life must be fun."

"But your car is fixed! That's great!"

"It *is* great," Mallory confirmed, "though your evil double still has my bag."

"Well, one victory at a time."

Mallory allowed a small smile to creep across her lips. "Do we have time to pick it up?"

"We do indeed."

Mallory nodded and leaned back in her seat. "Then take me to the mechanic's shop, Jeeves. I've got some gettin' the hell out of here to prep for."

X

"You're all fixed up. Alternator works. Car runs. I did what I said I'd do."

Mallory tried not to stare as thick globs of drool plopped down from Rufus' jaw and spattered on the blacktop. She sidestepped the liquid shrapnel of one especially large slobber bomb but still managed to get a drip of Rufus spit on her shoe. She decided to magnanimously ignore it, seeing as how an ancient evil had once scrambled his brain and all.

And also considering that he'd just made it possible for her to leave Anomaly Flats.

"This is great," she said. "Ahead of schedule and everything. Thank you, Rufus." She took his hands in hers and squeezed them in a manner that she considered appropriately nice. "Will it *keep* working?" she asked. "Is it magnetic field-proof now?"

Rufus snorted, which caused a sickeningly green glob of *something* to come rocketing up out of his throat. It missed Mallory's shoulder by an uncomfortable three inches. "Can't make it magnetic-proof. Field's low today, though. You'll want to get going soon."

"Couldn't agree with you more," Mallory grumbled under her breath.

Rufus pulled a handkerchief from his back pocket and wiped his greasy hands. "Didn't take as long as I thought, 'cause most of the parts in your old one were pretty good," he explained. "Guy who built the old alternator did a pretty good job."

"Guy?" Mallory asked, trying her best not to look condescending, and failing miserably. "You mean Chevrolet?"

"Whoever." He sucked back on a line of drool that had started to spill from his jaw. It reversed itself and crept back up into his mouth. "Fixed the dent in the door, too."

Mallory circled around the Impala and admired the smooth surface of the passenger door. "It looks really good," she admitted. "Like it never happened."

Rufus just stared at her. "Yup."

She ran her hand lovingly along the hood. "Ooooh, I've missed you," she whispered. Then she turned to Rufus. "So. I know you don't know me, like, at all…but how's my credit here? My wallet was hijacked by—"

But Rufus shook his head, stopping her with a little shower of flailing spittle. "Bill's been paid."

Mallory jerked her head back in surprise. "Sorry, what?"

"Paid up." Rufus reached into the pocket of his coveralls and fished out Mallory's keys. "You're all set."

Mallory eyed the keys suspiciously and did not reach for them. "Who paid?"

"Man in a white coat. Bow tie. Had a mustache."

Mallory grabbed Lewis by the elbow and dragged him over so he stood directly in front of Lewis. "Did he look like this?" she demanded.

Rufus shook his head. "He had a *mustache,*" he said, stressing the last word so hard that flecks of spittle flew from his teeth.

Mallory wiped the saliva from her cheek. "I understand that he had a mustache. *Besides* the mustache, did he look like Lewis?"

Rufus shook his head again. "Not the same at all. He had a mustache."

"He had a mustache, Mallory…it wasn't my clone," Lewis threw in, trying to break free of her grasp.

"You know…" Mallory began, shaking her head in exasperation. Then she sighed and waved her hands. "Never mind. Forget it. Why did he pay my bill? What did he say?"

Rufus shrugged, his shoulders ratcheting up slowly toward his ears. "Said he was a friend. Overpaid, matter of fact. Said he didn't care 'bout the change." Rufus dug a wad of bills out of his pocket and held it out for Mallory. She took the money uncertainly and peeled open the bills.

"$30," she said dryly. "I'm rich."

"It's all ready to go." He held the keys out and jangled them a bit.

Mallory swiped them out of his hand. "Looks like your evil clone wants me out of the picture," she said, turning to Lewis. "I like the way he thinks."

Lewis rolled his eyes. "It wasn't my clone, Mallory, he—"

"I know, I know, he had a mustache. Jesus, Lewis, you're the most selectively smart person I've ever known."

"What do you—?"

"Forget it," she said, cutting him off with a shake of her head. "Let's just go get my backpack so I can leave this crummy hell-hole behind."

"Oh," said Rufus suddenly, and loudly, as if he'd just remembered something very important. "*This* backpack?" He popped open the door to the back seat and pulled out a purple Jansport.

"My bag!" Mallory gasped, snatching it out of his hands and gaping at it. She turned her eyes to Rufus and screwed up her face in exquisite confusion. "He gave you my *bag*?" Rufus just nodded. Mallory whumped the backpack down on top of the car and unzipped it. "It's all here," she murmured, rifling through the contents. "He didn't take anything." *Why didn't he take anything?*

"Best of luck." Rufus tilted his head by way of goodbye as a little waterfall of drool poured down onto the asphalt. Then he turned and shuffled back into the garage.

Mallory turned to Lewis, her mouth hanging open. She held up the backpack, as if he might not believe it existed unless it was right in front of his face. "He brought me my bag," she said softly.

Lewis nodded grimly. "Maybe this mustachioed man *is* somehow connected to my clone," he said, fretfully rubbing his chin. "Mallory, I think for some reason, he wants you to leave."

Mallory zipped up the bag and hiked it onto her shoulder. "That makes two of us," she said. She turned and put her hands on Lewis' arms. "Look. I know we've got this major battle with an ancient evil that could mean the end for everyone in Anomaly Flats and might or might not destroy the entire world. So don't take this the wrong way. But I've got things to do. Things that aren't here. So I think I'm gonna go."

Lewis started. "Wait—you're *what?*"

"I'm leaving. I have my car, I have my bag...that's what I'm in this for, and now I have them. Therefore, I am getting the proverbial fuck out of Dodge." She pulled open the driver's door and tossed the backpack inside. "I'm sorry, Lewis. But really, I think you're gonna be fine." She gave his shoulder a little pat. "You got this."

"Mallory! You can't *leave!*" Lewis leapt forward and grabbed the frame of the door, pulling on it and refusing to let it close. "You have to help me! We shook on it!"

"No, Lewis, I don't *have* to help you. The only thing I *have* to do is get to Canada before the Missouri State Highway Patrol closes all the roads in a 50-mile radius." She attacked Lewis' fingers with her own, prying them back from the car door.

"Argh!" Lewis cursed as she twisted his fingers back. "*You're so sturdy!*"

"*Stop calling me that!*"

She slammed her fist down on his remaining fingers with a dull thud, and he howled in pain. He released his grip on the door and tried to shake the agony from his hands, hopping from one foot to the other and crying. "Don't do this!" he wailed.

"I don't owe this terrifying-ass town *anything*," she said, jabbing a finger into his chest. "I've put up with *way* too much shit in the last two days. There are tentacles, Lewis—*tentacles.* And portal farms, and plasma creeks, and hypnotic voids, and people with flies swarming out of their mouths." She tried not to vomit as she said it. "So get out of the way and let me leave, or I'm running you over." She climbed into the car and slammed the door.

"But you *caused* this!" Lewis screeched, smacking his hands against the window. "You *made the clone*, now you're just going to *abandon* us when he's about to let out the evil in aisle 8?!"

"Sorry about that," she said through the glass. "Really. Best of luck."

"Don't do this!" he repeated, his voice cracking with desperation. "I don't know if I can stop him alone! Don't just leave us to die here! You can't! Mallory, you *can't!*"

"Oh yeah?" she asked, turning the key in the ignition. It fired up on the first try. The Impala had never sounded so smooth. "And why's that?"

Lewis pressed his palms against the glass, looking like a young boy who just realized what it meant for a dog to be put down. "Because you're a good person," he said.

That was too much. Mallory threw off her seatbelt, popped the latch, and shoved her shoulder into the door. It slammed into Lewis' chest, and he toppled down onto the asphalt. "A good person?" she screamed, stepping out of the car. "*A good person?* You don't know *shit* about me, Lewis!" She snatched the purple backpack from inside the car and yanked open the zipper. She held the bag open so Lewis could see inside. "Look at this! *Look* at it! Is this what a good person carries around in a fucking *Jansport*?"

Lewis peered into the backpack. He gasped, and his eyes grew large. "Mallory," he said quietly, shaking his head slowly. "What is this?"

"This is one-point-three million dollars, in hundreds. And this?" she asked, unzipping the front pocket and tilting the bag so Lewis could see the pile of glittering diamonds inside. "This is another hundred thousand."

Lewis sat on the blacktop, stunned. He gazed up at Mallory, then back down at the bag, and then up at Mallory once more. His mouth worked itself into a silent frenzy for a good ten seconds before he finally said, "Mallory...you're a jewel thief?"

Mallory rolled her eyes. "No, you idiot, I'm not a *jewel thief*. I'm a woman who got sick of her boss' deprecating, chauvinistic, ass-grabbing bullshit and cleaned out the motherfucker's wall safe while he was in Barbados. And now I'm fleeing the country, heading toward a safe house in Canada with a slight fucking detour through the Twilight Zone." She zipped up the bag and threw it back into the car. "But the detour's over." She climbed behind the wheel and slammed the door. She rolled down the window and frowned down at the stunned scientist. "Good luck with your demon," she said. "I mean that."

Then she put the car into drive and left the repair shop behind.

X

Evil Lewis smiled behind his binoculars. This was going even better than he'd planned.

He giggled with glee as the silver Impala peeled out of the parking lot and left Lewis in a confused heap on the ground. He tweaked the dial on the binoculars and brought the other scientist's shirt into sharp focus. *The pink-and-green plaid*, he thought with a scoff. *Of course. And a purple tie? You look like a doofus, you doofus.*

He tossed the binoculars into the back of the Willys Jeep and struggled to haul himself up into the driver's seat. He made a mental note to steal something a little lower to the ground next time while simultaneously cursing the original Lewis for being so unreasonably short.

"And for having such terrible taste in clothes," he mumbled aloud. Though the good thing about Lewis' wardrobe choice for the day was that Evil Lewis knew where to find that shirt on the rack. He smiled as he fired up the Jeep and even started laughing as he turned onto the road to J. C. Penney.

Everything was working out nicely.

X

Lewis gazed up at the cloudy sky and resolutely refused to move. *If I stay here, someone will eventually run over me with a tow truck, and none of this will matter anymore.*

But that would, of course, guarantee the evil clone's success, and in no time, the demon would turn Anomaly Flats into a literal hell on Earth. Skin would be flayed, lakes would be boiled, and maggots would infest even the freshest cuts of pork. "Maybe it won't be so bad," he mumbled aloud, his words drying and cracking in the heat of the sunlight. He was a scientist; maggots were more of a curiosity to him than a source of disgust. But then he remembered the wood carving of the rectum poles. And rectal impalement was most certainly *not* a particular curiosity of his. "Yeah, okay. I should get up and go stop him." He sighed as he struggled to a seat. The RV was just a few parking spots over, but something so familiar had never felt so very far away.

He tried not to curse Mallory as he ambled to his feet. She'd let him down; she'd let all of Anomaly Flats down. That much was true. But of *course* she'd let them down. That was the nature of people out there in the world. Here in the Flats, folks looked out for each other. Those folks were mysterious and complex and, yes, often troubling…but they always stood by their own. When the eerie, green glow appeared behind the Del Taco and started turning everyone who looked at it into werecows, the town's oldest magician went into the center of the light and allowed himself to be swallowed by the source in order to sate the glow's weird hunger. When the old ruins near Highway 95 caught vapor fire, all seven members of the Tribe of Bahamut lent their crystal fish charms to help summon the only type of deathwind that could smother the blue and purple flames. When Farmer Buchheit's pet orca came down with a particularly bad case of sand cough, Trudy slung waffles for three days and nights straight, keeping the rescue teams nourished and fragmentally time-resistant.

And when a young, scared scientist had shown up in the middle of downtown with a suitcase of beakers in one hand and a handwritten letter from his future self in the other, the people of Anomaly Flats had treated him with all the apprehensive distrust and reluctant acceptance they could muster. He'd never felt truly integrated, but they hadn't chased him out, either.

After all, hadn't that been the main reason he'd stayed? Anomaly Flats was always meant to be a short diversion, a five-year experiment at most. But with each passing month, the differences between the world in here and the world out there became more and more exaggerated. Out in the real world, people gave him cautious looks and avoided him as best they could. Back at the university, his colleagues whispered and snickered about his disastrous particle acceleration experiments behind his back. Back home, his aging parents vociferously lamented the fact that their only child had dedicated his life to scientific advancement rather than something more comprehensible, like marketing, or construction, or "even community journalism, for crying out loud." But the people in this town didn't avoid him or jeer at him or tell their relatives they were disappointed in his chosen vocation.

It was small, and strange, and practically inaccessible to the outside world.

But Anomaly Flats had let him in.

Which was why his five-year plan had stretched into a twelve-year plan, and soon it would become a twenty-year, and then it wouldn't be a plan anymore at all, but a life, *his* life...his life in Anomaly Flats, where things were weird, and things were dangerous, but things were never as awful as they were in the rest of the world.

Hurricane Mallory had brought that outside awfulness with it. She was rude, and she was crass, her first language was sarcasm, and she acted without concern for consequence. She'd created the greatest threat to survival Anomaly Flats had ever seen—which was truly remarkable, given the circumstances—and then she'd turned and fled as soon as she had the chance.

But of course she had. It wasn't surprising at all. The world was full of cowards.

Which was why Lewis Burnish refused to be one.

He sighed as he climbed into the driver's seat of the RV. He didn't need Mallory. He had his pistol, and the Spear of Rad, and a good seven hours before sunset. He could defeat the evil clone easily enough. He didn't need her...and not only that, he didn't much like her, either. He could see that clearly now.

So why did he already miss her so much?

He tried to shake away the thought of her, and he reached down and clicked on the radio.

A familiar voice was just beginning its latest bulletin:

"Attention, Anomaly Flats: The time is currently 11:58 AM. The following hours will be replaced by minutes today: 12:00, 1:00, 2:00, 3:00, 4:00, 5:00, and 6:00. Be advised: The next seven hours will each be replaced by minutes. Attention, Anomaly Flats: The time is currently 11:59 AM. In nine minutes, it will be 7:01 PM."

Lewis gaped at the radio. "No," he whispered. "No, no, no, no, no! Not a time lapse! Not *now!*" He fumbled for his keys and couldn't quite get them to jam into the ignition. "No, no, *no!*"

Time was suddenly his enemy. Just like that, he had less than ten minutes to stop his clone from releasing the ancient evil on the town.

The keys finally found their slot. He fired up the Winnebago, ground it into drive, and squealed out of the parking lot.

He had to get to the Walmart.

CHAPTER 19

MALLORY'S EYES FLASHED up at the rearview mirror before she pulled out of the repair shop parking lot onto the road that led out of Anomaly Flats. There was Lewis, lying prostrate on the ground, sad and confused and probably questioning a lot of life choices. Mallory felt bad for him, but not *too* bad. Was she abandoning him in a time of great need? Maybe. Was she responsible for the great evil that was about to wreak havoc all through the town? Sure, okay. Yeah. But Lewis had a gun and a good six or seven hours to get into position. If he couldn't stop the evil clone with that sort of head start, the town deserved to melt. Or burn. Or get anally speared. Or all of the above. Whatever it was an ancient evil did to a town of people that locked it up beneath a Walmart shelf of canned beets for a few centuries or so.

In a way, Mallory sort of felt for the ancient evil.

And she didn't have time to deal with this particular disaster. Two days had passed; surely *someone* had noticed the theft by now. The secretary, the cleaning staff, the CFO, who Mallory was reasonably sure had siphoned off money from the accounts and stashed her boss's cut in the safe on Friday afternoons; surely someone had noticed that something was amiss. And even if the police couldn't bumble their way into Anomaly Flats, there was a good chance they had blanketed the rest of Missouri with an APB, and that net would get tighter every second. With any luck, the search was focusing on familiar places—her hometown, her sister's house, the family cabin at the Lake of the Ozarks—or they probably assumed that if she wanted to leave the country, she'd be headed for Mexico. People always fled to Mexico. Mallory didn't understand it. Mexico was hot, and dirty, and everyone spoke low Spanish. Canada was a much better choice. She just had to get there before the cops realized it, too.

Besides, who knew how long the alternator would hold out? She had to make it out of town before the magnetic field drank its coffee and starting pulsing again at full power. Being stranded for another two days in Anomaly Flats was unthinkable.

And the evil clone was a problem, sure…but he was *their* problem. A problem wholly specific to this dimensionally fucked-up town. She may have been a catalyst for the creation of the clone, but it was going to happen sooner or later. Eventually, *someone* would push *someone* into the lake, and the whole thing would have happened without her. She refused to hold herself responsible for something so inevitable. She refused to feel guilt.

Nope, she thought as she idled at the edge of the parking lot. *Leaving is the only option.*

She peeled out onto the road, thrilling at the tremble of the Impala's engine rumbling through the steering wheel. She'd never been so happy to be behind the wheel of a car. But as she left the auto repair shop, she caught a flash of Rufus in the rearview mirror as he slunk out of the shadows of the garage. Rufus, who had once been a brilliant surgeon, now reduced to a slobbering grease monkey in oil-stained coveralls. And from nothing more than touching a can of beets.

"Don't think about it," she warned the Mallory in the mirror.

Lewis was going into that same canned goods aisle, armed with a peashooter and a rusty crowbar. He should be able to stop the clone, yes…but if he couldn't? "He'll be at Ground Zero when the ancient evil tumbles loose," mirror Mallory said.

"I don't care," she replied.

If just touching a can near the evil could have such an impact on Rufus…what would the full power of the demon do to Lewis?

Stop it, brain.

She should keep driving. She knew this was her chance. If she didn't take the road out of Anomaly Flats now, she might be stuck there indefinitely. And if she ever did make it out, the long arm of the law would be waiting.

Images of Lewis flashed before her eyes, dark, flickering views of a simpering, brain-dead scientist, writhing on the ground, gaping hollowly at the fluorescent lights above as dented cans of beans fell from the shelves of aisle 8 and bounced off his useless head one by one.

"Is that what you want?" mirror Mallory asked.

A loud hiss and pop from the car radio made her jump, and she lost control of the car for a split second. The radio had been off, but the voice on the other end insisted on being heard:

"Attention, Anomaly Flats: The time is currently 11:58 AM. The following hours will be replaced by minutes today: 12:00, 1:00, 2:00, 3:00, 4:00, 5:00, and 6:00. Be advised: The next seven hours will each be replaced by minutes. Attention, Anomaly Flats: The time is currently 11:59 AM. In nine minutes, it will be 7:01 PM."

"Don't think about it," she said again. "Think about being rich and mounting a Mountie."

Even mirror Mallory couldn't argue that either of those was a bad thing.

She gripped the wheel and pressed harder on the gas, flooring it toward the city limits.

X

Lewis took a deep breath and tried to will his hands to stop trembling.

His trembling hands suggested that he mind his own business.

He had never been inside the Walmart before. It was practically suicide to pass through the automatic doors, no matter how chipper the Rollback Prices signs seemed. But avoiding the superstore was no longer an option. The sun was setting, and the clone would be here any minute, if he wasn't here already. Lewis took a deep breath and stepped up to the doors.

They slid apart with ease and grace, exhaling a gentle *pfffft* that set the scientist's nerves on fire. Doors weren't meant to go *pfffft*. They were meant to go *creak* and *slam* and *thunk*. *Pfffft* was all wrong. It was an abomination, even in a town filled with abominations.

He took one step into the entryway, and an impossibly old man lurched forward from the wall. Lewis hadn't noticed him; he had blended in so perfectly with the plastic bubble toy dispenser and coin-operated rocking horse behind him. He reached his papery, yellow hands out toward the scientist. Lewis screamed as the elderly man rasped, "Welcome to Walmart. Need a cart?"

"Get away!" Lewis shrieked. He leapt to the far side of the foyer and hoisted the Spear of Rad high above his head. "I'll smash your skull! *Get away!*" The old man hissed and retreated to the camouflage safety of the entertainment machines. Lewis skirted him and ran through the second set of automatic doors, giving the spear a good swing for emphasis, and to keep the old man at bay.

How could he have forgotten about the greeter? *Stupid, stupid*, he cursed himself. He'd have to be more careful.

Much, *much* more careful.

He crept backward away from the doors until they slid themselves closed again. He peered through the glass, holding the spear at the ready, in case the greeter decided to follow him in…but the old man seemed content to prop himself up in the foyer.

Lewis relaxed a bit and lowered the Spear of Rad. He glanced nervously over his shoulder and got his first good look at the inside of Walmart. It was clean—much cleaner than he had imagined. The linoleum floors sparkled under the bright, cheerful lights. A line of spick-and-span cashier stations spanned the front of the store to his left, but they were all unmanned. Lewis looked around the store and realized there wasn't a single Walmart employee in sight, other than the mummy in the foyer.

They're not used to customers, he realized. *They're probably on eternal break.*

Even so, something about the row of quiet cash register sentinels unnerved him, and he stepped cautiously to his right, into the produce section, so as to avoid the checkout lanes. He pulled the pistol from his lab coat pocket and tiptoed carefully through the impeccably stacked pyramids of apples. Honey crisp, gala, red delicious, Granny Smith—they all shone in the illusory fluorescent lights, as if they'd been polished to a high sheen with the most expensive name brand furniture polish the Walmart had to offer. Next to the apples sat the lemons and limes, bright and pleasant and genetically mutated to a few sizes larger than was natural. The pomegranates sat with their crowns pointed perfectly up; the avocados were all the exact same dark shade of green. The bananas were organized into an orderly pile, and their peels were just this side of yellow, prompting Lewis to wonder how the Walmart received such perfectly ripe produce. No delivery trucks ever entered Anomaly Flats. They couldn't if they wanted to. And yet, the produce was pristine.

Nothing here can be trusted, he thought as he skirted the vegetables. *This is the devil's playpen.*

He crossed around the onions and shallots and was sneaking past the leafy greens in the wall cooler when a crack of thunder sounded, and a flash of lightning ripped through the store. Lewis yelped in surprise and slipped on the polished floor. He landed hard on his back, and the pistol went off, blasting a bullet straight through the artichoke stand and into the soft loaves of bagged Wonder Bread in Aisle 1. The crack of the gun rang through the empty store, but not even the greeter came to see what had happened.

Lewis struggled to his feet, panting and sweating and waving the pistol around like a madman, searching desperately for whatever sorcerer had opened up the ceiling and caused a thunderstorm in the lettuce section. He was equal parts embarrassed and relieved when he realized the thunder wasn't *real* thunder at all, but a recorded sound effect. The lightning was just a flash of the small produce lights. Little water sprayers set into the cooler sputtered to life, sending a fine mist down over the cabbage and kale. The fake thunder and lightning were just for kitschy effect.

You were right, Rufus, he thought. *Getting misted is horrifying.*

He took a deep breath. If any store employees were lurking in the freezer section, waiting to pounce, at least they knew he was armed now.

At the very least, there was that.

He tiptoed past the cilantro and finally reached the far side of the store. He peeked his head around the freezer case and peered down the eternally long side aisle. Rows of soft drinks and outdoor barbecue supplies lined the right wall, even though outdoor barbecues were highly illegal in Anomaly Flats…as were soft drinks. And on the left side of the long walkway, the line of numbered aisles loomed, cold and silent, their number markers boldly and bluntly stating their horrible-but-standard grocery store contents: COFFEE, TEA, SOUP, TOMATO SAUCE, LARVAE, JELLY, STARFISH LEGS, COOKING OIL, SPICES, POND WEEDS, CHIPS, and, of course, CANNED GOODS.

Lewis took a deep breath. Soon, he'd either be a hero, or he'd be dead. There was no middle ground.

Well, there *was* a middle ground, but it involved rectum spikes, so it was best not to think about that.

As he crept toward the canned goods section, he became aware of gentle music playing above him for the first time. It was light, instrumental music, the piano-washed version of a song he knew but hadn't heard in many, many years. He couldn't remember the name of it. It was something by Lionel Richie.

It was nice.

He tilted his head in time with the gentle beat, and the tension melted away from his step. He passed the soup aisle, and he thought, *A can of tomato bisque would be good, with the chilly weather that's coming in.* He swayed gently toward the stack of Campbell's cans as the homage to Lionel tinkled serenely overhead.

He was reaching for a can of bisque when he looked up and saw a Walmart employee gaping at him from the other end of the aisle. She was middle-aged, with bleached-white hair frizzing out over an unnaturally tan face. She wore khaki slacks and a pink blouse beneath a blue Walmart vest with a smiling yellow face beaming out from the chest. She stared at Lewis with wide eyes, probably more surprised to see him than he was to see her. It had surely been years since she'd seen a customer. Many, many years.

"Can—I help you?" she croaked, her voice dusty and dry with disuse.

Lewis looked at his hand. It was in mid-grasp, just inches away from a can of soup. He gasped and yanked his hand back. "What am I doing?" he whispered, cursing himself internally. "*Grocery* shopping? What am I *doing?*"

The woman at the far end of the aisle cleared her lungs and smacked her lips together, trying to work up some saliva to lubricate her throat. "Special on Great Value-brand chicken noodle," she rasped, pointing awkwardly at the white and blue cans to her left. "Buy two, get one free."

But Lewis' soup spell had been broken. He staggered backward into the side aisle, holding his hands up as if in protection against the Walmart employee. "I'm not here for this!" he cried, working to convince himself as much as he wanted to convince her. "You'd like to get me off track, wouldn't you? You'd like me to lose myself down your plaintive aisles, with your Lionel Richie music and your bright lights and your well-stacked soups! You'd *love* me to grocery shop instead of saving the town! Stop weaving your magic on me, Walmart!" he shrieked, turning and jogging down the aisle, spear and pistol still in hand. "Stop weaving your horrible black magic!"

The Walmart employee sighed with relief. She feared customers and counted herself lucky that she had narrowly survived the encounter.

Lewis pushed on down past the rows of soft drinks, blinking hard and trying to keep his focus. The music, the lighting, the design, the layout…everything about this store was working against him, working to make him lose himself in a siren song of forgetfulness and consumer goods. "Just get to aisle 8," he whispered to himself, wiping sweat from his brow with the back of his pistol hand. "You just have to make it to aisle 8."

But then…all at once, it seemed…he *was* at aisle 8. It was as if the canned goods section had rushed up to meet him, and there he was, hesitating at the end cap, trying not to lean too close to the specially discounted and oddly-flavored K-Cups. His heart pumped diesel fuel through his veins, and his chest heaved and fell like a volcano ready to erupt. This was it. This was where it would all come to a head.

This was aisle 8, and it was where goodness would make its stand against the gruesome designs of a prehistoric evil.

It all suddenly seemed pretty high above his pay grade.

"There's no one else," he reminded himself, though his feet were practically screaming to run away. "It's up to you…your clone has to be stopped, and it's wholly up to you."

He took one more breath, held it, turned the corner, and fired blindly into the aisle.

The bullet whizzed through the canned goods section and buried itself somewhere in women's sleepwear. Aisle 8 was empty.

"Look first, then shoot," he reminded himself, whispering harshly over the mellow piano. "Look first, *then* shoot!"

Everything in aisle 8 appeared to be in order; which was to say, there was no portal to hell, no primeval blood demon slithering across the linoleum floor. He had gotten there in time. He had beaten the clone.

He exhaled relief...but that relief was short-lived. The clone may not have been there yet, but he would be, and very soon. It was starting to really sink in that Lewis would have to kill another human being—and yes, he did believe the clone was classified as a human being—which is something he'd intrinsically decided he would never do, somewhere along the way. And this human being just happened to be a perfect genetic replica of himself, which didn't make things any easier. But he had to; there was no way around it.

Evil Lewis had to be put down, and Regular Lewis was going to have to be the one to do it.

He decided that Evil Lewis was likely to approach from the center aisle. The direct approach. Lewis had tiptoed through the produce section to the *side* aisle because he didn't like the look of the cash registers, but he doubted they would give his clone much pause. Evil Lewis had a job to do, and he would head straight to it.

But so did Lewis. He had to make it to the other end of aisle 8.

He glanced nervously at the canned goods before him. Green beans stood on his right; pineapple towered on his left. The red Del Monte labels seemed to roil with blood, though he knew that was just his mind playing tricks on him. But he also knew there was an ancient evil living behind those cans, and that just touching one was likely to render him a brain-dead, slobbering mess. He could *feel* the hateful energy radiating from the aluminum as he looked down the aisle to the far end. It seemed that both rows of shelves were pulsing with anger.

No, not anger; breath...actual *breath*.

Aisle 8 appeared to be alive.

Maybe I'll just go around, Lewis decided.

He hurried to his right and jogged down Aisle 9, trying to avoid looking at the baking powder and cake mixes, even though the Lionel Richie song had melted into a jaunty Michael McDonald tune, and Michael McDonald was extraordinarily powerful baking music, and Lewis had a sudden and desperate craving for funfetti cake, and it seemed once again as if the whole world were conspiring against him. He kept his eyes down and hurried through, holding the Spear of Rad before him like a shield, lest any of the sacks of powdered sugar got any bright ideas.

But the sugar held its composure, and Lewis made it through the aisle safely. He peered around the corner, back down toward the entrance, but the way was clear. There was no clone.

"Phew," he sighed. His shoulders relaxed, and he lowered the Spear of Rad. He walked in front of aisle 8…and saw the clone out of the corner of his eye, sneaking up on the far end of the row, the end he'd just come from. In one choppy motion, he whirled to his left, gave a warrior's scream, raised the gun, and fired.

The bullet found its mark.

The abomination screamed. "What the *shit*, Lewis?!"

Lewis lowered the gun. He squinted down the aisle. Then he blinked. "Mallory?"

"Did you just *shoot* me?" she cried. She slapped down her body with her hands, looking for a perforation. "You *shot* me!"

"I think I missed," he corrected her.

"You fucking *shot* me!"

"I think I…shot *that*." He pointed to a bottle of Sun Drop just behind her and to the right. It had sprung a bright, fizzy leak.

"You *shot* me!" she screamed.

"I missed!"

"*You shot* at *me!*"

"Mallory, I think you might be in shock…" he said uneasily.

"I am not in shock!" she demanded. "I'm in pissed off!"

"I'm really sorry! I thought you were the clone!"

"*Do I look like your clone?*"

"Well…not upon closer inspection," he admitted. "What are you even *doing* here?"

"I turned around!" she said, seething. "I turned around to help you save your stupid goddamn town and also *so you could shoot at me!*" She brushed herself off angrily and side-stepped the growing puddle of electric-yellow Sun Drop.

"You came back," Lewis said, truly realizing it for the first time, now that his adrenaline was slowing. "You came back to help me."

"And this is the thanks I get." Mallory crossed her arms and shot daggers through her eyes at the scientist at the other end of the aisle.

"I'm really sorry. I really did think you were my clone. I figured you were halfway to Iowa, and who else would be creeping up on aisle 8 but the clone?" He thought for a second, and then added, "And why *are* you creeping? Why'd you take the side aisle?"

"I thought if I came up the main aisle, you might…I don't know…*shoot me.*"

"Makes sense."

"Uh-huh." They stared at each other for several long moments, Lewis delighted and relieved, Mallory supremely pissed off. But her heart eventually slowed its maniac pounding, and her breath relaxed to something like normal, and her face softened a bit. "Just… don't do it again."

"Sorry. Really. Sorry."

Mallory sighed and glanced around the Walmart shelves. There was a severe dearth of mayhem and hellfire chaos. "I take it we made it in time?" she asked.

Lewis nodded. "He'll be here any second, though. He'll likely come up the main aisle, but it's possible he'll sneak up the side."

Lewis' cheeks blushed rosy pink, and he looked down, trying to hide them, as he said, "I'm really glad you came back, Mallory. Thank you."

"If you start crying, I'll leave again," she muttered. "Now throw me a weapon. Unless we time-warped into a silent movie, I doubt this soda puddle is going to do much to stop a clone."

"I don't think anyone ever slipped in puddles in silent films," Lewis pointed out. "You're thinking of banana peels."

"Just toss me the goddamn gun, Lewis."

But Lewis clutched the pistol to his chest and shook his head. "I think I should keep the gun."

Mallory tipped her head at the puddle. "Yeah…you're really good with it."

"If he comes up the main aisle, a long-range weapon will be best," Lewis insisted. "If he comes your way, it'll be closer quarters, and you can lance him with the spear."

"*Lance* him?"

"It means to pierce or—"

"I know what it means, Lewis. Why can't you say 'stab,' like a normal person?" She shook her head irritably, but she held up a hand and flexed her fingers, beckoning for the spear. "Fine. Toss me the crowbar." Lewis gave a look down the aisle, to make sure the clone wasn't coming, then he tucked the pistol into the waistband of his pants. He grabbed the Spear of Rad firmly in his right hand. He took three steps back and bounced a few times, flexing his knees and wriggling his toes. He swung his arm forward, then back, then forward, then back, then forward again, then back again, warming up his shoulder and trying to pair his breath with the arm movement.

"For fuck's sake, Lewis, just throw it!"

The scientist nodded. He took a deep breath, ran three steps forward, and grunted mightily as he hurled the spear as hard as he could.

It clattered to the ground about halfway down the aisle.

"Are you kidding me?" Mallory demanded. She couldn't remember ever having been so disgusted in her life.

"I never took javelin!" Lewis cried. He didn't remember ever feeling more embarrassed.

"No one ever *takes* javelin; they just *throw* the javelin, because throwing is a *natural motion*!" She stared down at the spear, which lay sadly beneath the bright glare of overhead lights. Then she glanced up at the cans of garbanzo beans that towered over it on one side, and the stack of canned peaches on the other. They didn't necessarily look all that evil...but she could feel the darkness emanating from them like radio waves. There was something demonic behind those shelves, all right. She felt sure that if she stepped between the rows of cans, her soul would shrivel, and her eyes would blacken, and she'd be lost forever. "Come get it," she said.

"It's closer to you," Lewis pointed out.

"I'm not getting sucked into some low-priced hell-circle because you babied the throw," Mallory snapped.

"You won't get sucked into anything as long as you don't touch the cans."

Mallory crossed her arms in perfect defiance. "Prove it," she said. She was *not* stepping into that aisle.

Lewis bit his bottom lip nervously. Then he said, "Hold on. I have an idea." He pulled the pistol from his waistband, gripped it in both hands, and pointed it down toward the spear. "I'll shoot it over to you."

Mallory lowered her head and rubbed the bridge of her nose. "Lewis..."

"I can do this," he said, sounding surprisingly confident.

"No. You can't."

"I think I can."

"If you pull that trigger, I'm leaving."

"It's the only way," he said. His tongue poked itself out of the corner of his mouth, and he closed one eye, lining the other up along the sights of the pistol. "You might want to move. The bullets could ricochet."

"Lewis. Do not fire that gun."

"Are you going to get the spear?"

"No."

"Then I'm going to fire this gun."

"Lewis…"

"Quiet, I need to concentrate."

"That's it," Mallory said, throwing her hands up in the air. "I'm leaving."

"No, wait!"

"Hi there!" chirped a bright voice over Lewis' shoulder. He jumped and twirled around, firing the gun into the ceiling. He screamed and waved the gun in the direction of the voice, but it didn't belong to his clone. It was another Walmart employee, a man this time, wearing the signature blue vest and beaming through an impressively bushy mustache. "Can I help you folks with something?"

Lewis exhaled a sigh of relief and lowered the pistol. "No, thank you. My colleague and I are just…debating."

"Not sure what to do about dinner?" the employee asked jovially. "Got a sale on canned tuna this week. Three cans for just $2.49!" He leaned in close and whispered, as if it were some great secret, "We keep the tuna over in Aisle 3."

"We'll certainly keep that in mind," Lewis replied. "Thank you."

Mallory squinted at the Walmart worker from the other end of the aisle. Her eyesight wasn't what it used to be—her company had staunchly refused vision insurance, just another reason she had no choice but to rob the CEO blind—but there was no mistaking the face behind the mustache, even from the distance. "Lewis!" she screamed. "It's the clone! *Shoot him!*"

Lewis rolled his eyes and shook his head with a little chuckle. "Mallory! Why in the world do you think every man with a mustache is my clone?" He gave the man another look, and he did have to admit, there was something...*familiar* about him. Maybe it was the clothes; the Walmart employee wore the same gray slacks, the same pink-and-green plaid Oxford, the same purple bow tie as Lewis wore. He even had a pair of ratty old Keds on his feet and a spotless white lab coat under his standard-issue Walmart vest.

He was a very sharp dresser; that was for sure.

Maybe it was the hair that rang a bell; the mustachioed man had short, light brown hair that stuck up a little in the back, sort of like Lewis' short, light brown hair that stuck up a little in the back. Or maybe it was the glasses, which were square-rimmed and really rather handsome, in Lewis' estimation. Or maybe it was the man's height, since he was exactly as tall as Lewis.

Yes, the similarities were curious. They were even a little unnerving. But there was one very distinct feature that just couldn't be ignored: A man just can't grow a full mustache in a matter of hours.

"I'm sorry," Lewis said, holding his hands up apologetically, "my friend is a little confused, and—" As he spoke, he noticed something exceedingly odd. The corner of the other man's mustache seemed to be sliding down over the edge of his mouth. It moved slowly at first, then picked up more speed as it crested the top lip and plunged down toward the chin, leaving a sticky, stringy trail of spirit gum behind it.

Lewis gasped. "*It's a false mustache!*" he shrieked.

"No shit," Mallory sighed.

The scientist raised the pistol, but Evil Lewis was ready for him. He socked Lewis in the jaw, and the poor man went tumbling into the end cap, knocking over the display and sending a tidal wave of Tang canisters spilling across the linoleum.

"That was pathetically easy," Evil Lewis sneered. He ripped off the drooping mustache and flung it as his original. Then he grinned across at Mallory as he shrugged out of his vest. "You should have gone for the spear," he said.

Mallory gritted her teeth. Getting lip from one science dork was bad enough; she'd be damned if she took it from his double, too. She reached for the soda shelves behind her and ripped open a case of Orange Slice. The cans came tumbling out, and she snatched two of them as they fell through the air. She hurled first one, then the other down the aisle. Evil Lewis shrieked and ducked behind his arms, but he was too slow; the first can flew wide, but the second smacked against his cheek with a sickening *thunk*, knocking the evil clone onto his back.

"Don't tell me what to do," Mallory spat.

Lewis rolled over like a frenzied turtle and brought the butt of the pistol down toward Evil Lewis' nose, but the clone blocked the attack with his forearm and grabbed the pistol with his other hand. Lewis cried out and threw himself on top of the clone, and they rolled around the floor, each grasping for the gun and trying to rain kicks and headbutts down on the other, but neither one succeeded very well. Limbs flailed and shrieks flew, and watching the two men wrestle was like watching two drunk kittens trying to play.

The clone knocked Lewis against the ear with a fist; Lewis delivered a knee to the evil clone's ribs, and then they were rolling around on the far side of the aisle, knocking into display crates and tumbling over each other like laundry in a dryer.

Suddenly, Mallory lost track of which Lewis was which.

"Goddammit," she said under her breath. "Not again."

The Lewises flew at each other with whatever limbs they could swing. The one on the left landed a slap; the one on the right threw an elbow. Left Lewis bit Right Lewis on the hand; Right Lewis lowered his shoulder, drove forward, and pushed them both into a pile of women's sweaters across the way. Sensible polyester blends flew through the air as the scientist and his evil clone screamed and punched and kicked and bit, and then they screamed some more.

Through it all, both Lewises fought for control of the gun.

Mallory had to take action. She closed her eyes and took a deep breath. She held the air deep in her lungs. She opened her eyes.

She ran for the spear.

Maybe it was the cloud of evil shrouding the canned goods, or maybe it was just Mallory's mind playing tricks on her...but as she sprinted into aisle 8, she could feel the temperature drop by good twenty degrees at least. A chill prickled through her arms, and when she exhaled the hot air from her lungs, she could have sworn it puffed out in a little cloud. After just a few steps, she heard something rustling from behind the cans. *Leaves,* she thought subconsciously. *Branches.* But as she reached down to grab the Spear of Rad, she realized the rustling sound wasn't leaves *or* branches. The sound wasn't a rustling at all. It was a chorus of whispers.

The canned goods were speaking to her.

Maaaaaaallory, rasped a can of Goya mixed vegetables, *touuuuuch meeeee.*

Put me in your caaaaaart, hissed a can of Libby's peeled potatoes. *I'm an excellent vaaaaaaluuuuue.*

We're buy-one-get-one, Maaaalloryyyy, whispered a whole stack of Bush's baked beans. *Come cloooooser and graaaaasp uuuuuuuus.*

An icy hand closed around Mallory's heart, and it wasn't the sudden temperature drop. It was the fact that she could hear the cans beckoning, and that she actually *wanted* to do as they said. She knew it was wrong—she knew that if she touched a single can, she'd end up like Rufus, or worse. She *knew* without a single speck of doubt that if she so much as brushed her fingertips against a label, she'd be rendered brain-dead. She would be forever lost. She *knew* that.

But even so, she wanted to touch those canned goods like she'd never wanted to touch anything in her life. They controlled her desire. They propelled her forward. Mallory felt herself slipping toward the shelves...

Then she tripped on the Spear of Rad, fell down hard, and cracked her head on the sparkling linoleum floor, on the same exact spot above her right eye where she'd discovered a bump just a few days before. "Ow!" she yelled. A hand flew immediately to her forehead, and already, the little lump was burning with a stinging, bruising vengeance beneath her fingers.

On the bright side, though, the pain seemed to clear her head. She could no longer hear the whispers of the canned goods over the red buzzing in her own head. She grimaced as she reached out and snatched up the Spear of Rad. Then she pushed herself to her feet and strode down the aisle, toward the pair of flailing Lewises.

Time to end this, she decided.

The Lewis on the left had control of the pistol, and he drew a bead on the other Lewis' chest, but the other Lewis caught Left Lewis' gun hand in both of his own and twisted. Left Lewis screamed, and the two men struggled over the gun. The Lewis on the right pulled Left Lewis' hand back, then launched it forward, and something in Left Lewis' hand popped. He let go of the gun, and it clattered down the aisle, sliding to a stop at Mallory's feet.

Mallory dropped the glorified crowbar and picked up the gun. *Yes,* she thought. *This is better.*

She pointed the pistol in the air and fired a shot. A light exploded overhead and rained shards of glass down on Mallory from above. She did her best not to move and to act like shooting out a light fixture was precisely what she meant to do.

The Lewises stopped fighting and both raised their hands instinctively. "Mallory!" they cried in unison. "Shoot him!"

"Isn't *this* a familiar scene," she muttered. It occurred to her then that the safest thing to do would be to shoot both of them. She was not entirely opposed to the idea.

"He's the clone!" Left Lewis cried, and he whirled around and socked Right Lewis in the stomach.

"I am not!" Right Lewis gasped as he crumpled to his knees. He lunged forward and sank his teeth into Left Lewis' calf. Left Lewis howled in pain, and just like that, they were back on the floor, grappling and screaming and tumbling about. Mallory squinted at the flailing pair, trying to determine which one was the real Lewis, but

222 | ANOMALY FLATS

it was impossible. Of *course* it was impossible. They were genetically identical.

And they were both wearing the same stupid shirt.

One of the Lewises launched himself on top of the other Lewis, and the Lewis on bottom caught the other Lewis with his feet. He grunted as he gave his legs a mighty push, and the Lewis on top flew backward, straight toward Mallory. He screamed as he flew through the air, limbs spinning and slipping. He spun around on the slippery floor, making eye contact with Mallory for only the briefest moment...and that moment was all Mallory needed. In that split second, she could see the rage and the murder in his eyes. She squeezed the trigger three times, and three red holes blossomed in Evil Lewis' chest. He fell to his knees and gazed up with clouding, astounded eyes as blood seeped through his lab coat and pooled onto the floor. "No," he whispered. Then his body fell limp, his eyes tilted back, and the evil clone was dead.

"Oh, thank God!" Lewis cried, struggling to his feet. His face was covered in bruises and lacerations; his right shoulder had been dislocated, and he walked toward her with a limp. "You saved my life," he said, tears welling up in his eyes. "I thought you'd left, but... Mallory...you saved everything."

"I'm a hero," she agreed, smirking as she gave Lewis a hard pat on his good shoulder. "And now I'm gonna go."

Lewis grinned, despite his pain. "I guess you've earned that right," he said happily. "Although I was hoping you'd at least stay for a—" But his voice trailed off as he slid his gaze to the shelves over Mallory's shoulder. The corners of his mouth fell, and the blood drained from his face, leaving his cheeks powdery white.

"What?" Mallory asked, tilting her head. "Are you having a stroke? Do you smell burnt toast?"

"Mallory..." Lewis raised a finger slowly and pointed to the shelves.

Mallory furrowed her brow as she turned. "What—?" But she didn't have to finish her question. She saw what made Lewis blench.

The clone had knocked a can of green beans off the bottom shelf as he fell.

"Oh…" she said, exhaling sharply. "That's…not good, is it?"

Before Lewis could answer, a low thrumming began emanating from the shelves. The hum grew louder, and it grew more powerful, until the quick *whump-whump-whump* became so fierce that more cans began rattling off the shelves and falling to the floor below. A strange red light whispered itself to life, burning into existence like a slow ember somewhere in the center of the aisle, near the canned asparagus and spreading like wildfire until every shelf in aisle 8 glowed red with hellfire and heat. The cans began whispering urgently again, their gentle urgings replaced with a thrilled chatter of ends reached and destinies fulfilled. The temperature dropped another twenty degrees. There was no doubt that Mallory's breath was now pluming out in a thick, billowing mist. She instinctively reached for Lewis' hand and found it already open and waiting. Each clutched the other as they waited for the end of the world.

"What happens now?" Mallory whispered, her voice hollow and strange in her own ears.

"I don't know," Lewis answered. The honesty pulled at his voice like a boulder.

Then the shelves exploded, answering at least a part of the question.

Cans burst apart and rocketed to the far reaches of the Walmart, and a syrupy tsunami of canned fruit and vegetables rained down from above. Peaches splattered against the juice boxes in aisle 10. Peas pelted the Hawaiian rolls in aisle 1. Corn kernels peppered the ladies' hosiery. Globs of sauerkraut plopped down on the antiperspirant aisle, destroying all hope of deodorization.

One entire half of the store became the victim of culinary bombardment.

Mallory shielded herself from the food explosion by throwing up her arms, and they were pelted by Spaghetti-O's and a surprisingly wide assortment of beans. She grimaced at the onslaught, but she bore it with an appropriate amount of dignity.

Once it stopped, she lowered her dripping hands and peered into the new and awful landscape of aisle 8. Every single can had been launched clear, and the shelves had burst into shards that now littered the floor like shrapnel from some Great War of Capitalism. The frames of the shelves had remained bolted to the ground, but the backs of the shelving units, which had so recently been made of thin metal, now glowed with red and yellow swirling mists. They roiled behind the shelves on both sides of the aisle, but the mists did not break the plane into the aisle itself. And there, on the right side, not far from where the Spear of Rad now lay beneath a haphazard heap of shelf debris, there stood an innocuous wooden door, strong and unsupported, and wholly unaffected by the churning hell-mists that surrounded it.

Aisle 8 had shown itself for what it truly was: a portal to the lair of an ancient and powerful demon.

"Lewis," Mallory whispered, forcing her voice to choke itself out, even though her throat was staunchly against the idea. Lewis made some sort of questioning whine in his chest, which was all he could muster under the circumstances. "I want you to know something." She gave his hand a squeeze.

He tapped his thumb against her fingers and managed to say, "What?"

Mallory closed her eyes. She leaned her head down so her lips were close enough to his ears that there was no danger of being misheard. "I blame you for everything."

They stood like that for several long minutes, in total silence, waiting for the ancient evil to emerge from his weathered wooden door. Lewis didn't try to pull his hand away, and Mallory didn't bother releasing it. No matter who was to blame, they were in this together, here at the end of things.

But the door remained closed. The mists kept swirling, and the thrumming kept humming, but the door did not open. Mallory didn't know how long they stood there, hand-in-hand; time didn't exist here, in aisle 8 of the Anomaly Flats Walmart. It might have been minutes, or it might have been hours, but after a certain amount of time, however long that time was, it became abundantly clear that the door was not going to open.

"What's happening?" Mallory asked. She supposed that perhaps she should be glad that there wasn't a writhing, oozing evil slithering out of the old oak door, but somehow, the creature's total absence was even more terrifying. "Why isn't it coming out?"

She felt Lewis' hand tremble within her own. "It's waiting for us," he whispered.

Mallory snorted. "It's waiting for *us*? To go down *there*?" She finally released Lewis' hand, only to find that her fingers had cramped and needed to be pried loose. "Perfect. He can keep waiting. Forever. I'm going to Canada."

She handed him the pistol. But she didn't make a move to leave.

"This needs to end," Lewis said, his voice quiet and trembling, but unmistakably resolute. He turned and looked Mallory squarely in the eyes. "You can end this," he whispered.

"Me?! No, no, no, no, no. You, sure. We, maybe, though probably not. But me? No way. You want to go down and fight the demon? Be my guest."

"I couldn't fight a child in this condition," Lewis said sadly, clutching his dislocated shoulder and tilting his bruised and beaten face so that the fluorescent lights gleamed off the swollen welts. "Not that I would ever fight a child. But you know."

"This isn't my fight," Mallory snapped. "I may have made the clone, but the beet-demon was licking its lips down there in its stupid dungeon *way* before I came to town and pushed you into a lake."

Lewis sighed heavily. "I know," he said. "But you're the only one with the strength to end it once and for all."

Mallory squinted down at him, sniffing at his words for another jab at being sturdy. She decided to let it slide, if for no other reason than Lewis would probably be wearing his skin around his waist soon, and that seemed like punishment enough. But that didn't mean she was ready to sacrifice her life to try to kill the thing waiting for them on the other side of that door. "You know," she said, "I'm not particularly convinced Anomaly Flats is worth saving."

Lewis looked up at her, his eyes sad but firm. "If you really thought that, you wouldn't be here."

Mallory crossed her arms. "You think you know so much," she said, annoyed. And the part that was so annoying was that he was right. She *had* come back for a reason. Or maybe for a lot of little reasons that added up to one big, stupid, ill-advised ball of reason: she felt guilty; she didn't want Lewis to die; she didn't want to be single-handedly responsible for the decimation of an entire town; and she couldn't deny that Lewis had been right when he said the people of Anomaly Flats were worth saving. They were weird, and they were scary, and some of them had swarms of flies coming out of their throats…but they didn't deserve to be flayed alive.

She reached down and snatched up the Spear of Rad. "Fine," she said, testing the weapon by giving it a few stabs through the air. "But if I die in there, I'm going *Poltergeist* all over this stupid town."

"Honestly," Lewis said, pushing his glasses up his nose, "dying should be the least of your worries."

CHAPTER 20

MALLORY STOOD before the weathered oak door, holding the spear so tightly in both hands that her knuckles glowed white. She frowned. "Do I just knock, or...?"

"I think you just go in," Lewis said from his hiding spot behind the end cap.

"*You* go in," she grumbled under her breath. She tapped the pointy end of the spear against the door three times. It made no sound whatsoever. "If I save the town and destroy the all-powerful, indestructible demon, can I go?"

"Not *if*," Lewis said, trying to sound encouraging and failing all the way. "*When. When* you destroy the indestructible demon." He thought about this for a second, and then he added, "I'm not sure 'indestructible' is an appropriate adjective for a demon that you're going to destroy."

"That's what worries me," she said.

She reached out, grabbed the knob, and pulled. The door swung open on its hinges, perfectly silent. She peered into the darkness of the doorway; a set of stone steps wound around to the left and down, down, down, along a curving stone wall that was sparsely lit by small torches spaced unevenly down the staircase. Mallory glanced around the doorway, which was set into the shelving unit. Behind the shelves was another unit, and another aisle, and there was no way the stone steps *actually* went back into that space. But looking through the door, there was no mistaking it; the ancient evil's dungeon went back much farther than the Walmart shelving unit should have allowed.

It was very disorienting.

Adding to the unease that permeated the air was the fact that the torches on the wall looked eerily familiar. "If this leads to the Check Into Cash, I'm letting the whole town burn." She turned and raised an eyebrow at Lewis. "I don't suppose I can just nick the bastard and run?" she asked.

The scientist shrugged. "It's been a while since I read the manual. But I'm pretty sure you have to drive it all the way through his heart."

Mallory shook her head and gazed sadly down at the crowbar. "Drive it through his heart. Got it." She took a deep breath and stepped through the doorway into the darkness.

There was an unmistakable chill in the air. Mallory drew her arms up against her chest as she crept carefully down the stairs, holding the point of the spear out and trying her best to peer around the curving staircase into the darkness below. "This is stupid, this is stupid, this is stupid," she whispered. Her voice did not echo, like she'd thought perhaps it would. And then she noticed all the other sounds that weren't there; the torch flames didn't crackle, the walls didn't drip, and her footsteps didn't make so much as a single scrape. It was as if someone had muted the volume on the entire world.

But she could still hear herself whispering, and that gave her a strange sort of comfort.

"Stab the heart, run away," she instructed herself. "Stab the heart, run away. This is stupid, this is stupid, this is stupid, this is stupid. Stab the heart, run away. This is stupid, run away." But instead, her feet kept moving forward, easing themselves down the stone steps.

Before she knew it, Mallory was standing at the foot of the staircase, in the lair of the ancient evil of Anomaly Flats.

"Hello?" she whispered. She didn't know *why* she whispered it; she didn't want to hear a response from whatever else might be down there, and she wasn't particularly keen on announcing her own presence to it. But her entire body seemed to be operating on autopilot now, and she couldn't really fault it; this was nothing if not uncharted territory.

Her heart dropped into her shoes when she heard a voice from the back of the chamber say, "Hello."

It seemed like a good a time as any to vomit in the corner.

So, she did.

"Are you all right?" the voice asked as Mallory wiped her arm across her mouth. It was a man's voice, and it sounded unreasonably sincere. She found a strange sort of vindication in the fact that the ancient evil was, indeed, male.

"Fine," she said sourly, returning her full attention to the Spear of Rad and holding it defensively in front of her chest. "Do me a favor and impale yourself on this crowbar, will you?" She tried to keep the quaver out of her voice, but she was under no illusions that she was actually managing to do it. She could feel her throat vibrating with every syllable.

"I'm afraid I can't," the voice said, slow and syrupy-sweet as honey. "Though I'm not sure I would if I were able."

"What do you mean?" Mallory asked, squinting into the darkness. She couldn't see anything beyond the halo of light thrown by the torch bolted to the wall above the bottom step. She had a feeling that the chamber went much, *much* farther back. She waved the point of the spear in a slow arc before her, in case the ancient evil decided to pounce. She didn't know if the movement of the spear would help, but she also didn't know that it wouldn't.

The voice in the darkness chuckled. "I'm in a bit of a fixed state," it admitted. Then, "Where are my manners? I imagine you'd do well with a bit of light."

On his command, an orange glow with no discernible source filled the chamber. It was warm, and welcoming, and Mallory felt her shoulders involuntarily relax a bit. She could see the entire room now, and it wasn't nearly as large as she'd imagined; it was just about the size of a basketball court...which meant she had no trouble seeing the ancient evil where he stood at the far end of the room.

He was tall, but not overly so, and his clothes were surprisingly plain and hellfire-free. He wore brown linen pants and a white, long-sleeved waffle shirt with the sleeves pushed up to his elbows. He wore a dusty brown cowboy hat, and with his head tipped down, she couldn't see his face beneath the brim. He was slim, and in good enough shape to send an involuntary flutter through Mallory's stomach (*Seriously? Now?* she scolded herself), but it was the man's chains that really demanded most of the attention. He had shackles around each wrist, and another pair clamped tightly on his ankles. Thick, heavy chains linked them to gleaming stakes in the stone wall behind him. Even from the distance, there was no mistaking the finality of those bonds.

"I hope you won't think me a poor host for not greeting you at the door," the creature said, raising his hands as far as he was able, the chains clanging until he had pulled them taut. "I'm not quite as mobile as I'd like to be."

"Who *did* that to you?" Mallory blurted. She had a strong feeling that she shouldn't provoke a primeval demon, but seeing him in chains was such a shock, she couldn't help herself. Besides, odds were she was going to meet a horrible, painful end down in this dungeon, and if she was going to die, by God, she was going to die a well-informed woman.

"Protestants," came the easy answer. He said it as if the idea was terribly amusing to him. For all she knew, it was.

Mallory took a deep breath. Her life had rocketed so far past surreal, it wasn't even worth wondering how she'd managed to find herself in this particular predicament. She decided just to roll with it and see how it all played out. But even so, she wasn't quite ready to approach the imprisoned creature. Not yet.

"So you're just stuck there? A bunch of Protestants overpowered something like *you* and locked you into the wall?" she called out.

The ancient evil snorted. "People…can surprise you," he said, with a little laughter in his voice.

Mallory frowned. "You sound awfully chipper about it. All things considered."

"I suppose I shouldn't be," the man admitted. "But when you've lived as long as I have, any bit of surprise is an opportunity to smile."

Mallory glanced down at the ancient spear in her hands. Then she looked back up at the man chained to the wall. He looked pretty spry for being a few million years old, restraints notwithstanding. "This might be a weird question…but you *are* the ancient evil, right?"

The man on the other side of the room smiled. Mallory couldn't see it, but she could *hear* it, somehow. "I suppose that's as accurate a description as most of the others," he assented. "I wouldn't go around calling myself evil…but I see where others might get that idea."

"And you're the one responsible for…all this?" She waved her hand up in the general direction of the town above. "For Anomaly Flats?"

"It may be more accurate to say that Anomaly Flats is responsible for me. I found myself helplessly drawn to its singular qualities some time ago. I've become a bit bonded to the fabric of the town over time, it's true. But Anomaly Flats was a dimensional oddity long before I came to town."

Mallory took a step toward the creature. "Look, don't take this the wrong way," she said, trying to sound braver than she felt, "but I'm supposed to stab you through the heart." She cleared her throat. "With this magical crowbar from space."

The ancient evil shrugged. "Makes sense," he admitted. Then he raised his head, and his dark eyes bored into Mallory's, a sneer creeping up along his lips. "I'd probably be more surprised if you'd said you came here in peace."

Mallory gazed into his face. His features were confusing; that was as specifically as she could describe them. His dark eyes seemed to almost radiate light, but that might have been an optical illusion caused by the fact that they were constantly changing size and shape. First almond-shaped, then round, then up at the corners, then down, and on and on and on, as if they couldn't make up their minds. His nose, too, blurred through a series of various shapes and sizes, and his mouth flickered above his ever-shifting chin, trying on a different set of lips each half-second that passed. He was a never-ending slot machine of features.

"What's wrong with your face?" she blurted.

"I've always liked it myself," he said, pretending to be taken aback by her brazenness. Then he smiled through his shifting lips. "I just can't seem to settle on any one look. I often try to assume features that appeal to the person I'm addressing, to put her at ease... but I confess, I'm having a hard time pinpointing what exactly those features might be for you, Mallory. And in any case, wearing a mask is disingenuous; and I think I owe you a bit more than pretense."

"Ah," she said, as if that all made perfect sense, although it made absolutely none whatsoever.

"Does it bother you?" he asked.

"It's not what I expected," she admitted, taking another step closer.

"And what did you expect?" he asked, clearly amused. "Slime? Entrails? Pus and blood and sulfur and ooze?"

"I mean...yeah." She shrugged.

"I would imagine so," he smiled. "I've seen the drawings they've made of me."

"And the wood cuttings?" Mallory asked. She took yet another step in his direction.

His pulsing eyes gleamed with interest. "Someone made wood cuttings? How wonderful."

"Wonderful isn't...*quite* the word." Mallory shifted the weight of the Spear of Rad, and she was almost close enough for its ages-old but razor-sharp point to pierce his chest. *Just another few steps*, she thought.

"Do you really mean to run me through?" He asked this calmly, almost passively, as if he'd just asked if she wanted cream in her coffee.

"I can't really think of a reason why I shouldn't," she said, working hard to keep her voice even. "You know. All things considered."

"How about because I'm fettered to a wall and completely helpless?" He spread his hands again and jangled the chains.

"Something tells me you're probably a little less helpless than you let on."

The ancient evil clucked his tongue. "The things people must think of me up there..." he mused.

"They *think* that you shove hot sticks up people's asses and skin them alive and sew their heads onto decapitated deer bodies," she snapped. She knew she probably shouldn't take such a cavalier tone with an old demon, but the scenes from the woodcuttings disturbed her so, *so* much.

The ancient evil laughed, a loud, long, throaty chuckle. "I see why you brought the spear," he said. He shrugged one shoulder up to his face and wiped the tears from his eyes on his sleeve. "Humans are so...imaginative," he said gleefully.

"Are you saying you *didn't* do those things?" Mallory said, squinting and trying to seek out his face for lies. It was a difficult thing, since the entire *face* was a lie. It cycled through its seemingly endless array of options and gave nothing away.

"It's not really my style," he grinned. Then he bobbed his head a bit and added, "Well, the impaling. I *did* do that. But you have to understand, that was a different time. That sort of thing was expected. It wasn't even my idea; it was the suggestion of the town's mayor at the time. He said, 'I suppose you'll be shoving red-hot pokers up our arses now,' and I thought, 'Sure, yes, I suppose I can do that.' But I'm really more of a slash-and-burn kind of guy, to be honest."

"I'm not sure splitting hairs over which *type* of eternal hell you prefer is really all that important." Mallory took one more step, and she was finally close enough to reach the evil with the spear. The stakes that held the chains into the walls glittered more brightly, to the point of blinding Mallory if she looked directly at them. It was almost as if they were made of light.

"You may be right," he admitted. "I'm sorry. I don't mean to upset you, Mallory. I just want to be honest with you." He peered directly into her eyes and said, "I will never lie to you."

His gaze had a strange effect on her knees. They suddenly felt watery, and she had the overwhelming urge to collapse. She closed her eyes and shook her head, shaking the memory of those eyes from her mind. "You know my name," she said without opening her eyes, trying to change the subject. "What do I call you? Just… Ancient Evil?"

The demon laughed lightly. "You're right. I'm being a terrible host; I completely bypassed proper introductions. You *can* call me the ancient evil if you'd like. But I'd much prefer it if you called me Chad."

Mallory blinked. "The great and powerful ancient demon is named Chad?"

The ancient evil raised an eyebrow. "Is it really that surprising?" he asked.

Mallory thought back to all the Chads she'd known throughout her lifetime. She shrugged. "No, not really," she admitted.

Chad indicated the weapon in her hand. "I assume that's the Spear of Rad?" he said. Mallory nodded. "How wonderful," he smiled. "I've heard stories of its power, but I've never seen it up close." He jangled the chains again. "I've been a little tied up."

"Prison humor," Mallory muttered. "Hilarious."

"You have to find joy where you can," Chad said. "Would you mind...could you hold up the spear? So I can get a decent look?"

Mallory hesitated. She assumed this was some sort of trick. But his bonds did appear to be incredibly secure, and while Lewis had told her to pierce the ancient evil through the heart, she assumed that driving the spear through his skull would probably do the trick, too. So she raised the weapon, but she kept the tip pointed at the demon.

He tilted his head so he could read the engravings on the side of the spear. In the strange, source-less light, the etchings almost seemed to be written in flames. "Sponsored by Dish Network," Chad read. He nodded sagely. "I should have guessed."

"Wait, it *really* says that?" Mallory asked, incredulous. She pulled the spear back and examined the runes along its shaft. She couldn't make heads or tails of the markings, but a nerdy scientist and an ancient evil couldn't both be wrong. "That is the stupidest thing I've ever heard."

"It is truly a weapon of extraordinary power," Chad said, leaning back against the stone wall. "It would definitely do the trick."

"Well," Mallory said, shifting the spear in her hands, "what're we waiting for?" She gripped the shaft and took a series of deep breaths, trying desperately to work up the will to stab a well-mannered, human-looking demon through the heart.

"I assume you've been told what to expect when you run me through?" he said.

Mallory snorted. "I expect you'll die a pretty painful death."

Chad smiled. "Yes, I imagine that's likely true. But the future doesn't look good for you, either."

Mallory tensed. Was this some sort of ancient evil trickery? It seemed likely. "What do you mean?" she asked.

"This room is a cell meant for keeping me locked away. That is its only purpose. Once that becomes no longer necessary, the room has no more reason to exist. When I die, it will collapse in on itself, compressing into literal nothingness." He gazed up at the heavy stones set into the ceiling. "How much do you think each one of those weighs?" he mused.

"Come on," Mallory scoffed. "You really expect me to believe that?"

"I told you I would not lie to you," he said simply. "If you want proof, I can deliver it. The spear is sharp enough; cut me."

Mallory raised an eyebrow. "Cut you?"

"Cut me," he nodded. "Anywhere you'd like."

She tapped her teeth together, thinking. It was almost *certainly* a trick...but then again, if he was telling the truth, she needed to know. A collapsing dungeon might change the game a bit. And besides, slicing open a hell-demon could only win her a few karma points. Quickly, before she could change her mind, she slashed the Spear of Rad across his arm. A long trickle of blood welled up and began dripping onto the floor.

Something above her head shifted, and the entire room groaned.

Little puffs of dust filtered down through the ceiling. Tiny pebbles tumbled to the floor.

The dungeon shuddered like an old barn in a windstorm.

"You see? Not that I think it should necessarily change your mind. I believe a person's own destiny should always be fulfilled. If you're meant to end my existence, then postponing that end is fruitless. I just want you to know what you're in for when it happens. I want you to have all the information."

Mallory glanced nervously over her shoulder at the staircase. It wasn't really *that* far away. "I can make it," she said aloud.

"Maybe," he agreed. "I suppose we'll find out."

"I suppose so," Mallory said. But there was no mistaking the uncertainty in her voice. It was a perfect match for the uncertainty in her brain.

The ancient evil surely heard it, and he seized his opportunity. "Would you permit me a bit of theatre before the end? If I'm destined to die, I won't fight it, but we do all have our parts to play and our scripts to read. Do you mind?"

Mallory groaned. She hated actors, and allusions to theatre. But she wasn't necessarily opposed to postponing the self-sacrificial slaughtering of a demon. "Sure, Shakespeare. Knock yourself out."

He nodded, pleased. "I assume you've noticed the stakes that hold me here?" He gazed fondly at the huge nail above his left shoulder. "You see how it sparkles? Have you considered why it does that?"

Mallory shrugged. "It was born that way?"

An amused little smile played across Chad's lips. "You're correct, in a sense. There are rules, Mallory, about demons and angels and what can hold them and what can set them free. That," he said, nodding down at the Spear of Rad, "is one of the things that can set us free. In a manner of speaking. And this," he said, indicating the glistening stake over his shoulder, "is one of the things that can hold us. Take a closer look. Can you not see what the stakes are made of?"

Mallory brought her eyes closer to the spike, but not so close that she was within reach of the man's fettered hand. The nail was monstrous—the head alone was three inches in diameter, at least—and it was clear, but faceted, so the light played off its surface and sparkled like sunlight on a river. "Cubic zirconia?"

Chad laughed out loud. "Close," he said. "Each one is a solid diamond, fashioned into a stake many years ago."

"Solid diamond?" Mallory asked. A warm flush crept up the back of her neck, and the edges of her vision blurred a bit, so that all that remained in focus was the gleaming head of the spike. She lowered the spear and felt herself being helplessly drawn to its light. She reached out and brushed her fingertips against the smooth surface.

It was cool to the touch.

238 | ANOMALY FLATS

"I wonder if you know the monetary value of a diamond of that size, in today's market," Chad said. The hushed tone of his voice couldn't quite conceal his mirth.

The truth was, Mallory didn't know the value of a diamond that was probably at least a foot in length. But she knew the value of the tiny diamonds in her backpack, and it wasn't very hard to extrapolate the figures to such an incredible degree.

A diamond like that would be worth hundreds of millions, she knew. Probably more. It was, quite possibly, a billion-dollar diamond.

And there were four of them down here, just sticking out of the wall, collecting dust.

Mallory realized she wasn't breathing. She instructed her lungs to work, but they refused. So she just stood there, breathless.

"I'll tell you how the rules are written," Chad said. He eased himself back against the wall, and his iron chains rattled, startling Mallory from her reverie. She found her breath again and drew herself back, once again out of reach...but her eyes remained focused on the diamond. "One diamond anchor is enough to hold even the most powerful demon. Some people might use two, just to be on the safe side, which I don't really fault them for. A third anchor is redundant, though, to say the least. And a fourth...well, a fourth is just overkill, if you ask me."

Mallory snorted. "So in other words, who would miss one little diamond stake?"

"Now that you mention it, I'm not sure anyone would know the difference," he said with a grin. "Except for me, of course. And you."

"So, what—I pull a pin, become rich beyond my wildest dreams, and you remain here, locked up for all eternity?"

"Eternity is a long time," Chad pointed out. "All I need is three other would-be slayers who understand the value of an extremely precious gem. I estimate that in another six thousand years or so, I'll be free."

"And I'll be long gone."

"In every way imaginable."

Mallory considered his words. She glanced uneasily between the diamond, which gleamed, and the demon, who flickered. "You're telling me that I could free one of your chains, and you'd still be trapped down here? I think you're lying," she said.

"No you don't. Nor should you. I don't find much point in prevarication, Mallory. The truth is easier, and almost always more convincing."

"And what's to stop me from pulling a pin, *then* killing you? And getting out before it all comes crumbling down?" She wondered if she sounded as tough as she meant to. Probably not.

Almost *certainly* not.

"That is definitely an option," Chad agreed. "You're welcome to try to outrun the destruction."

Mallory blinked hard. She tried to reason with her brain, but the more she thought about the proposal, the more sense it seemed to make. Reason was losing by winning. "And how am I supposed to get it out? Just give it a good yank?"

"Well, you *are* sturdy, aren't you?" he teased. Mallory glowered, and he held up his hands defensively. "I apologize," he said with a laugh, "You *could* try to pull them out with your bare hands, though I doubt you'd have much luck. If only you had some sort of mystical tool of great power that could pull a stake from a stone as easily as a plum from a pudding..."

Mallory looked down at the Spear of Rad. In truth, she had almost forgotten that she was holding it. Now she snorted out a little laugh. "The thing that kills you is also the thing that can set you free? That's a little convenient, don't you think?"

"Is it?" the ancient evil asked, raising an eyebrow. "I find that the things that set us free are quite often the same as the things that cause our demise. I'm sure if you think about it long enough, you'll agree..."

Mallory shook her head slowly. She ran a hand through her tangled hair and pushed it back from her face. "If I let you live, you'll eventually destroy the town. And all of the people in it."

"And, most likely, the entire planet," he added. "I'll turn the whole thing into a literal hell on Earth, if I can."

"Anguish, pain, torture, fire—all that?"

"Oh, certainly. For starters, anyway."

"But that won't be until long after I'm gone," she said quietly, almost to herself.

Chad nodded slowly. "I can't guarantee the timeline, but the odds are in your favor."

Mallory chewed her bottom lip as she thought. "What would I tell Lewis?" she said.

The ancient evil shrugged. "Lies aren't really my purview, as I've said. But I suppose you could tell him you completed the task." He lowered his eyes to the rusty point of the spear. "My blood *is* on the blade, after all."

Mallory couldn't even comprehend the type of life she could have with that much money in the bank. Forget Lenore's safe house. Hell, forget *Canada*. She could buy her own *island*. Fencing a diamond spike the size of her arm might be tricky, but surely Lenore would know somebody. You didn't become an international source of awe in the business of providing safe houses for criminals if you didn't have a few good contacts in your Rolodex. And even at an exorbitant handling fee—and there would *surely* be one—just *a single stake* from the demon represented more money than Mallory could possibly have hoped to spend in her lifetime.

She clapped a hand to her head and tried to let a little bit of reason into there, because surely this was nothing but madness... wasn't it? Who in their right mind would sentence all of mankind to excruciating torture and eternal, flesh-stripping damnation? The image of the naked men impaled upon the glowing hot iron rods burned before her eyes. That would only be the beginning, she knew. No matter how well-mannered and easy-going he portrayed himself, that's how he would warm up...by playing with an unlucky few, using them as an example of why it was pointless to even try to stand up to his hateful, barbaric omnipotence.

Anomaly Flats would be the epicenter; the murder and chaos would start here, then gleefully spread across the state. The nuclear power plant in Callaway would have a meltdown and spread radiation through the entire country; the Mississippi would boil over and flow red with blood; the Ozark Mountains would crack and split wide open, and the meth-addicted hill people would fall into the eternal swirling darkness of the chasm, and that would be just about the only upside to the whole ordeal.

The rest of the Midwest would follow; acid would rain down upon the plains, and peoples' skin would slough right off their flesh. Temperatures would rise, and eyeballs would roast and pop in their sockets. Children would split right down the middle, and their organs would fall out of their bodies and writhe, steaming, in the dust. Unfathomable creatures would emerge from beneath the ground—huge, stinking monsters with the gigantic heads of wolves or tarantulas or cuttlefish, and they'd scoop up the survivors with their tentacles or spindles or whatever they had attached to their monstrous torsos and crunch them down their gullets.

Then the entire country would be plunged into darkness. The earth would shake and tear itself apart. The Grand Canyon would fill with boiling tar. Water would transmute into venom, fruit would rot and bear swarms of locusts, and scorpions would spill forth from every corner of every home. The oceans would rise, skyscrapers would collapse; liquid fire would gush from every sidewalk crack.

And after that...the people. The world's population would melt, burn, shrivel, decay, but they would be kept alive, every single human being; they would, each and every one of them, experience the sheer excruciating pain of decimation, and when humans had been reduced to simpering puddles and wailing cinders and breathing piles of ash, the demons would descent upon the world, and then the pain would truly begin.

The full power of Chad would be unleashed, and misery and pain didn't come close to describing what awaited those future generations if Mallory pulled the diamond stake from the wall.

And she could not be responsible for that.

"Yes I could," she said softly.

Of *course* she could. She didn't have much of a choice, really. She had already made her decision two days ago, when she took the cash and diamonds from the safe. She meant to amass a small fortune, trample every person who stood in her way, and live her life on her own terms, independently, and without regret. What *wouldn't* she do to secure that future for herself?

Of *course* she would take the diamond.

"A deal with the devil," she whispered.

"Yes," Chad admitted. "But you have to admit, it's a pretty good deal."

It was most certainly that.

Mallory spun the Spear of Rad in her hand and jammed the forked end beneath the head of the nail. She forced it in as far as she could, then pushed at the spear shaft with all the strength she could muster. As it turned out, the spear was mystical enough to do all of the work on its own; the diamond spike slid out easily, and her force took her into a face-first collision with the stone wall.

"Son of a bitch!" she cried, feeling her face for bruises.

"I may have forgotten to mention that particular rule. Mystical tools are usually overly-effective. Sorry about the lip. Worth it, though, I think." He nodded down at the loosened diamond, which now lay glittering and flawless on the dungeon floor. Then he hitched up his shoulder and sighed happily as he swung his arm freely in a circle for the first time in centuries. "For both of us."

Mallory suddenly realized she was within easy grabbing distance of the demon, and she slipped backward, out of reach. Chad grinned as he flexed his wrist and wriggled his fingers. "Smart girl," he said, every bit of his constantly-changing face gleaming with victory. "It wouldn't do for either of us if I ripped out your throat; it'd bring all the wrong sorts of attention. But an evil being does have its urges."

Mallory reached down and picked up the diamond. It was perfectly clear, and somehow polished, despite having spent the last several centuries buried in stone. It glittered and gleamed in the orange glow, casting dizzying refractions about the room. The light sparkled in Mallory's eyes, and she was so hungry for the precious gem in her hands that her stomach actually rumbled at the sight of it.

I wonder if there's something wrong with me... she thought.

If there was, it wasn't anything a few hundred million dollars couldn't fix.

"Don't break free for at least a thousand years," she warned him, giving the spear a little jab in his direction. "Or I'll come back and finish the job."

Chad smiled. "Sure."

The air in the chamber suddenly felt hot, and a little thin. It was time to go. Mallory tucked the diamond stake into her back pocket and fluffed her shirttail over the top to hide it. There were no mirrors in the dungeon, but a quick assessment with her hands told her that the overall effect was something less than covert. But she decided it probably didn't matter. For a scientist, Lewis was shockingly unobservant.

She backed away from Chad, holding the Spear of Rad before her, ready to strike. But the demon didn't move; he just flexed his wrist and watched her go, his face filled with a flicking amusement, his smile presenting itself in an ever-changing series of lips.

She reached the staircase and set her foot on the bottom step. The torches still flickered, and she could see a watery wash of light coming in from the Walmart doorway above. She turned and gave the demon one last look. The blood of billions would someday be on her hands. Some people, she knew, would lose a little sleep over that. But she took a grave comfort in the knowledge that the ancient evil's face wouldn't haunt her dreams.

She didn't even know what his face really looked like.

She hurried up the stairs, leaving Chad alone to his patient and gruesome plans.

"Mallory!" Lewis cried as she emerged through the doorway at the top of the stairs. "You're alive!"

"Try not to sound so surprised," she said irritably.

"I'm sorry!" he gasped. His eyes grew wide, and they were coated over by a film of tears. "It's just—I didn't—the ancient evil, and—I'm just…" He removed his glasses and wiped his eyes on his sleeve. "Just…welcome back." He limped forward with his arms out, aiming for a joyful embrace.

Mallory put out her hand and stopped him with a palm to the forehead. "Personal space, Lewis," she said, gesturing in a general circle around herself with the spear.

"Right," he said, clearing his throat uncomfortably as his cheeks flushed red. "Sorry. So what happened? Did you…you know?"

Mallory skirted sideways down the aisle to keep the poorly-hidden diamond stake out of his view. "It's done," she said.

"You killed it?" he asked, his voice quiet with wonder.

"Yep. Right through the heart, as instructed." Mallory held out the tip of the spear as she crept backward so that Lewis could see the drying blood.

Lewis shook his head in wonder. "Mallory," he said. His voice caught in his throat, and he cleared it a few times. He didn't want to choke up in front of her, but honestly, after all that had happened, how could he not? "I don't know how to thank you. For coming back. For finishing it. For…for saving Anomaly Flats."

"Yep. I did it. I saved the town and all its weird, carnival-side-show people. I'm a hero." She reached the end of aisle 8 and backed out of it, stepping over the exploded canned goods, the ruined shelving, and the lifeless body of Lewis' evil clone. "And I think I'd like to go now."

"Just like that?" Lewis' face fell. "Not even a goodbye drink? We could stop by the Dive Inn—"

But Mallory cut him off. "I'm not really a goodbye kind of gal, Lewis." She set the Spear of Rad on its hilt and leaned it against the end cap. "Let's just call it good, and maybe I'll see you later."

He gave her a sad little smile. "No you won't," he said.

"No," she agreed with a nod. "I definitely won't."

Then she turned, hurried down the aisle, and left Lewis alone in the Walmart with a half-dozen employees and a primeval demon that would someday rise up and swallow the world.

CHAPTER 21

EVIL LEWIS SNORTED as Mallory ran toward the exit. "Good riddance," he said, spitting on the floor.

He looked down into the blank, staring eyes of Lewis Burnish, a mediocre scientist in life and a useless lump in death. "Sorry about how this played out for you," Evil Lewis said, nudging Lewis in the ribs with the toe of his shoe. "I mean, not *very* sorry, but *sort of* sorry." He reached down and grabbed Lewis' cheeks. They were already turning cold. He squeezed his hand to make the dead man's jaw work. "I forgive you, Evil Lewis," he made the scientist's mouth say in a squeaky voice. Then he stood up and gave Lewis' body a good, solid kick. "I don't need your forgiveness," he spat.

Evil Lewis limped his way over to the doorway and peered inside. He couldn't hear the ancient evil below, but he could *sense* it. He could feel its energy radiating up the stairwell. It was still alive, then. Everything had gone quite nicely to plan.

"I was worried for a minute," Evil Lewis called down as he descended the stone steps. "I thought she might actually kill you." He hopped down off the last step and gave the ancient evil a wide grin.

"And she might very well have," Chad agreed. His features—his *true* features—were slowly shifting into their proper positions on his face...if one could really call it a face. His skin blistered, and little boils popped and hissed and spat streams of yellow goo onto the dungeon floor. His flickering nose sank into its cavity, and his eyes crusted over with sulfur. His ears dropped away from the sides of his head and melted onto the stone below, leaving nothing but vapors trailing into the air. His hair grew long and ragged beneath his hat, and then it fell out altogether, and that, too, vanished in a sour-smelling puff of smoke. He continued to rotate his new-ly-freed shoulder, working the feeling back into it after the long years of restraint. The fingers on his hands melted themselves into a cloven flesh hoof. "But if there's one thing you can count on, it's that greed makes people foolish, and almost everyone is a slave to it."

"Must we have let her get away?" Evil Lewis asked. "I wish you'd let me kill her as soon as she resurfaced."

"Death is rarely the best punishment," Chad said.

Evil Lewis nodded. He approached the demon and bowed low. "You know best," he said.

Chad reached out and placed his free hoof tenderly on the back of Evil Lewis' head. "You've done well."

Evil Lewis raised his head, and his eyes burned with shame. "You only have one bond loosed," he said, his voice small.

"We don't write the rules," Chad said simply, giving a little shrug. "Only outsiders may loose the stakes, and only one each, at that. It is writ in the fabric of the universe. There's no sense upsetting oneself over it."

"But we could have used the scientist," Evil Lewis said bitterly. "I'm...I'm sorry he was killed before he could be put to use."

But Chad shook his head. "I have a sense that Dr. Burnish was one of the incorruptible sort. I don't think he could have been per-suaded, and then I might be dead, or fixed to all four chains yet. No; things worked out as they should have, I think."

Evil Lewis sighed. Perhaps it was true; maybe it all *had* worked out for the best. Everything certainly went much better than it could have. "I wish the process wasn't so long."

"Time hands down its own justice," Chad said simply.

Evil Lewis nodded. That much was true; time would eventually set the evil free, and it would punish the arrogance of the natural citizens of the world. He had no doubts about that. He, a simple clone, had played a large part in that, and he had played it well. There was much pride to be taken in that. "Still," he sighed, "I wish I could be there with you for your reign."

Here, Chad's bubbling, popping lips twisted themselves into a sly grin. "The rules of time in Anomaly Flats are quite unique, my friend. I think together we will discover how to properly use them to our advantage."

"We may," Evil Lewis said. Then he brightened considerably. "We *will*! I *know* we will. One day, I'll write the letter that leads Lewis Burnish here."

Chad nodded. "Indeed. The secrets of time will allow us much freedom...eventually. So don't fret. You've done well, and you'll be rewarded."

Evil Lewis smiled.

"Now listen carefully, my friend," Chad continued, "for we have much work to do, and I am eager to begin..."

CHAPTER 22

FACING LEWIS HAD BEEN HARDER than Mallory expected. She scrubbed at the tears that threatened to spill down her cheeks as she hurried to the Impala in the parking lot. "It doesn't matter," she muttered sternly to herself. "He'll be long dead by the time the demonic shit hits the fan."

She popped open the door to the car and tossed the diamond onto the passenger seat. Even here, in the darkness of the Anomaly Flats night, it glittered and sent sparkles of light around the interior of the car. It was almost as if it was being lit from the inside.

The purple Jansport was still tucked safely beneath the driver's seat. One quick pat of the bag was enough to reassure her that the money was still inside, although it hardly mattered anymore. Still, *more* was always better than *enough*.

"Please start," she prayed, slipping the key into the ignition. "Please, please, *please* just start." She turned the key.

The engine started.

"Yesssss," she whispered. She threw the car into drive and hit the gas.

The roads were quiet, of course, and the highway out of Anomaly Flats took her away from downtown, so she was spared the sight of the citizens whose descendants she'd doomed to an excruciating fate. But then, the people in Anomaly Flats were all sterilized, weren't they? There would *be* no descendants to kill off. That made

Mallory feel better about her recent decisions. "Keep drinking that coffee," she said.

She rolled down her window and let the cool, humid night air whip her hair into a frenzy. The further she got from the Walmart, the lighter she felt. She smiled out over the headlights, and then she actually laughed. She was headed out, and she had the net worth of an oil well, and she was *alive*. She'd survived an ancient evil and plasma and flies and waffles and roaches and tentacles and corn and clones and Mars and portals and a predatory lender and vaporization and magnetism and an honest-to-goodness cross-dimensional nexus, and she'd been justly rewarded. She had no more fear of running into the police; surely a five-figure bribe would encourage any patrolman to look the other way. *And here, a few thousand more, to buy your wife something nice,* she saw herself saying, flinging a bundle of bills into the air as she peeled out into the night, up toward the Canadian border.

Even the city limits of Anomaly Flats couldn't stop her. As she neared the peeling wooden billboard that read *WE'RE SURPRISED THAT YOU'RE LEAVING*, she felt a little tug in the pit of her stomach that said, *There's no way they'll let you go.* But she stomped her foot on the pedal, the engine roared, and the Impala rocketed past the boundary of town and kept going strong. The radio sprang to life as she tore down the road, and a familiar female voice came through the speakers. *Attention, Anomaly Flats,* it crackled. But the signal was weak, and the rest of the message was lost in a flurry of static, and then the station went dead altogether.

Mallory laughed out loud. She was free.

She squealed at the top of her lungs and beat her hands against the steering wheel in sweet, unadulterated triumph. "Too bad about the future!" she screamed gleefully into the woods that blurred past her open window. "Sorry, year 10,000!" She screamed again and did a jerking little dance of celebration in her seat.

It was going to be a good life.

By the time she was a few miles down the road, any remaining heaviness about what she'd just done in Anomaly Flats had completely melted away. She put the town, and its people, out of her mind, and she was shocked—and delighted—at just how easily they faded. Like the radio station, the strange town of Anomaly Flats was already becoming static, and soon the air would clear, and there would be nothing left.

Nothing but the world's biggest diamond.

She wondered for a brief moment if perhaps one of the other three spikes had been bigger, and she felt a pang of regret for not making a more careful choice. Maybe she could have squeezed out an extra few million dollars if she'd just taken a minute to gauge their sizes. She cursed herself for being so hasty. A strange sadness settled over her then, but she figured it would evaporate as soon as she converted her diamond to cash.

She kept one hand on the steering wheel and reached over to the passenger seat with the other. She picked up the stake and held it up to the moonlight that filtered in through the windshield. It was positively entrancing. Dazzling. Sparkling. Gleaming.

Glowing.

The diamond was *actually* glowing.

Mallory screwed up her face and peered into the depths of the stone, keeping the road in her periphery. There was a brilliant white light breathing itself to life in the center of the diamond, growing brighter and brighter until the blinding glow filled the entire spike, and little rays of light shot out in all directions. And the diamond was growing warm, too. No, not warm; *hot*. Suddenly, it was burning her hands. Mallory cried out and tossed it from one hand to the other, fighting to keep the car straight with her knees. The stone emitted an angry hum, and the light took on a dark shade of red. It was actually smoking now, its heat intense and unbearable. Mallory screamed; it felt like her hands had been plunged into a lava pit. She looked up and saw that she had veered over into the wrong lane. She gave her legs a jerk, and the car squealed across the road. It skidded across the shoulder and slammed into the guardrail. Metal squealed on metal, leaving a long gash along the passenger door. Mallory dropped the diamond and grabbed for the wheel. The stone clattered off the window ledge and fell onto the street, where it shattered into a million glowing red pieces.

She yanked the car back onto the road and tried to brake, but something was stuck under the pedal, and the car continuing barreling down the road. She fumbled beneath her feet with shaking hands, trying to keep the car on the road. She found the thing that was stopping her from braking.

It was the purple Jansport.

She clawed it out from beneath the pedal and hurled it across the car. It fell down onto the floor in front of the passenger seat. Mallory slammed on the brakes, and the car squealed to a halt, but there was really no point in going back. She had seen the diamond—or *whatever* it was—shatter against the pavement. There was no sense in going back for it. She'd been tricked by the demon; the shattered pieces of glass were worthless. She seethed behind the wheel, feeling the blood course angrily through her veins like acid. Then she stomped on the gas, squealing farther away from Anomaly Flats.

"*Fuck!*" she screamed. Then she screamed it again. Then she screamed it a third time, because how could life be so goddamn unfair?

She stabbed at the button that rolled up the window. She'd had enough Missouri air to last her a lifetime. She took deep breaths, trying to calm the roiling ocean in her veins. She still had the backpack. She still had the cash, and she still had the small diamonds. The *real* diamonds. She still had Lenore's safe house, and she still had her car. She would be fine.

Everything would be okay.

She drove on through the night, and slowly, her disgust began to dissipate. She was back on the road, and she had broken even, and that was no small thing. Before long, she had convinced herself that she was better off without a giant diamond anyway, because it could only draw nothing but unwanted attention, and as she neared the next river crossing—the whole reason for going through Anomaly Flats in the first place—she had already forgotten all about it. The farther she got from the city limits, the less of it she seemed to be able to hold in her mind, and that was just fine with her. A few more miles on, and she couldn't even remember the name of the little town where she'd spent the night before.

Or was it two nights?

Maybe she hadn't spent a night there at all. No, how could she have? She'd just left St. Louis earlier that morning.

Hadn't she?

She glanced over at the passenger side of the car, at the purple backpack that held her future—a future she'd stolen from a man who'd abused her one too many times.

"Karma really is a bitch, isn't it?" Mallory scoffed.

"The bitchiest," mirror Mallory scoffed back.

Then she grew calm. Everything was fine. No one was looking for her. In all likelihood, it would be Monday at the earliest before anyone at the office realized the safe had been broken into, and that gave her plenty of time. Soon, she'd cross the Missouri River, and then it wasn't far until she was out of the state. In a couple of hours, she'd be in Nebraska, and she doubted they'd be looking for her there.

But fate seemed to be making other plans as Mallory drove.

She came to the river crossing to find that the bridge had collapsed. The local sheriff's department was there, so she sank down in her seat and draped her hair over her face and prayed the deputy wouldn't recognize her. "What's the problem, officer?" she asked, wondering why the words sounded so familiar.

The deputy leaned down and spat a stream of brown liquid onto the highway. "Bridge's out," he explained, his mouth full of tobacco. "Gotta turn around."

254 | ANOMALY FLATS

The officer directed her to head back the way she'd come, and she was only too happy to oblige.

A new road opened up on the left, and she pulled the wheel. The Impala squealed against the pavement and cut off down the backwoods highway. The road wound deeper and deeper into the heart of nowhere, and the trees loomed high above and crowded her in, blotting out what little sunlight was left. For the hundredth time since leaving Ladue, her fingers itched to turn on her phone and check the Google map. But phones could be tracked, and she didn't know if anyone was keeping an eye on her signal, but she didn't want to find out. Honestly, she wasn't even sure that turning the phone off made it untraceable. *NCIS* had been mixed on that point. "Thanks for nothing, Mark Harmon," she grumbled.

The highway twisted through the woods, and Mallory started to feel uneasy, passing through what felt like two solid walls of trees. "This is the Midwest," she said aloud, frowning at the tall, dark shapes spread out on either side of the road. "Where the hell are all the fields?"

A vague sense of déjà vu whirled in Mallory's head as she gazed at the stars ahead. Millions of stars...*hundreds* of millions of stars...

Almost more stars than Mallory had ever seen before in her life.

She rounded a curve and saw a sign at the edge of the highway that read ANOMALY FLATS – 2 MI with an arrow pointing to the left.

Flats, she thought. *Flats sounds fieldish, right? Flats sounds good.*

She turned on her blinker, slowed down the car, and pulled onto the road that led to Anomaly Flats.

ACKNOWLEDGEMENTS

FIRSTLY, I'd like to thank my amazing wife, Paula, whose constant encouragement and tireless belief in good things around the corner are the ink that keeps my pen flowing. Or the condensed air can that keeps my computer keys clacking. Whatever, you know what I mean. Paula Pia, thank you for your support, in everything. I love you like bacon.

A very special thanks is also due to my dear friend Steven Luna, who not only managed seventy billion rounds of edits for this book, but who played a major role in the story's conception. Steven was a reliably stalwart sounding board for the storyline and for Mallory's character, and he's also responsible for the very idea of the time loop. Steven, you made this story sharp as Anomalian rain, and you gave me the perfect opportunity to finally write the time-mucking tale that I've always wanted to write. You're the best Viscount a writer could ask for!

I'd also like to thank Missouri. What a weird and wonderful state. You're a truly beautiful place, Missouri, even if you're downright terrifying sometimes, and I wouldn't change you for the world. Thanks for imprinting my brain with all of your charming oddities throughout the course of my formative years.

Finally, special thanks to Victor Mazzeo, who inadvertently sent me spiraling down a rabbit hole of weird and wonderful inspiration, without which Anomaly Flats would never have been born.

ABOUT THE AUTHOR

Photo by Emily Rose Studios

CLAYTON SMITH is a writer of speculative fiction living in Chicago, where he has become exceedingly good at cursing the winters. His work includes *Apocalypticon*, *Death and McCootie*, *Pants on Fire: A Collection of Lies*, and *Mabel Gray and the Wizard Who Swallowed the Sun*. Some of his nonsense has been featured on such popular Internet sites as Write City Magazine and Dumb White Husband, and his plays have been produced rather mercilessly all over the country.

He would like very much to hear from you. You can find him on Facebook, Twitter, and Instagram as @claytonsaurus.

And if your computer hasn't succumbed to the terrible powers of magnetism, you should join his email newsletter! It's fun there. There's cake! (There's no cake.) Find more information at StateOfClayton.com.